IGNITE

Tracy Lawson

IGNITE

BOOK THREE OF THE RESISTANCE SERIES

© 2016 by Tracy Lawson

Cover design by EbookLaunch.com
Back cover image by Jamie Buchsbaum

First Print 2016

978-1-948543-36-1

DysCovered Publishing
TracyLawsonBooks.com

To my Bexley Theatre Arts family
faculty, staff, students, and parents
past, present, and yet to be

IGNITE

Chapter 1

9:35 PM
Wednesday, November 29, 2034
Quadrant OP-439

The fire alarm's wail ceased abruptly, and Careen Catecher's rapid, shallow breathing fogged up the oxygen mask that covered her face. Velcro straps and a neck brace immobilized her on the rescue backboard as two grim-faced paramedics rushed her gurney through the rubble inside the demolished building. Her whole body began to shake as they emerged into the cold night air. Floodlights positioned above the scene dazzled her eyes, and she had the impression of a large crowd of people pressing forward as the paramedics loaded her into a waiting ambulance. *They're taking me to the hospital. Someone's going to recognize me.* Her teeth chattered, and her eyes darted frantically back and forth. *Where's Tommy? Where's Wes?*

As soon as the doors closed, she clawed at the straps and struggled to sit up, fighting the hands that sought to soothe her. Her fingernails found skin and drew blood.

"Hey! Take it easy! I'm trying to help you."

A needle jabbed her arm, and within seconds, everything faded to black.

TEN MINUTES EARLIER

Quadrant Marshal Henry Nelson clenched his nightstick and resisted the urge to strike out at the crowd that pressed against the barricade. In the few minutes since firefighters summoned paramedics inside the rubble of what had been the university's student center, curious onlookers gathered until they outnumbered the squad of marshals by at least twenty to one. A large crowd could turn into a violent mob at any provocation, and Nelson felt trapped between two potentially dangerous situations. Smoke still wafted from the wreckage behind him, and debris floated on the chilly breeze. None of the firefighters or members of the investigative team said it out loud, but he knew everyone was thinking the same thing: could it have been some sort of accident, like a gas leak? Or were more bombs set to explode? There had to be some explanation other than terrorism, because terrorism didn't happen in OP-439.

The crowd shifted and craned their necks to get a look at the paramedics who emerged from the gaping hole in the building and rushed a gurney toward a waiting ambulance.

Nelson glanced over his shoulder at the victim—a student? She was dust-covered, bloody, and bandaged, her face obscured behind an oxygen mask. He caught a glimpse of pink highlights in her dark hair, but that did nothing to distinguish her from thousands of other girls who had adopted the trend made popular by one of the leaders of the Resistance. While the paramedics shoved the gurney into the ambulance and prepared to leave, he and another marshal moved the barricade and shouted at the crowd to make way. The ambulance's siren faded away and an uneasy silence fell over the crowd as another paramedic crew wheeled out their gurney.

They, in contrast, were in no hurry. Nelson threw a questioning look at one of the paramedics, who subtly shook his head and motioned him over.

"He's one of yours. He was gone before we got to him. Looks like internal bleeding from blunt force trauma, and there were some shrapnel wounds." The paramedic lifted a corner of the blood-spattered sheet, and Nelson nodded slowly. "Dammit, Wes," he muttered. "You weren't even on duty today. How the hell did you end up in there?"

He turned away to compose himself. There was a murmur and a ripple in the crowd, and Nelson whirled around, tensed for some kind of confrontation. Instead, the crowd parted for a campus security guard who staggered drunkenly, bouncing off the onlookers. Nelson let him inside the barricade. The guard paused, his bloodstained face just inches away, and shouted, "You see a kid—blond guy—maybe six-one, with a scar on his chin? He attacked me. Took my service weapon."

Nelson took a step back. "No. Are you all right?"

"What?" The guard stuck a finger in his ear and winced. "Can't hear a dang thing. I was too close to the blast."

Nelson raised his voice. "EMTs just brought out two vics, but neither match that description. I haven't seen anyone else inside."

"That kid might be the perp. It was the darndest thing. He jumped me in the hallway and hustled me out of the building just before it blew." He looked dazedly at the gun in his hand. "When I came to, it was beside me, in the ivy." He brandished it as he spoke, and several people at the front of the crowd screamed and ducked out of the way. "He could've killed me or left me inside. But he didn't."

Nelson felt around in his pocket for latex gloves. "That could have prints on it! Give it here." He took the gun by the end of the grip, motioned to a member of the crime scene investigation team, and handed the gun off to her. She bagged it and took the security guard aside. Then he called to the nearest marshal. "We're going to need backup to secure the market. He could have escaped over there and blended in with the crowd."

"Who?" Nelson turned toward the voice and found himself nose-to-nose with a PeopleCam news crew. The camera operator turned on the unit's floodlight, and Nelson squinted and shielded his eyes against the glare.

The reporter signaled the camera operator to get some shots of the crowd and drew Nelson a few steps closer to the building.

"You said the bomber escaped into the market? Have you initiated a manhunt?"

"No, it's not clear what happened yet. We haven't begun to follow up on leads."

The reporter headed toward the demolished building, but Nelson grabbed him by the sleeve. "Stay out of there. You'll contaminate the crime scene." The reporter shook him off and stalked over to the crowd at the barricade.

9:40 PM

Eduardo Rodriguez worked his way toward the front of the crowd. Just minutes before, he'd heard a loud boom, and his apartment had trembled so violently that he'd run outside, thinking it might be an earthquake. He'd spotted the cloud of smoke in the sky and hurried toward it, wondering what new catastrophe had befallen his once-quiet home quadrant, and arrived at the smoldering ruin of the university's student center in time to watch an ambulance pull away from the scene.

He caught most of what the security guard said. He was no fan of the QM, but he felt sorry for the marshal who was simultaneously trying to question the guard, keep the crowd under control, and rein in an overeager PeopleCam reporter. The camera operator turned the lens his way, and Eduardo moved behind the guy next to him.

The reporter pressed the marshal. "Could the explosion be related to the fact that people are right across the street selling food without government licenses?"

A curly haired young man standing near Eduardo had scrawled the symbol *CXD* on his sweatshirt with a Sharpie; he snorted and then raised his voice, as though hoping to rile up the crowd. "The OCSD's not above blowing up a building to scare us away from the market ... or better yet, distract us from how badly they handled the food shortage. They don't seem to care that we have to trade our stuff so we can eat. The meals people paid for haven't been delivered because Essential Services can't get their heads out of their—"

The reporter held out his microphone, and someone else in the crowd shouted, "Maybe it was the Resistance that blew up the student center!" Eduardo's pulse quickened, and he scanned the crowd for familiar faces.

The marshal motioned to the camera operator with a finger across his throat, but instead he zoomed in on the young man in the sweatshirt, who spoke louder, defying anyone to silence him. "No chance! Careen's latest message said to avoid doing anything violent or destructive. I'm betting it was the QM trying to make sure we know our place. They and the higher-ups in the OCSD have plenty of food while we wait for deliveries that never come. The people who died at OP-441 last week were just trying to get something to eat. You can't make problems go away by turning off a video camera. You can't ignore the truth!"

He raised his right fist in the air. "Enough for us!"

The crowd picked up the chant. "Enough for us! Enough for us!" The marshals inside the barricade closed ranks. One of the students at the front vaulted over the barrier into the open space, and within seconds, the wave of people surged forward and engulfed the marshals' inferior numbers. Eduardo, heart pounding, fought to stay on his feet and avoid being swept into the epicenter. Since he'd become involved with the Resistance about a month ago, he'd been in too many tight spots and brawling mobs. He was one of the lucky ones who'd escaped unharmed from that food riot in OP-441 the week before.

Three patrol cars, sirens blaring, edged their way onto the scene, prompting most of the people at the rear of the crowd to head back to the market on the university green and escape the emerging marshals' nightsticks.

Eduardo took advantage of the momentum shift and braced himself against a battered car to let the crowd flow past. It was the same make and model as the one he'd loaned to a friend, but this one was dented and scratched on the side and rear panels, and the trunk was bashed in. He peered at the license plate. *¡Dios mio! Tommy told me he knew how to drive.* Even as he shook his head over the damage, he smiled at the thought of seeing Tommy and Careen. After they'd busted through the quadrant marshals' roadblock and escaped the capital together, he'd lent them his car so they could continue on their search for Tommy's parents. He threaded his way against the thinning crowd and headed for Tommy's house, hoping to meet them on the way.

Fifteen minutes later, he glanced around for signs of trouble as he approached the Baileys' white clapboard house. A dim light burned on the ground floor, and the television screen flickered behind the drawn blinds. He crossed the unlit front porch and tapped softly on the door.

There was no response. He tried again.

"What do you want?"

He took a step back at the harsh greeting. "Tommy? It's Eduardo. Let me in."

"Eduardo?" The door swung open, and Tommy Bailey stood silhouetted in the light from the living room, clutching a baseball bat. Eduardo stepped over the threshold, and Tommy locked the door behind him. "How did you know we were here?"

"Saw my car parked in front of the student center. What's left of it, that is. Looks like you used it in a demolition derby. It's inside the marshal's crime scene tape, so I figured you must've walked home."

Kevin McGraw was there, too. Eduardo hadn't seen him since they'd infiltrated the OCSD together. Kevin had been a nervous wreck that day, and so had he. Now, Kevin looked tougher, and not just because he was smeared with mud and blood.

"You need someone to take a look at those cuts. Both of you. Is *Carina* with you?" He glanced around expectantly, but Tommy dropped the bat on the sofa, shook his head, and disappeared upstairs.

"*¿Qué pasó?*"

"Careen and Wes were in that building when it blew. We couldn't get close enough to get a look when the EMTs brought them out."

Eduardo whistled. "Another one of Carraway's plans?"

"Yeah. PeopleCam reported a quadrant marshal was killed in the blast. We're pretty sure it was him."

"*¡Dios mio!* What can I do to help?"

Kevin pointed toward the stairs. "Could you?"

"*Claro.*"

A door at the end of the upstairs hall stood ajar, and Eduardo stuck his head into the room. Tommy sat slump-shouldered on the edge of the rumpled, unmade bed. "Come on, let's get you bandaged up. Then we need to get out of here." Tommy followed him into the bathroom. Eduardo rummaged in the medicine cabinet and wet a washcloth at the sink. "Look, there's one thing I learned since all this started: you have to try and do what you think is right. Sometimes it's gonna work out; sometimes it won't."

Tommy winced as Eduardo dabbed at the worst cut on his cheek. Eduardo continued, "It was my idea to let those people into the hub at OP-441. I pushed Carraway and the hub director to do the right thing, and I'm partly responsible. I have those people's blood on my hands."

Tommy's chin trembled, and he squeezed his eyes shut. Eduardo finished applying a gauze bandage and closed the medicine cabinet.

"But it's not my fault; do you understand? It's not my fault any more than what happened tonight is yours. People will get hurt and people will die whether you and I try to do the right thing or not. I'm going to keep trying. So should you. Come on, let's go."

Eduardo hurried downstairs to where Kevin waited in the Baileys' darkened front hall, Tommy trailing behind. There was no need to whisper, but Eduardo kept his voice low. "Anything else on the news?"

Kevin shook his head. "Nothing about the explosion, but People-Cam's showing video of protests all over the country."

"What're they protesting about?"

"Actually, they called them nonviolent gatherings to raise awareness and help bring an end to the food shortages."

"I bet the nonviolent thing won't last when the QM shows up to disperse the crowds. Hey, speaking of crowds, did you see all the CXD graffiti and stuff? People got it written on their hands and shirts. Know what it means?"

"No idea." Kevin looked over at the comfortable sofa in the living room. "We could stay here tonight and make a fresh start in the morning."

"No, we should get outta here. I don't know how long it'll take the QM to get the whole story out of that security guard. He was kinda loopy, you know? I didn't realize it at the time, because I didn't know you were here, but he described Tommy to that marshal. If they get Tommy's prints off the gun, they'll come here looking for him."

"Yeah. Guess we'd better move." He extended his hand. "Take it easy."

"You, too, *amigo*." Eduardo clasped his hand, picked up the keys to the truck, and steered Tommy out the door ahead of him. They and Kevin went their separate ways into the night.

Chapter 2

10:00 PM
Quadrant DC-001

"Madam Director?"

Madalyn Davies looked up from the file on her desk and glared at her assistant. *What was her name again? Oh, right. Mousy Nicole.* The woman clutched the doorframe and cowered, half out of sight, as she delivered the news.

"There's been an explosion at the university in OP-439."

Madalyn's livid expression made the timid woman shrink further away. *Dammit.* That was one of the few quadrants where nothing bad ever happened. Until recently. "Well?"

"The details are still sketchy, Madam Director. Besides the explosion, umm, there are also riots and protests."

"In OP-439?"

"All over the country."

"Turn on my television."

Nicole let go of the doorframe and crossed the room to click the television remote that lay on the desk, less than an arm's reach away from her boss. The television powered up, and Madalyn watched her assistant's eyes grow wide. Nicole dropped the remote and scurried out before Madalyn could spin around in her chair.

A photo of Madalyn, photoshopped into a Marie-Antoinette-style costume, bore the caption "Let Them Eat Cake."

How had she become the most hated woman in the country?

Six weeks ago, she'd been perfectly happy with her position as the assistant director of the Office of Civilian Safety and Defense.

The OCSD was the most important government agency in the United States, created to oversee all aspects of the nation's domestic security. Since its inception in 2019, the OCSD had implemented Civilian Restrictions to protect people from dangerous situations.

Though limiting access to cars and social media might seem extreme, Restrictions were necessary to curtail the ever-present threat of terrorism.

In 2024, the Restriction that created the Essential Services Department and banned the sale and distribution of food items by anyone else went into effect. For a time, it faced strong public opposition. But the food supply was vulnerable to attack. People who were afraid to shop for their own food organized, started a petition drive in support of the Restriction, and soon drowned out the dissenters. It was all for the best, and people soon grew accustomed to having food delivered to their doors once a week.

The Essential Services system had worked without a hitch for ten years, unless you counted the skyrocketing costs.

The Marie Antoinette meme wasn't fair. How could she have predicted the events that led to the nationwide food shortage?

The problems with CSD were completely unrelated. And now they were inexorably snarled. No one would remember anything good about these security programs.

Six weeks ago, the OCSD had mandated that everyone take the Counteractive System of Defense antidote daily to protect against a chemical weapons threat. The people, used to a never-ending stream of danger, had complied.

There was no chemical weapons threat. But that was a secret only a few people in the top echelons of the OCSD knew.

The antidote's hallucinogenic side effects helped people cope with the stress. Of course, some people—higher-ups in government and those with jobs considered essential—received a placebo formula that allowed them to keep delivering the mail, packaging and delivering food, and manufacturing more of the antidote.

The next phase of the drug increased people's suggestibility and blocked their memory. People blindly followed government-issued messages ordering them to spend money, which the government believed would stimulate the sluggish economy. Teens and younger adults obediently reported for nightly combat training and remembered nothing the next day.

Phase Three was supposed to complete the people's transformation into malleable soldiers and civil servants who were devoid of free will. Lowell Stratford, who had been the OCSD director at the time, desired a strong and fearless military force that could crush any threat—be it from without or within.

It should have worked—but spies and saboteurs, part of a resistance group, had infiltrated the OCSD. They'd ruined the batch of Phase Three and somehow deleted all record of the formula.

During a live press conference, Stratford had toasted the success of his program with what should have been sugar water—but instead dropped dead on camera. Someone had tampered with his vial and substituted poison.

Trina Jacobs, a doctor who'd been on the research team, and Careen Catecher, a college student who was part of the Resistance, were accused of his murder, and were now fugitives from justice.

Without the new batch of CSD, the people all detoxed and became clearheaded just as the Resistance mounted a smear campaign of propaganda videos, most of which featured pretty, young Careen Catecher. The Resistance's interference threatened to ruin the public's confidence in the OCSD's ability to manage the country's security issues.

Let them eat cake, indeed. None of this is my fault. Well, that wasn't exactly true, whispered a tiny voice inside her. She dismissed the pang of conscience. *It's more Lowell's fault than mine. When he died, I was left behind to take the blame.*

Maybe no one believed CSD was necessary to protect against chemical weapons anymore, but she had hoped people would crave the comfort of the low-grade high. Compliance was the key to getting things back under control, and people on CSD were remarkably compliant.

She countered the Resistance's messages by dangling free Transitional CSD and the promise of blissful oblivion in front of the confused and frightened people.

Transitional CSD became a top priority, but one week ago, on the day of the first delivery, nearly every postal carrier took the stronger dose and was incapacitated by the side effects. She'd forgotten that postal workers had all been on the placebo dose before.

Madalyn had done the only thing she could do. She'd ordered the Essential Services Department to delay food deliveries and help distribute the CSD. Her decision caused a ripple effect that left about one-sixth of the population without their weekly allotment of food. Instead of waiting for Essential Services to sort out the problem, people had panicked, hijacking trucks bearing food and breaking into each other's homes to steal from one another.

Essential Services struggled to get back on track, while black market providers swooped in like vultures and took advantage of the situation. Madalyn suspected the illegally traded food was either stolen from authorized government networks, or substandard. Unsafe.

The president, heedless of her warnings, had rescinded the Restriction that protected the Essential Services monopoly, and black market dealers became legitimate food providers overnight. They had absolutely no licensing, and worse yet, they were selling food that should have been reserved for distribution by Essential Services.

On the television, Madalyn's image had been replaced with amateur video of the explosion in OP-439.

Chapter 3

6:45 AM
Thursday, November 30, 2034
Quadrant BG-098

Fifteen-year-old Jaycee Carraway peeked out the diner's front window and watched as her father walked four quadrant marshals out to their Jeep. He lifted his hand in a brief wave, but as soon as they pulled out of the parking lot, his shoulders slumped, revealing just how much the news of the disastrous bombing mission in OP-439 weighed upon him.

His brother Wes had been killed in the explosion. Things were bad, but at least the marshals hadn't discovered the Resistance members hiding in the boardinghouse about a hundred yards from where they'd just eaten breakfast. Mitch shuffled toward the barn, and Jaycee sighed and squared her thin shoulders before she set to work lugging stacks of dirty dishes to the sink and scrubbing at sticky dribbles of syrup on the counter. She was so intent on what she was doing that she jumped when the bell on the diner's door jingled. Two marshals stepped inside. The young one, sandy-haired and freckled, looked fresh out of cadet school. He stood up straight, his glance flickering uncomfortably between her face and the faded linoleum floor. The other, gray-haired, obviously a veteran of years in law enforcement, seemed to sag inside his uniform, spilling over his belt in a way that made his belly look much broader than his shoulders.

"I thought you all had left. Need some coffee to go?"

"Josephine Cecilia Carraway?"

Jaycee, confused, was slow to react to her given name. "Umm, yeah?"

The young marshal spoke as though he'd memorized what he had to say. "I'm Quadrant Marshal Seamus Owens. We're here about your uncle, Wesley Jefferson Carraway. Badge number 52068010."

Jaycee knew she had to act surprised, even though she'd known about Wes's death for hours. She pulled her face into what she hoped was an appropriate expression.

"We regret to inform you that Quadrant Marshal Carraway was wounded in the line of duty last night. He was transported to a hospital, where every effort was made to save him, but his injuries were too severe, and they lost him." He bit his lip. "I mean, he died."

She'd never been much of a crier, but as Seamus Owens struggled through his speech, her chin began to tremble, and she didn't have to force the tears that coursed down her cheeks.

"He named you next of kin. We need to know if you want his body brought here for burial. You'll receive the rest of his pay and his death benefit, too. There'll be papers to sign. Stuff like that."

"Yes. He should be buried here." The finality of it all washed over her and she began to sob in earnest.

"I'm real sorry for your loss. I'm sure your uncle was a great man." The distress in the boy's voice was genuine; he was watching her in a way that made her wish her face wasn't all red and blotchy beneath her freckles. She dabbed at her nose with the cuff of her hoodie and sniffled.

The older marshal regarded her with sympathy. "Are you all right? Do you need us to call someone to stay with you?"

Jaycee shook her head. Seamus looked back at her as he followed his partner out the door. She'd always assumed that someday she'd inherit the family diner, that she'd be stuck behind the counter forever. She couldn't change the fact that Wes was dead, or that her father's grief had made him gruffer and more remote than usual. But maybe things could change for her. She wiped her tears and blew her nose on her apron.

Chapter 4

8:45 AM
Quadrant DC-001

Madalyn looked at the girl on the video monitor as she spoke on the phone. "Are you sure it's her? I mean, absolutely sure?"

"Yes, Madam Director. We checked her DNA against the database of samples collected on Distribution Day."

"And how serious are her injuries?"

"Surprisingly, nothing major. She has cuts and abrasions from flying debris and a possible concussion. No internal injuries, though. Looks like she was sheltered from the full impact of the blast."

"Is she stable enough to be moved?"

"Yes. She's been combative, though. It would be best to keep her sedated."

Madalyn nodded. "Have her transferred here immediately."

She disconnected the call and turned to Art Severson, who lounged in one of the wing chairs facing her desk. "I can't wait to tell the world that Careen Catecher is finally in custody—and that she was responsible for that bombing. I was right all along about her being a criminal!"

"Madam Director, might I advise you to proceed with caution?"

"Why?"

"Wouldn't it be better to wait before you make any kind of announcement? Criminal or no, she seems to wield a certain amount of influence with the public. No sense in making her a martyr to the Resistance's cause."

She crossed her arms and glared at him, but he dismissed her frown with a wave of his hand.

"You have to admit that ridiculous pink hair thing went viral. I suggest you avoid any announcements that will cause teenagers with pink highlights to start setting off bombs all over the country."

Madalyn took a deep breath as if to prepare for battle. She stared at Careen's image on the monitor. "Yes. You're right. For some reason I cannot fathom, she's more influential than I am. That has to end."

"Either eliminate her or turn her to your side; doesn't really matter which."

"Trust me, she's not seeing the light of day until she's no longer fit to lead a rebellion. I'm going to break her. That'll end her influence, once and for all."

9:00 AM
Quadrant BG-098

If Careen was in OCSD custody, Dr. Trina Jacobs was now Public Enemy Number One. The assembled members of the Resistance had kept an all-night vigil at the boardinghouse in BG-098 waiting for news of Wes and Tommy's mission. The blackout shades kept the thin winter sunlight outside, and it still seemed like night to Trina as they remained in front of the television, hoping for some information about Careen's condition.

She never could have predicted her life would take this course.

It had all started when she accepted a medical research position at the OCSD the previous September and was assigned the top-secret task of developing an antidote that would render any kind of airborne poisons ineffectual.

The Counteractive System of Defense drug, developed by her boss, Dr. Lowell Stratford, was really nothing more than a hallucinogen mixed with scopolamine, so instead of a nation of cowering, frightened victims, he'd have a nation of complacent, suggestible victims. Trina had vehemently opposed the whole plan and had ended up sedated with a heavy dose of the antidote and locked away in the OCSD building so she couldn't interfere. Luckily, Kevin McGraw, another employee, had rescued her. Kevin was working with the Resistance, and together they'd sabotaged the production of the third and final phase of the drug.

One of her early batches of potential antidotes had been deadly; someone had stolen it from the lab and used it to poison Lowell

Stratford. Trina was accused of the murder, and she and Kevin had made a hasty escape to Resistance headquarters in the remote mountains of Quadrant BG-098, where they now worked to destroy their former employer's grip on the people.

Early yesterday, Kevin had headed back to the capital to infiltrate the OCSD. He was her closest friend and confidant; she didn't think she'd be able to sleep until she knew he was all right.

When she'd first met Mitch Carraway, the Resistance leader, she'd thought he was just some overzealous hillbilly playing war games. She'd accidentally overheard him on the phone, making plans to buy the CSD formulas from Madalyn, and called him out for making deals with the enemy. Once he'd shared more about his plan and the scope of his clandestine network of spies and freedom fighters, her respect for him had grown.

David Honerlaw and Grace Hughes, the retired political science professors who'd also been rescued from OCSD custody, were dozing in armchairs. Eduardo Rodriguez, the newest arrival, sat awkwardly on the sofa; he didn't know anyone but Tommy, who had disappeared upstairs as soon as he got back. Lara Bailey, Tommy's mother, had her arm around Jaycee, who had recently come in from the diner and curled up beside her on the sofa.

Danni Carraway, Mitch's cousin and the Resistance's connection for black market food and weapons, had supplied the blocks of C-4 Wes and Tommy had used to destroy the student center. Danni had never spent any time ingratiating herself with the group, and now she sat in a sagging recliner in a far corner of the room. No one had any words of sympathy for her, and her shame was a chip on her shoulder.

They all watched the television in silence. "Acts of defiance have become commonplace across the country. Citizens have refused to abide by the established curfews and are ignoring the Restriction that forbids congregating in public. In the aftermath of the university bombing, videos of parties and gatherings are pouring in from quadrants all over the nation. The symbol CXD, which appears both in graffiti and on the persons involved in acts of disobedience, seems to be inspired by the most recent communiqué from Careen Catecher, spokesperson for the Resistance.

"In other news, the OCSD has released updated information

regarding last night's terrorist attack in OP-439. The unidentified young woman pulled from the rubble is in critical condition. The identity of the quadrant marshal killed at the scene is being withheld pending notification of next of kin.

"We'll be taking you back to OP-439 shortly for continuing live coverage of the tragedy there."

Trina turned away from the television. "Oh, Lordy. If Careen's really still unconscious, she's got serious injuries. Are they giving her proper medical attention? Surely they wouldn't withhold treatment even if they think she—"

Danni spoke up. "If she dies before she regains consciousness, we don't have to worry about her spilling all our secrets."

Jaycee jumped off the sofa. "Shut up! She's not going to die." She burst into tears and ran out of the room, Lara close behind.

David waited until Jaycee was out of earshot. "Wes and Tommy created the wrong kind of distraction. It allowed the OCSD to discredit the Resistance and blame the bombing on Careen. She was our most effective link to the public. I'm not sure it's even worth it to proceed with our original plan, now that her fate and future are uncertain."

Grace had lost her take-charge attitude. "I'm so upset about what's happened to the children that I can't even think. What should we do?"

Danni stood up. "In case anyone cares, I'm headed out to spread the gospel of Careen and make sure hungry people have something to eat." She swept out of the room.

"We're going to have to take a different tack to advance our work." David lowered his voice. "I suspect Mitch has something cooking on the side. Anyone know what?"

Trina shifted her weight but said nothing.

9:20 AM
Quadrant DC-001

A greasy-haired janitor bobbed his head to the music that pulsed through his earphones as he wheeled a vacuum cleaner into the

OCSD lobby. He plugged it in, and it snored like a slumbering beast as he pushed it back and forth in a slow, hypnotic motion. Anyone who was watching would assume he was some mindless drone, doing his job on autopilot. His half-closed eyes belied the fact that he was fully aware of the bald man in torn, muddy clothing who came in through the visitor's entrance, signed in, and crossed the lobby to the elevators.

As the janitor guided the vacuum across the spotless carpet, he rubbed his nose with the back of his free hand and spoke into a tiny transmitter on his watchband. "He's here."

9:30 AM

Alone in her office at last, Madalyn broke into a happy dance. Finally, *finally* something was going her way. With Careen in custody, she could push Hoyt Garrick to focus all his efforts on apprehending Trina Jacobs. Once she had a chance to interrogate the girl, it wouldn't take much to round up the members of the Resistance.

Careen was sedated and en route, expected to arrive at the nearby naval hospital by midafternoon. Madalyn sank into her leather chair and spun around, as excited as a child anticipating a birthday party with lots of gifts.

"Madalyn?"

She put both hands on her desktop to halt her rotation. The last person on earth she expected to see stood in the doorway. She straightened her skirt as she moved out from behind the desk. "Kevin? Where in the world did you come from?"

He looked awful—scratched and bruised, in torn and muddy clothing. He wavered on his feet as if he were about to faint and croaked out, "Trina ..."

He drew back in alarm as she advanced upon him. "What about Trina? Where is she?"

"She's gone crazy. She kidnapped me and dumped me in the middle of nowhere. I've been trying to get back here for a week. I was on foot until I managed to steal a car yesterday."

She sighed and put on a look of concern. "You poor thing. Come sit down."

She returned behind the desk and he sank wearily into one of the wing chairs. She folded her hands on the glossy, varnished surface, trying to control her eagerness and keep her voice calm. "What happened to Trina? Do you have any information on her whereabouts?"

"I have no idea where she went after she let me go."

Then I don't have time to deal with this now. She smiled benignly. "Do you want some coffee?" She pushed the button on her desk to summon security.

"Thank you. I'm so tired. So glad to finally be safe."

It was awkward waiting, and Madalyn jabbed the button again. *Someone please come get him out of my office. I have more important things to think about.*

Nicole opened the door for two guards, who pulled Kevin to his feet and patted him down. One swept him with a metal detector, which beeped as it moved past his shirt pocket.

The guard pulled out a roll of candy. "What the—? These wands are pretty sensitive. It must be reacting to the foil wrapper."

Madalyn's eyebrows went up. "Candy? Where did you get candy? It's not on the approved foods list."

Kevin looked crestfallen. "You have no idea how long I've been saving that."

"Well, I'm afraid I'm going to have to confiscate it. Sorry." She dropped it in her desk drawer, and he sighed.

"I understand. But I'm not sure what to do next. I'm afraid to go home. What if Trina … well, what if she comes after me?"

So much the better. "There are the guest suites on the third floor. Why don't you go up and get some rest? You'll be safe there."

She spared him a cursory glance as he followed Nicole out of the room. At the moment, Careen Catecher was her only priority.

Chapter 5

9:45 AM
Quadrant OP-439

Henry Nelson believed that people needed strongly enforced rules to protect them from each other—and from themselves.

His family had instilled in him a sense of order and a patriotic love of country. He'd been a member of the Junior Marshals as a teen and had applied to quadrant marshal cadet school on his eighteenth birthday. He'd proudly served Quadrant OP-439 for the past ten years and took his duties seriously. He knew the name and occupation of every adult in the quadrant and where every child went to school. He paid regular visits to elderly residents to make sure they knew they were remembered and protected.

It was a plum assignment, safeguarding the occupants of a wealthy quadrant. Aside from the rare instance of property crime, little happened in OP-439. When he'd learned a terrorist cell had been operating there, he'd taken it as a personal affront.

Henry did his job with precision and efficiency. How had these terrorists escaped his notice? He wished he'd discovered and neutralized them before they'd destroyed the university student center.

Usually he looked forward to hitting the hay at the end of an overnight shift, but on this morning, sleep was the furthest thing from his mind. Back at the marshal station, he changed out of his dirty, smoke-permeated uniform into civilian clothes and then made his way down the hall, glancing over his shoulder before he stepped into the records room and closed the door behind him.

Wes Carraway had been kind of a cowboy, a rebel. No denying it. Wes had said himself, the first day they'd met, that the instructors at cadet school hadn't been able to train the troublemaker out of him. Well, looks like trouble found him this time. Even though they hadn't exactly been friends, he felt the loss of a comrade in arms.

Quadrant marshals were in more danger than they'd ever been, with those lunatics in the Resistance stirring up trouble. Last night it had ticked him off when that punk behind the barrier said the QM was responsible for setting off the explosion. No way that could be true. At least he could try to make sure the real culprit took the blame for that explosion—and for Wes's death.

He logged on to the computer, pulled up last month's files, and soon found the name he was looking for: Bailey, Thomas Jr., who matched the description given by the security guard.

Henry had been with Wes at the Bailey house twice in the last month. The first time there'd been a problem with a bottle of CSD that allegedly hadn't been delivered. Together, he and Wes had followed protocol and forced a dose on Tommy Bailey, who'd resisted; that alone was enough to get him pegged as a dissident. Then, a few days later, they'd gone back to his place to arrest a girl for failing to take part in the mandatory combat training. He scrolled back through the arrest records but found nothing except the report of the undelivered antidote. *That's strange. I fingerprinted and processed Tommy Bailey myself, while Wes processed the girl.* He searched the computer for all the reports Wes had filed since he'd been transferred to OP-439, with no luck. *Where could that record have gone?*

Nothing came up when he cross-checked under his own name for the statement he'd taken from Art Severson, the witness who'd seen the girl run away from the training exercises and enter the Bailey house. *I could've sworn I'd filed it properly. This is a fine time for a glitch in the computer system.*

Wes hadn't mentioned anything about losing his prisoners. But then again, he hadn't seen much of Wes since the day they'd arrested the pair. Soon after, the OCSD director was killed, and during the CSD riots, everything had seemed to spin out of control. No wonder he couldn't remember the last time he'd seen or talked to Wes. Had Wes been killed by a so-called Resistance member who was really nothing more than a terrorist?

There was one more angle to check, so he pulled up the file for the pending investigation into the previous night's bombing. Only a few documents had been uploaded, but he found what he wanted—the artist's sketch done from the security guard's description of the perp. It was a perfect likeness of Tommy Bailey.

11:03 AM
Quadrant BG-098

Tommy laughed as Careen led him along the shadowy path to their cabin in the woods. She danced ahead, just out of reach, until he put on a burst of speed to catch up to her on the trail, and her squeal of mock fear heightened his primal need to pursue her. He swept her into his arms, pinning her against the rough bark of the nearest tree, and buried his cold nose in her neck, making her squeal again before he claimed her lips. The fruity smell of her shampoo mingled with the tang of the pine needles that hung like a curtain around them. Her arms slid around his neck, and their kiss produced so much heat that he wouldn't have noticed if he'd been standing in a foot of snow.

"We don't need to go all the way to the cabin. Right here's good." He was only half-joking as he ran his hand down her side and along her hip.

She blew out a frosty breath. "No way! It's freezing! You're gonna have to build me a fire first."

He tightened his hold on her. "I'm working on it."

She squirmed, laughing, caught between him and the tree.

A yellow flashlight beam spotlighted them in the darkness. "Quadrant Marshals. Freeze!"

He ducked out of the light, pulling Careen with him, and tried to blink away the after-image burned on his retinas as he groped along the trail. They hadn't gone far when Careen faltered. Were there more lights in the woods, or were his eyes still playing tricks on him? She clutched his arm, and her whisper seared on his brain. "They're going to make me tell. I'm so sorry. Don't let them catch you."

He opened his mouth to speak, but before he could do so, she threw an impressive shoulder-check that caught him off balance. He arced through the darkness and off the trail in slow motion, watching the flashlight beams play against the trees above him as the marshals converged on her.

Tommy's body jerked as if he'd really hit the ground, and he lay tangled in the blanket, drenched in sweat. He hadn't had a dream that completely enveloped his senses like that since he quit taking CSD.

He fumbled in the gloom for the bedside lamp and switched it on. He was in his parents' room at the boardinghouse. He felt groggy and disoriented, as if he'd only been asleep for a few minutes. The clock said 11:15, but with the blackout shades drawn, he couldn't tell if it was still morning, or if he'd slept a whole day away.

A soft tap at the door made him jump.

"Tommy? May I come in?"

A lump formed in his throat at the sound of his dad's voice. "Yeah," he croaked, and rolled over so he was facing away from the door. He'd cried like a little kid with his mom when he'd arrived back at the boardinghouse early that morning, but he couldn't break down in front of his dad. He'd ignored Tom's counsel and insisted on accompanying Wes on the bombing mission; he didn't feel entitled to any display of weakness. Certainly not tears.

The door clicked shut, and he felt the other side of the soft, old mattress dip as his dad sat down. He dreaded what his father might say to him so much that he swore there was a vise clamp tightening around his guts. "I should've listened to you."

When there was no response, he stumbled on. "I don't know why we thought it was a good idea. Nothing went the way we planned, and I'm the only one who came back." He took a shuddering breath that was dangerously close to a sob. "Again."

His dad cleared his throat. "You know that your mother's memory spontaneously returned yesterday, and while you were gone, she and I talked over everything that's happened since the accident. She refused to consider the possibility that she'd lose you now. We're glad you've come back to us."

A tear rolled out of the corner of Tommy's eye. He clenched a fistful of pillow but kept his voice steady. "I'm glad Mom's back, too."

There was a long pause. "Do you need anything?"

Besides Careen and Wes? Nothing else mattered. "Umm, could I stay here a while longer? I don't want to go back to my room at the diner. Not yet."

"Of course."

The mattress shifted again, and Tommy heard the door open.

"Dad?"

"Yes?"

"I'm sorry."

"You acted on your convictions. What's done is done."

He heard the door close, and his dad's footsteps faded down the stairs. The tears he'd held back wouldn't come, and he lay, eyes stinging, wishing it had been his convictions rather than his cowardice that had led him astray.

12:10 PM
Quadrant OP-439

Nelson waved the sketch of Tommy Bailey at his post commander. "This is big. I mean *really* big! Should we call the Chief QM in to start an investigation?"

The post commander hesitated. "It's gonna look bad that the Resistance has been operating right under our noses and we didn't know anything about it. This quadrant has had an awful lot of bad publicity lately, what with the riots and the protests and now this bombing. I can't draw attention to the fact that the Resistance has an active terrorist cell here." He shook his head and scooped up the file Nelson had brought into the office.

Frustrated, Nelson jumped to his feet. "They killed Carraway! He was one of your men! You should want to catch those rebels and see them brought to justice!"

"I'll handle it." Apparently the matter was closed.

"One more thing, sir. I want to attend the funeral."

"Remains have already been shipped back to his home quadrant."

"Where?"

"BG-098."

He'd never known where Wes was from. "Then I'd like time off and permission to make the trip."

"I'll consider it. It depends on whether the situation here stabilizes." The post commander ushered him into the hall and closed the door.

Nelson swore under his breath and stormed out of the station, zipping his jacket against the chill as he headed for the university. He ducked under the crime scene tape surrounding the blast site and ventured into the rubble, crunching through broken glass and other debris. The inside of the building was unrecognizable—metal rebar and wires dangled from the shattered walls, and the comfortable furniture that had occupied the lounge was crushed under the rubble that had rained down from the upper floors.

Had members of the Resistance lured Wes here and killed him? Was it retribution for arresting Tommy Bailey, or had Wes stumbled onto more of the rebel group's secrets?

"Can't believe this, can you?" Nelson heard more footsteps disturbing the rubble and froze out of sight, listening.

"It's crazy. I was here, man—sitting, like, right over there. I'd just gone over to the market when I heard the explosion. If I'd hung around much longer, who knows?"

"Yeah, close call. And that's not even the best reason to come to the meeting with me tonight. You know that hot girl from calculus class? She'll be there, too. So you gotta go. I did some trading at the market and had a major score, so come over about dark, and we'll have a couple of beers first, 'kay?"

Once the voices faded and the two young men left the building, Nelson picked his way out through the mess. He hunched his shoulders against the cold and shoved his gloved hands deeper into his pockets as he followed them into a large group of students gathered at the open-air market on the green. The young people were huddled together, mostly in twos and threes. The guys he'd followed joined a pair of girls. He saw one of them slip something into a girl's hand, and as they moved away, Nelson watched out of the corner of his eye as she unfolded the piece of paper, glanced at it, and passed it to another boy. *Helps that I'm invisible to this age group.* He kept his eyes trained on the piece of paper until finally someone crumpled it up and tossed it in a trash bin.

He looked over his shoulder before he retrieved it and pocketed it as he walked away.

Chapter 6

2:05 PM
Quadrant BG-098

Eduardo stayed hunkered down on the sofa in the boardinghouse and stared at the television, his eyes gritty from lack of sleep. Tommy had been silent most of the drive, unwilling to talk about what had happened. When they'd arrived early that morning, everyone had been eager to know what was happening back in OP-439, but Tommy had disappeared upstairs with his mom, and hadn't talked to anyone else. Eduardo himself had little information to share. What he'd managed to discern from Kevin left him sick with worry over Careen's fate. If he thought he could help her, he'd leave for the capital right now.

Mitch came into the room and paced behind the sofa without acknowledging Eduardo, who eyed him critically. This was the man who had raised Carraway, shaped him and influenced him. He wasn't sure he could be trusted.

On television, Jeremy Howard, the young reporter who'd broken the story, looked rumpled and a little dazed as his live coverage approached its sixteenth hour. Eduardo pointed at the television and spoke to no one in particular. "I saw that reporter last night, right after it happened. I can't believe he's still there!"

"Pete, Sheila, the initial investigation into the explosion at the university student center has sparked more questions than answers.

"Witnesses claim a young man in his late teens or early twenties attacked and disarmed a security guard who was patrolling the building just prior to the explosion. The guard claims his attacker rushed him out of the building with seconds to spare and then disappeared into the crowd."

Sheila broke in to the conversation. "Excuse me, Pete, Jeremy. We can now confirm that the dead marshal is twenty-one year-old

Wesley Carraway, who was assigned to the post in OP-439 just two months ago."

Pete chimed in. "Jeremy, I see a large gathering behind you. Can I assume it's some kind of vigil for the dead marshal?"

The reporter looked over his shoulder at hundreds of students sitting cross-legged on the green. "I've been told they're here to honor the victims; I understand someone is about to say a few words."

Eduardo recognized the curly haired young man who'd led the chanting at the barrier the night before as he stood up and came forward. He'd traded in his CXD-emblazoned sweatshirt for a button-down shirt and navy blazer and seemed subdued and respectful. The reporter offered him the microphone.

"I'm Jude Monroe, president of the Interfraternity Council and Communications Chair for the Student Senate. We, representatives of the student body of this university, send our condolences to the family of the marshal who died. But we cannot ignore that this explosion was planned—meant to distract us from the food shortages that continue nationwide and especially to turn our attention from the civilian deaths that occurred during the food riot last week in our neighbor quadrant, OP-441. This tragedy happened on our campus, and it's our duty as citizens to call attention to the real problem.

"The marshals at OP-441 were more concerned about having enough food for themselves than about helping the people who were there to claim the food that was rightfully theirs."

The hapless Jeremy Howard tried to retrieve his microphone, but several members of the crowd rose to hold him back.

"Essential Services still hasn't resumed deliveries here, so no one's getting any food except through markets like the one over on the green. The president lifted the Restriction, so the QM can't legally shut it down, but they're trying to intimidate us and keep us away. Without the market, how are we supposed to eat? This emergency has prompted us to take action. We will occupy this space and declare the university green a Restriction-Free Zone!"

He raised his clenched left fist to show the CXD symbol written on his hand. At his signal, people in the crowd raised banners and signs showing the CXD symbol and everyone began to chant, "Enough for us!"

The reporter broke free from his captors as Jude shouted over the crowd, "Anyone who wants to trade is welcome here!"

After a brief tussle, he reclaimed the microphone. "Umm … this is Jeremy Howard reporting live in OP-439. Back to you, Pete."

Chapter 7

3:45 PM
Quadrant DC-001

President Christopher Wright looked out his window at the protesters that had gathered on the sidewalk outside the White House gate. Though they were behaving peacefully, he felt a need to circle the wagons. Lifting the Restriction on food sales and distribution had been a bold move, but it wasn't going to be enough to solve the problem.

He summoned his personal secretary. "I want an update on the food shortages. Not the update Essential Services gives to reporters; I want the actual facts and statistics, and a breakdown of the death toll. How many died from malnutrition or starvation? How many have been killed fighting over food? And how many perished in the riots at OP-441? Tell them I'm expecting a response within the hour." The secretary hurried out, closing the door behind her.

How could he have continued to eat regular meals in the midst of the food shortage? Maybe at one point in his career that wouldn't have bothered him, but now it certainly did. He'd skated through his presidency, trusting the OCSD to respond to all crises—until now. Since Lowell Stratford's death, he'd resolved to spend his remaining months in office shaping a respectable legacy. He didn't want to be remembered as the guy who was in charge during the debacles of November 2034. He wanted to be remembered as the leader who got the country back on track.

Ten years ago, after a particularly nasty strain of bacteria was released in one hundred grocery stores, it had seemed necessary to let the OCSD oversee food distribution. People had clamored for more safeguards on the nation's food supply; they'd been enthusiastic about not having to spend time shopping at supermarkets. In accordance with Lowell Stratford's recommendation, retail grocery stores passed into the control of the newly formed Essential Services Department. Convenience stores and gas stations were no longer allowed to sell food. He'd had no idea the Essential Services Department's food delivery system was vulnerable to collapse until it was too late.

Lifting the Restriction was sure to create disorder in the short run. Many people couldn't afford to buy supplemental food, and there was no system in place to refund the automatically debited payments for food that people had not received.

He should have lifted the Restriction as soon as the Essential Services deliveries were delayed. Now the only thing he could do was attend the upcoming memorial service for those who lost their lives during the riot at OP-441. It felt like too little, too late.

President Wright was one of the most powerful people in the free world, but he was never meant to be the sole decision-maker in any crisis. That sort of presidential power only existed in schoolchildren's politics. When he was newly elected, it had been a relief to let Stratford, the experienced OCSD director, take the lead on the nation's never-ending security issues. It had been a jolt to realize that, over time, Stratford had usurped most of his power and attained so much influence over the other branches of government that no one dared challenge his authority.

Madalyn Davies lacked her predecessor's ability to micromanage any situation, but her lust for power eclipsed Stratford's, and that made her a dangerous adversary. She didn't hesitate to make threats when she was challenged or criticized. He couldn't afford to have her challenge his decision to lift the Civilian Restrictions. She'd recently threatened to fabricate a terrorist attack so she could lay the blame for lax security standards on him.

He'd feared the bombing in OP-439 was exactly that—Madalyn's retribution for his lifting the Restriction. But what else could he do? People had been in danger of starving. Madalyn was insisting the Restriction be put back in place, because the private food distributors were hampering the government agency's efforts to get back on track.

Would it be possible to oust her? She'd come into that position only because Stratford had named her his assistant director, a post that had been vacant since she became director of the OCSD by default. Stratford had been too powerful. He could've had Wright impeached—or assassinated—with a wave of his hand.

It would be prudent to appoint a new assistant who was qualified to take over should Madalyn be forced to step down. Right away, Brandon Renald came to mind. Renald was a six-term senator from the Southwest who chaired the Subcommittee on Crime and Terrorism and did two tours in Afghanistan during the Fourth Gulf War. He would be a true asset to the OCSD, bring some actual experience to the job. A new, energetic presence at the OCSD was just what was needed to shake things up a little.

Chapter 8

4:00 PM
Quadrant BG-098

Tommy came downstairs from his parents' room and lurked in the back of the sitting room. He hoped he could catch an update on PeopleCam before anyone else noticed he was there.

Pete Sheridan led off at the top of the hour. "Authorities continue to piece together what really happened last night in OP-439. The nation's interest centers on the young woman discovered in the rubble after the blast, who is believed to be the bomber. She is reportedly still unconscious, in critical condition. There is no telling when she will be well enough to answer questions."

Sheila Roth added, "Until then, we'll just keep rehashing all the pieces of the puzzle until they start to make sense."

Pete nodded. "Though there is a suspect in custody, members of the grassroots organization known as CXD support the theory that it was actually quadrant marshal Wesley Carraway, acting on orders from the OCSD, who set off the explosion to frighten people away from the barter-friendly market that had just opened across the street. Though this has been stringently denied by a spokesperson for the OCSD, we must ponder the possibilities presented by that theory. Was Carraway the perpetrator of the bombing and an accidental victim of his own actions?"

"Most perplexing, Pete."

"We'll have more on the story as the investigation continues."

Tommy glanced across the room; Mitch was leaning against the doorway to the back hall, staring daggers at him.

The last thing Tommy wanted was a confrontation. He retreated upstairs.

Madalyn Davies led the way down a hospital corridor and stopped outside the door flanked by two armed guards. She barely glanced at her companion. She was in a hurry to see for herself the girl who lay inside. She pushed open the door and stepped into the dimly lit room. It was her. Undeniably. She recognized her regardless of the cuts and bruises and the bandage that covered part of her head. Madalyn felt a rush of triumph as she crossed the room to stare down at Careen Catecher, darling of the Resistance, fettered in soft restraints and hooked up to an IV line and a softly beeping monitor. She was no longer a threat to Madalyn's power. More like a mouse to be toyed with before the kill.

"Welcome, Careen. It's a pleasure to meet you under these circumstances."

Careen kept her gaze down and her breath came in short gasps, which made it easy to visualize her as an animal caught in a trap.

"You dirty little terrorist," Madalyn whispered, leaning over the bed. "Thought you had everyone fooled, didn't you? But you made a big mistake when you set off that bomb and killed a quadrant marshal."

"Was it really only one?" Tears spilled down her cheeks.

What does she mean by that? "Wasn't one enough to make your point?" When Careen didn't answer, Madalyn dug in with wicked glee. "Your capture is the biggest news since Lowell Stratford's murder. When it came to light that you were nothing more than a common terrorist, the public quickly changed its opinion of you, and I'm pleased to inform you that you've fallen from popularity. Even your criminal cohorts in the so-called Resistance don't want anything to do with you." Madalyn reached out to touch the strands of hair that peeked out from the bandage. "Pink highlights are *so* out of fashion."

The girl's trembling silence fed Madalyn's desire to flaunt her power. "Your fate rests with me, Careen. I could see to it that you stand trial for the murder of Wesley Carraway and the university bombing, and also for conspiring to assassinate Lowell Stratford. I could have you locked away for the rest of your life. You could be put to death for your crimes. I could even say you were killed while trying to escape from prison. But you'd be much more valuable to me in another capacity."

"I don't understand."

Either way, I win. "You could come work for the OCSD." She paused for effect. "As the spokesperson for the OCSD's new safety initiative."

Careen's face contorted and Madalyn sneered. "Oh, don't look so devastated. The Resistance is finished. The new security program encourages people to take responsibility for their actions. You'll be doing exactly what you were doing before. You'll just be doing it for me. So let's write the next chapter in your story, Careen. What's it going to be? Convicted terrorist … or celebrity?"

She was silent much longer than Madalyn expected. When she raised her head, one last tear slid down her cheek. "All right. I'll do it."

Madalyn nodded. "Fine. Let's begin right now."

Careen gulped and held up her gauze-swathed hands as best she could in the soft restraints. "Could you please take these off?"

Madalyn shook her head. "You've been combative. It says on your chart that you pose a danger to yourself and others. I'll need to see some cooperation first. How long have you been a member of the Resistance?"

"I'm not."

Madalyn pressed her lips together in a hard line before she spoke. "We both know better than that, don't we? If you're going back on our bargain already, I'll have you transported to prison. Now give me the name of every member of the Resistance."

Careen kept her eyes averted. "I can't."

"You were in hiding with them for weeks, weren't you?"

"It's just … well, I wasn't allowed in any of the meetings. I worked in the kitchen at their headquarters in exchange for a safe place to stay. They used code names when they referred to each other in front of me. They used me in the videos because I was already … umm, sort of well known. All I did was read those scripts they gave me."

"So the Resistance exploited your notoriety to gain sympathy for their cause? Of course they did. But how did you find them?"

"They found me. After the press conference at the OCSD, I escaped from the security guards and got out of the building. I was running across the parking lot when a black car pulled up, and a man jumped out and grabbed me. They took me to Resistance headquarters."

"Where?"

"I don't know. We drove at night and arrived when it was still dark. Once I was there, I wasn't allowed to go outside."

"Did they force you to bomb the student center at the university, or did you volunteer to do it?"

"I don't know." Careen glanced up, and Madalyn glared at her until she shrank back against the pillows and began to babble. "I'm sorry! That part's all mixed up. I heard someone say I was in an explosion? Is that why I'm in the hospital?"

Madalyn pounced again. "How do you explain the photo of you with three girls that posted on PeopleCam? Were they members of the Resistance, too?"

"Oh, that … no. They were just … we stopped for gas and—"

"I find it difficult to believe that the Resistance's security detail let you be photographed with a bunch of teenagers. During the day. When you just told me you traveled at night."

The girl quailed even more. "I only remember that it didn't seem like a big deal at the time."

"Think hard, Careen. You must know the names of some of the people in the Resistance—like Tom Bailey, for instance?"

Her eyes flicked away. "No."

"I see." Madalyn turned on her heel and stalked out of the room. Art Severson was waiting where she'd left him in the hall, and as soon as the door closed behind her, she spat out, "She's lying. How dare she lie to me! Tom Bailey is on the loose and he's a huge liability. You came crawling back here with information about Careen, but I haven't forgotten that you were the one who let the Baileys get away. You were supposed to report back after you completed the job, and I never heard from you!"

"How many times do I have to explain that I was locked up in that Podunk jail for over a week? You could've sent someone to look for me."

"I had enough to worry about, don't you think? What if Tom goes back to his verbal attacks on the OCSD? What if he blabs about being detained? Do I tell Garrick to send marshals out to arrest people who are supposed to be dead? I need to get him back in custody ASAP. And the girl obviously knows where he is."

"Why don't you just dose her? Surely there's still a bottle of CSD around here somewhere. That'll speed things up."

"No. I want her to remember every single humiliating moment of her interrogation. I don't want her to have any excuses for betraying her friends and bringing about the demise of the Resistance. CSD won't be necessary by the time we're through with her." She called a nurse over. "When we're finished with this patient, sedate her and prepare her to be moved."

Art opened the door and followed Madalyn back inside. Careen's eyes grew wide at the sight of him.

"Hello, Careen. Surely you remember me?"

The heart rate monitor in the corner began to beep rapidly.

Art smiled. "I understand you're confused about a few details? Maybe I can help. You weren't traveling with strangers the day we met. You were with the Bailey boy. In fact, unless I'm mistaken, you'd known him long enough to be living with him. Long enough to infiltrate the OCSD building with him to try and rescue his parents."

Madalyn raised an eyebrow. "Tell the truth or our deal's off."

Her tears started again. "All right—yes! Tommy helped me once, and in return I went with him to the OCSD to help rescue his parents. When we didn't find them there, we left and kept looking." She addressed Art. "A security guard told Tommy that Tom and Lara were with you. When we got back to OP-439, he went to see someone who told him where you'd taken them."

Madalyn sneered. "And somehow you found the time to murder Lowell Stratford while you were trespassing inside the OCSD building. Where is your accomplice? Where is Trina Jacobs?"

Careen's arm tensed against the restraint. "I don't know."

Chapter 9

5:00 PM
Quadrant BG-098

Mitch had grown weary of the hushed voices and sympathetic looks from the group assembled at the boardinghouse, and he'd gone back to the diner where he could watch the news in peace. The programming was all coverage of the university bombing, with inferences designed to malign the Resistance and signal that the OCSD had things under control. Mitch didn't worry too much about hits to the Resistance's reputation. There was no such thing as bad press, after all. The bright spot in this debacle was that the OCSD's hold on the people was starting to crumble. Those little cracks and fissures would eventually topple the OCSD once and for all. Away from the others, he was free to rejoice in the progress.

Lara arrived to prepare dinner, and he followed her into the kitchen. When she faced him, he saw in her eyes the spark of extraordinary intelligence that had been absent during her episode of amnesia.

He smiled down at her, something he could only do when they were alone. "I didn't know if you'd *ever* remember."

"I remember everything."

"Then I wasn't sure if you'd be able to play it cool. I was afraid you'd—"

"Mitch, I was an amnesiac. I was never an idiot." She turned on the oven. "Although it's probably lucky my memory came back when you weren't around, or I might have slipped up."

"Do you still have you-know-what stored someplace safe?"

She smiled wryly. "My own head wasn't safe enough, was it? But to answer your question … yes. I do. I hope." Her demeanor changed. "We can't access it now, so let's deal with the current crisis.

I'm very concerned about Careen. It surprises me that you don't seem to feel the same."

"Hell yes, I'm worried about her. I'm worried she'll spill her guts and ruin everything. I'm worried that when they announce they've got her in custody, people will either feel sorry for that poor, defenseless girl or convince themselves she was a terrorist all along. Either way, they'll forget how ineptly the OCSD handled the food shortage."

5:28 PM
Quadrant DC–001

Chief Quadrant Marshal Hoyt Garrick waited impatiently in Madalyn's outer office. She had demanded a five o'clock meeting to discuss the manhunt down in the BG quadrants. He'd arrived on time, but she was nowhere to be found.

Marshals had combed the rural, mountainous area for Resistance members after Careen Catecher's phone pinged off a communication tower two days ago. But it was just a blip, active for about two minutes. There was no way to tell which way she was moving. There were nearly a thousand two-mile-square quadrants in the sparsely populated BG sector. That was a lot of rugged ground to cover in a house-to-house search, especially without a solid idea of where to begin.

Garrick had decided Madalyn's obsession with finding and arresting Trina Jacobs was fueled by her need to perpetuate the lie that it was Trina, and not Madalyn, who'd poisoned Lowell Stratford.

He wandered into her office, opened up the fully stocked bar, and mixed himself a Manhattan.

He'd poured a second drink by the time Madalyn strode in, phone to her ear.

"As I've stated before, Transitional CSD was meant to foster a calm, cooperative atmosphere. The riots and uptick in crime in response to the food shortage were the exact opposite of the intended result. Yes. Now that people have stopped panicking, everything's going to be just fine. Please direct further inquiries to Victor Martel at Essential Services." She disconnected the call with an impatient sigh.

"Essential Services up and running again?"

"Should be in a few more days."

"What's the holdup this time?"

"Deliveries cannot resume until more food becomes available. Essential Services doesn't have what they need to provide meals that meet the established nutritional standards. Many of the suppliers they rely on began working with former black market dealers."

"The reports of problems and shortages have fallen off to next to nothing. You should be glad everyone's got something to eat. Aren't you glad they've stopped rioting and panicking?" He took a gulp from his glass. "You wanted to see me? Half an hour ago?"

She dismissed his questions with a flick of her wrist. "Something took longer than I expected. Finding Trina Jacobs is also taking longer than I expected."

"They're searching BG as fast as they can. What else would you suggest?"

"That's *your* job! I've been questioning the suspect in the university bombing."

"Got a name yet?"

"Of course I do. It's Careen Catecher."

He whistled. "How about that?"

"I've decided not to release her identity yet."

"Forensics found traces of blood on the gun, and they rushed it through DNA matching at the lab. One sample was the security guard, but the other belonged to Thomas Bailey, Junior, age eighteen, from OP-439."

"Really?" Madalyn sat on the edge of the desk. *Tom's son was the third person at the scene?* "About Tom Bailey ..."

"His father was an activist, outspoken against Stratford's policies. He and his wife were killed in an auto accident last summer. It made the news. Do you remember?"

"Yes, I remember." She'd hoped she'd never have to deal with this particular issue. "What if I told you the Baileys are alive?" She went on in a rush before he had time to speak. "They faked their own deaths. They've been in hiding, and Tom is leading the Resistance.

Obviously, we have to make sure we control how the Bailey name … umm, finds its way back into the media."

"How'd you find out about all this?"

"I have my sources. Now that we know their approximate location, we must apprehend them. If Tom Bailey decides to make any kind of public appearance, he could be an even greater threat to the OCSD than Trina Jacobs."

"So what about a BOLO on the kid?"

"Hold on that. It won't be long until Careen tells us exactly where to find the Resistance."

Chapter 10

6:41 PM
Quadrant DC-001

Kevin spent the day locked in a room so luxurious that he could almost forget his freedom had been taken from him, except that doing nothing was driving him crazy. There was no television. No books. Not even a clock. He was exhausted but afraid to let his guard down and sleep.

His stomach churned and his mouth watered—a sure precursor to nausea. He tried to think of something else, but his stomach was at the forefront of his concerns. He couldn't recall when he'd last eaten. The OCSD had gone to a lot of trouble to make his prison look like an upscale hotel room. They could've at least put in a minibar and stocked it with some candy and nuts. Alcohol would be good, too. And Alka-Seltzer.

Trina and Mitch must be wondering why he hadn't checked in. He sank down on the tufted velvet sofa, heedless of the dried mud and grime that clung to his clothes. At least he was finally dry. He relaxed into the deep cushions and leaned his head back.

The click of the lock brought him back to full alert, and he leapt to his feet.

A woman in a brown suit came inside and closed the door, a Styrofoam to-go box and a bottle of water in her hands. She set the food on the coffee table and shrugged, almost like an apology. "She forgot about you. But I didn't."

He sat down again. "You're her assistant."

She nodded. "I'm Nicole. You used to work here, right?"

"Yeah."

"So I guess you understand what it's like, don't you?"

He looked at her for a long moment. "Yeah, I do."

She perched on the edge of the sofa and dropped her voice to a whisper. "Madam Director doesn't think about anyone else." What she'd just said was treacherous, even if it was true. "What I mean is, she's so busy trying to protect *everyone*, she doesn't think about *anyone*." Her eyes darted around the room. "I don't know how to explain it, exactly."

"I know. She doesn't focus on individuals—other than herself. Thank you for thinking of me. I was getting hungry."

"The staff eats all their meals here. There's plenty."

Of course there would be. He forced the horrors of the nationwide food shortage to the back of his mind and opened the bottle of water. "Can you stay for a while? Keep me company?"

"Oh, I shouldn't. She'll be angry if she needs me for anything and I'm not there." She hugged herself for a brief moment and consciously relaxed her shoulders.

"Is there any way you could get me some clean clothes? It's been a rough week."

"I'll see what I can find." She left the room, and he opened the container of food. There was a generous scoop of chicken salad on a bed of lettuce and tomato ready to be transferred onto a split croissant, a shiny red apple, and corn chips. *Corn chips! I've been craving them since ... forever. Have they had them here all along?*

He was halfway through the meal when she returned and laid a folded uniform on the sofa beside him. He almost choked on a mouthful of food. "I was thinking you'd bring a pair of coveralls or scrubs and a lab coat. Do they just leave security guard uniforms lying around?"

"My friend works in the laundry. This was all they had ready right now."

"Well, then I guess it'll do."

Chapter 11

9:02 PM
Quadrant DC-001

The cymbal crash was so loud and unexpected that Careen jerked convulsively. Her head rolled from side to side on the pillow as if to escape the noise, but her eyelids were too heavy to hold open more than a slit. She could see nothing in the dark space. The crashes increased in volume and intensity.

"Turn it off." Her voice was slurred, muted. "Please turn it off."

A stinging slap came out of the heavy darkness; Careen's eyes flew open, and, still disoriented, she squinted as someone shined a light in her face.

"Wake up!"

She turned her face away and whoever it was slapped her again, harder, across her other cheek. She tried to put up her hands to defend herself, but the metal links on the restraints clanked against the bed rails and kept her from lifting her gauze-wrapped hands more than a few inches. When the cymbal crashes stopped, a woman's voice came from the darkness beyond the flashlight beam, harsh and unfamiliar.

"Let's start with something easy. Who bombed the student center?"

"I—I did."

"What kind of explosives did you use?"

"I don't know."

"Who helped you prepare the explosives?"

"No one."

Another slap.

"Why are you lying to protect people who don't care about you? The Resistance won't help you. They were just using you. Were you really that stupid?"

Stop listening, a calm inner voice whispered. *Tommy won't leave you here. Lara and Tom won't leave you here. They'll figure out a way to help you. You just have to hang on until then.*

Another slap silenced her thoughts.

"Who bombed the university student center?"

Careen drew a sobbing breath. "I did."

"What kind of explosives did you use?"

"Umm … dynamite."

"Who helped you?"

"I don't know." She could sense another slap coming so she cried, "I never knew her name!"

"Where is Trina Jacobs?"

"I don't know."

"Where is the headquarters of the Resistance?"

"I don't know."

"You must know what quadrant?"

"No one ever told me where we were."

"What kind of explosives did you use?"

"I don't know."

"You don't know? Does that mean you lied before?"

Careen pressed her lips together and steeled herself for a slap that didn't come.

Instead, the woman stepped into the light and unbuckled the straps across Careen's legs and abdomen, unhooked the soft restraints from the rails, and dragged her out of bed.

Chapter 12

9:30 PM
Quadrant OP-439

When Danni had arrived in OP-439 that afternoon, she'd avoided getting anywhere near the PeopleCam news crew set up outside the Caution tape. She unloaded a shipment of food that was immediately put out for trade in her customers' stalls. Marshals made their presence known outside the taped-off area but kept their distance.

She hung around as the day went on, watching the crowd swell inside the Restriction-Free Zone. When students who'd been reluctant to be part of the initial takeover saw nothing bad was happening to the CXD members who'd organized the flagrant act of defiance, they joined in, and by dinnertime the Zone took on a party atmosphere. Someone ran an extension cord from a nearby building and rigged up a sound system, and music blasted across the college green. Footballs and Frisbees sailed over the crowd. When it grew dark, people stood in groups around trash-barrel fires, some sipping coffee and eating from vendors' stalls, others passing flasks.

Now, Jude Monroe conferred with the PeopleCam reporter before he raised the yellow tape and allowed him and the camera operator to enter. Danni followed them, eavesdropping.

"CXD is about nonviolent civil disobedience plus community spirit—like, helping each other. Careen Catecher said to avoid breaking the law, but when the laws are unjust—or just plain stupid —we must respectfully choose a different course of action. That's why we've created this Restriction-Free Zone here at the university."

The camera operator panned across the crowd gathered inside the designated space. "What goes on inside the Restriction-Free Zone?"

"We're not doing anything wrong—just ignoring rules that curtail our personal freedoms. This market is always open, and we can meet friends here and stay out past nine o'clock. We're organizing live music for tomorrow. This is exactly the kind of thing Careen meant when she encouraged civil disobedience in her last message.

"We expected her to condemn the university bombing. She was a student here, and we're proud that one of our classmates has taken on such an important role in the fight for our personal freedoms."

"Isn't personal freedom just breaking the law?"

"No. It's much more than that. Jeremy, you've been on this story from the beginning. You know the real issue is the food shortage. Essential Services was our only way to get food. But that's not protecting us right now. It's hurting more people than it's helping." He addressed the camera operator. "Make sure you get a shot of all the food. Show how well we eat in the Restriction-Free Zone."

11:00 PM

The Zone showed no sign of shutting down. Danni was sharing sips from her flask with a couple of guys when she saw Jude duck under the Caution tape and stride off into the shadows. She excused herself and followed him as he left campus, headed down a deserted side street for several blocks, and turned into an alley. *This kid needs to take a lesson in self-preservation. I'm not even trying to hide the fact that I'm tailing him.*

"Jude."

Danni chuckled as he whirled around, startled. Most people didn't like it when you sneaked up on them in dark alleys, but Jude Monroe had more reason to be jumpy than most.

"Oh, hey. I'm gonna set up for the meeting. You coming?"

"Yeah."

He unlocked a padlock on the back door of a building, and she followed him inside. He pulled a lighter from his pocket and lit several candles, casting a soft glow around the neglected storeroom.

"I'm not gonna hold meetings in the Zone, you know? Most of the people there are just checking it out, seeing what it's like to break the Restrictions. And that's cool. CXD meetings are for people who are serious, you know?"

Danni perched on an upended crate and offered him the flask. "You totally surprised me. I didn't think you were serious at all. I thought you were just a candy-ass frat boy, especially when you asked about becoming affiliated with our national organization—like the Resistance and CXD are campus clubs or something. But you killed it on the news. And the Restriction-Free Zone thing is brilliant. The Resistance is wishing they thought of it."

He took a swallow. "When I decided I couldn't just sit around doing nothing anymore, I called my grandpa. He was involved in tons of protests when he was young, and he gave me some great ideas. Two of my best friends have disappeared since Distribution Day. One's dead; the other one's just gone. Ben and Drew weren't activists or troublemakers or anything. They were just regular guys. Drew's parents have made inquiries, but the QM isn't required to give them any information. For all we know, Drew's in a jail cell somewhere, or worse—dead, like Ben Sheridan."

She nodded, wondering what it would be like to talk about her own loss with someone nice, like Jude.

"Even after I literally lost my friends, I didn't speak out until Essential Services stopped feeding me. I was ticked that I had to come to the market and trade my vintage vinyl collection for something to eat. I kept waiting for someone else to do something, until I couldn't wait anymore. But you—you're doing something."

Danni shrugged. "Someone's got to rally the troops while the others get the glory."

"I can help. I belong to a couple national campus organizations, and that means I have contacts all over the country. If you want them, you'll have more willing protesters than you know what to do with. Everyone's heard of Careen."

Man, I wish I could say she was stupid enough to get herself caught and accused of something she didn't do for the second time this month. "She hasn't been around long enough to actually get her hands dirty."

"But she knows what she's talking about."

"You seem to think she's, like, model student by day, superhero by night. But she's not. Trust me."

A girl and two guys burst through the door, setting the candles flickering. All three were out of breath, but one of the guys gulped and spoke.

"QM. After you left … came and tore down the Caution tape. Scared everyone away."

"Was the news crew still there?"

"Yeah. They filmed the whole thing."

10:30 PM

Henry Nelson crept up to the vacant storefront. This was the perfect clandestine meeting spot—on a side street, in a cluster of boarded-up buildings, half a block from the nearest street lamp. It was more than an hour past curfew, so no one was about. No one who was obeying the law, anyway. He'd arrived after the time noted on the slip of paper he'd retrieved from the trash that morning, so as not to tip off whoever was gathering there. Now that the Zone had been shut down, he hoped he'd be able to trap the instigators and shut down this nonsense for good.

The glass in the front door was dirty; he couldn't get a good look inside. It was risky to go in without his service weapon, but he was there undercover. Unofficially, of course.

He grimaced as he pushed open the door and stepped into the darkness. Wes would have relished this kind of investigation. As his eyes adjusted, he could see a faint glimmer of light, somewhere deep in the recesses of the building. He pulled out his flashlight and, covering most of the beam with his hand, pointed it at the floor as he worked his way past office furniture and storage shelves that loomed eerily in the shadows.

The hum of voices rose as he approached the rear of the building. He moved forward a little too eagerly and brushed up against a desk. Something—a stapler, maybe—crashed to the floor, sounding ten times louder than it would have in the daytime. The voices hushed, and he heard a flurry of movement. Nelson cursed himself as he hurried to the door at the back of the main room. A rush of cold air hit him as he opened it.

Crates and plastic chairs were arranged in a cluster, and the sulfury smell of recently snuffed candles hung in the air. An apple core that had been picked nearly clean lay discarded on one of the crates. The draft was coming from the rear door, which stood ajar.

He crossed the space and poked his head out into the alley. No one was there. As he turned to go back inside, he saw the symbol CXD spray-painted on the cinderblock wall.

Chapter 13

10:40 PM
Quadrant DC-001

Careen's legs wobbled, barely supporting her, and the thin hospital gown afforded little dignity. The links of the short chains dangled from Careen's wrists until her captor cinched them together behind her back and steered her through the darkness. She stumbled, and the woman yanked her arms backward so viciously that she cried out in pain, afraid she wouldn't stop until her arms popped like a doll's from their sockets.

"Shut up!"

Four overhead spotlights powered up, one by one, until Careen was bathed in a circle of light. The rest of the room receded, and she couldn't see into the darkness. The concrete floor chilled her bare feet.

"Next time I ask you a question you're going to tell the truth."

Tommy is still alive. I have to protect him and the Resistance. She waited for the question that never came. Her knees began to shake, and it wasn't long before the trembling spread through her body.

The first time she wavered on her feet it earned her a slap and a barked order: "Hold still!"

She waited for the questioning to start again, but there was nothing but the blinding light. Her legs began to ache and cramp, and she shifted her weight from one foot to the other, seeking relief. That helped for a while, but then she leaned too far, lost her balance, and stumbled a step or two as she tried not to fall.

"Hold still!" Her interrogator was right behind her, shouting in her ear, yanking her upright. Careen winced and let out an involuntary shriek as the woman pulled a black hood over her head. Soon the air inside was stale and suffocating.

"Where is Resistance headquarters?"

The shouted questions became a senseless babble as she repeated over and over, "I don't know."

7:45 AM
Friday, December 1, 2034
Quadrant BG-098

Jaycee, lugging a plastic tub crammed with food and a carafe of coffee, followed Mitch into the boardinghouse. Eduardo and David were asleep in front of the television. She roused them and went upstairs to knock on the others' doors before she set up breakfast in the kitchen. Tommy was the last one to join the group. She tried to catch his eye, but he leaned against the wall and focused on the floor.

Mitch addressed the group. "Look, it's critical that you stay inside until I give you the all-clear. I guess I fed that squad of marshals too well yesterday, because they came back again. Said they'd be here tomorrow, too. We can't take a chance that they'll show up when we're in the middle of a meal or a meeting. Can't have them catching sight of any of you, so you're on lockdown until further notice."

Tom asked, "What exactly does that mean?"

"It's pretty simple. Nobody goes in, nobody goes out except Jaycee. Keep the blackout shades drawn. Have your getaway bags packed and stowed."

"Stowed? Where?"

"There are secret compartments in each of the bedrooms. Jaycee will show you. And she'll bring food."

"What if the QM comes here?"

"We have an advance warning system set up, but it's not a hundred percent foolproof, so you need to have at least one person awake and on watch all the time."

He pointed to a rotary dial phone on a side table in the sitting room.

"If the phone rings twice and then stops, it means they're coming."

Eduardo glanced at Tommy before he spoke. "What about Carina?"

"There's nothing we can do to help her now." Mitch held out his hand. "And I'll take the keys to the truck."

Jaycee saw Tommy grimace as Eduardo tossed the keys to her father.

Mitch pocketed them. "Can't have anyone striking out on their own and bringing the law down on all of us. Sit tight. Pray Careen can't—or won't—tell the QM where to find you."

Jaycee scowled as her dad left the room. He didn't have to frighten everyone like that. "Come on." She motioned for them to follow and led the way downstairs to a padlocked wooden door set in the cellar's stone foundation. "If the phone rings, hide in here."

Tom regarded her skeptically. "How can we lock ourselves in if the lock's on the outside?"

"That's what the QM will think, too. Daddy's sure they won't look closely enough to figure this out." She pulled at a clothesline strung on hooks under the rafters, and the door swung open to reveal a narrow passageway. She stepped inside, and they crowded after her. "Once you're all in, pull this lever here to lock it down."

Trina protested. "But we'll be standing elbow-to-elbow, with the QM just inches away. What if someone sneezes or something?"

In answer, Jaycee slid her fingers into a crevice in the stacked-stone foundation, and part of the passageway's wall slid back. She reached in and turned on a light switch.

David was first into the space and rubbed his hands together in delight. "The perfect spot for a bootlegger's secret cache!"

"Yessir, that's exactly what it is. Daddy always says our family's been bred to enjoy breaking the rules. A secret room like this comes in handy from time to time."

They ran a few practice drills, with different people releasing the catches and locking the doors. When Tom was satisfied they all knew what to do, they went back upstairs.

Jaycee packed the dirty dishes back in the plastic tub. "You gotta keep this place looking like no one's living here. Best you can, anyway. Be ready to hide at a moment's notice." She hefted the tub onto her hip. "I can't leave you any extra food, but I'll bring lunch when I can."

As soon as she was gone, Tom organized a watch schedule.

The first day, Tommy took his turn without complaint and then retreated to Kevin's old room. He couldn't bear sitting in front of the television with everyone else. They'd tell him if there was news of Careen. He tried, without success, not to think about her or Wes.

There was nothing he could do about Wes being dead. But was there really nothing he could do for Careen? The OCSD had yet to announce the bomber's identity, but it had to be her. Where was she? Locked up at the OCSD in the same room his parents had occupied? What were they doing to her? If Mitch hadn't taken the keys to the truck, he'd sneak out and head for the capital on his own.

In the days that followed, the boardinghouse nearly vibrated with nervous tension. Everyone seemed to be sitting on the edge of their seat. Tommy hadn't made his bed since he'd come home from the hospital after the accident the previous August, but now he, like the rest, left his room in spotless order and stowed his spare clothes and personal items out of sight. It was almost a relief when the phone rang during his second watch, and everyone hurried to the secret room just as they'd practiced. They huddled there in complete silence for hours, until Jaycee came to tell them it was safe to go back upstairs.

It took several more hours for his fight-or-flight urges to abate, but as time passed, the sense of urgency and the need to do something gave way to mind-numbing boredom. He lost track of what day it was.

Quadrant DC-001

Careen's entire world was now defined by light and dark. In the past, she'd feared the dark, but now her time in the light brought slaps and shouted questions. Her only means of escape was to retreat inside her head and hope she could hide there until her interrogators gave up. But they never gave up. When they left her alone in the dark, it was just long enough for her to doze off and wake again, disoriented, to loud noises and rough hands dragging her back into the light.

She prayed for strength not to fail. She couldn't betray the Resistance. She owed that much to Wes.

She saved her memories of Tommy for when she was alone, in the dark in-between times. Each time they came for her, she left Tommy behind in the darkness. She didn't want him there with her in the harsh light.

She'd once watched an old movie with her dad about a boxer who was about to fight the reigning champion. He was sure he couldn't win, but he confided to his girlfriend it would be enough if he were able to go the distance. Then he'd be able to respect himself. He wouldn't have failed.

If I go the distance, what's at the end when I get there?

Once, a lifetime ago, she and Tommy had run out of antidote, and they'd been sure they were going to die. She'd cried, and they'd wondered if they'd go to a place like heaven when it was over. They'd been too paralyzed with fear to fight for their lives.

Now that seemed like a joke.

She had to go the distance, even if it meant taking the Resistance's secrets with her into the dark silence of the grave.

10:00 AM
Monday, December 4, 2034
Quadrant BG-098

The marshals didn't show up for breakfast that morning, and by noon Mitch had confirmation that the squad had been called to another part of BG. Lockdown was over, and everyone but Tommy ventured out into the fresh air. Mitch and Jaycee served meals at the diner.

10:50 PM

Jaycee found Tommy lying on his bed in Wes's old room above the diner, staring at the ceiling. She stood in the doorway, waiting for some kind of greeting, but if he'd heard her approach, he gave no sign.

"You didn't eat today."

"Not hungry."

"Well, that's two words you've said to me since you got back." He didn't answer, and she bit her lip. "You don't have to go downstairs. I'll bring you some food from the diner. Whatever you want."

He shook his head.

"Are you all right?"

He kneaded his face with both hands before he spoke. "Everyone keeps asking that. I don't know how I am. I keep wondering why I'm the only one left—again."

She crossed the room to stand at the side of the bed and reached out her hand. "You're not alone."

He sat up and pulled her down beside him, enfolding her in a crushing hug. She caught her breath as he buried his face in her curls and wondered if he noticed how her heart was pounding. *I didn't know a guy could smell this good.* She didn't dare move or do anything that would cause the moment to end.

When he released her, he searched her face in a way that made her wonder what he was looking for. She lifted her chin a little, just in case, hoping he saw what she wanted him to see, but then he mussed her hair the way an older brother might.

"Were you serious about bringing me something to eat? I'm starving."

She hid her disappointment. "Sure. I'll go make you a cheeseburger."

Chapter 14

11:02 PM
Quadrant DC-001

Something prodded Careen's shoulder, and she groaned before she remembered where she was. Rough hands yanked off the hood, pulling her hair. She drew in a grateful deep breath, blinking in the light.

"Get up." It was a man's voice behind her this time.

At first her body didn't respond, but a sharp blow across her back made her try harder. She managed to kneel by pressing her forehead against the floor for balance. She wobbled as she tried to stand and fell onto her already-bruised knees. Getting up was impossible with her hands secured behind her.

"I need help."

He grasped her upper arm and hauled her roughly to her feet. Then he shoved her before she could get her balance, and she cried out as she sprawled on the floor again.

"Why would I help you when you won't help us?"

She curled her knees into her chest, prepared to try for a sitting position, but he placed his boot between her shoulder blades and pressed down hard. She fought, panicking, the pressure of his foot forcing her to take tiny breaths. Before long, black snow flew around the edges of her vision, and she felt herself sinking, yielding, as the darkness closed in. *It's okay. Just … let it happen.*

Then the weight was gone, and she gasped for air, feeling as panicked and helpless as a landed fish.

"The Resistance hasn't come to save you. They've given you up for dead. It's just you and me." Again she felt his boot against her back. "Who bombed the student center?"

"Me."

"Why did you kill the quadrant marshal?"

"That was an accident." She couldn't hold back the tears of regret that flowed for Wes.

"Where is the Resistance's headquarters?"

"I don't know."

"Where is Trina Jacobs?"

"I don't know."

He pressed his boot down, and she whimpered as her bones shifted in ways she knew they shouldn't.

"Where is Trina Jacobs? Where is the Resistance?"

"I don't know." He removed his foot just long enough for her to fill her lungs and then pressed down harder still. She was barely conscious when he released the pressure and kicked her onto her side.

11:15 PM
Quadrant BG-098

Jaycee laid the cheeseburger next to a pile of golden French fries in the Styrofoam to-go box. She'd never thought of using food to show someone she cared about them—until now. She grabbed a few napkins and was about to push through the swinging door to the dining room when she heard her dad's voice.

"My whole base of operations is here. I won't just go someplace else."

"Won't? Or can't? Is it true what Danni said about you being agoraphobic?"

She crept back to the other doorway to peek through the crack, unable to resist the opportunity to eavesdrop on her dad and Mr. Bailey.

Her father sat at the counter while Tom paced the aisle beside him.

Mitch grunted. "I don't go to town. So what? Lots of people don't like being around other people. Everything that's important to me is right here." He gestured about grandly. "This is the main communication hub of the Resistance."

"This is a run-down diner in the middle of nowhere. We're sitting ducks if the QM comes back."

"Even if you happen to get caught, I'll be fine."

"What makes you assume you won't be caught, too?"

"I've got a network of locals who'll protect me. Besides, I'm too smart to get caught, which is more than I can say for the rest of you. The only one you've got to protect you is me." He smirked. "No one's ever heard of Mitch Carraway. I'm just some hick who owns a run-down diner in the middle of nowhere. When the QM comes snooping around, will you rat me out and show them all my high-tech gadgets and toys? No. You can't, because I've never shown them to you. You can't prove I'm involved in the Resistance any more than you can prove I—"

"What?"

"Aww, nothing."

Jaycee shrank back from the doorway as Mitch got up from the counter. He poured himself a cup of coffee, and the clatter of the carafe against the burner masked the swish of the swinging door as Jaycee grabbed the to-go box and headed for the back stairs.

11:34 PM

Ever since Tommy's return, Tom's instinct had been to evacuate everyone to someplace safer. The lockdown system was bound to fail eventually. But where could they go? A wrong move would further jeopardize the safety of his family and everyone in the Resistance. But Mitch had been obstinate in his refusal to consider leaving. Tom knew the OCSD would interrogate Careen, and he was all too familiar with their methods from his own time as their prisoner. It was only a matter of time before the OCSD knew exactly where to find them.

When Mitch turned back from the coffeepot, his face was alight with something like a patriotic fervor. "It was you who gave me the idea. This revolution was set on course the first time I heard you speak. All of a sudden, I knew what I had to do. You were going to make us *both* legends.

"You said: 'When we relinquish our freedoms and liberties, we should not believe the loss is temporary. It is very difficult to regain them once they are taken. A wake-up call to the public is long overdue. We must be prepared to spin, deceive, or manipulate if it champions the cause. Revolution means breaking the law and using force if necessary. Casualties are to be expected.' I knew if I was out there working the same angle, I could push you and our cause to even greater heights."

"How do you remember that speech? It was years and years ago."

Mitch chuckled. "I never forgot it. I was surprised how much it bothered me when you got all the notoriety, though. You were taking on Stratford toe to toe, and I wanted to be in the fight with you. But then I realized I could accomplish my part behind the scenes. I was better off here.

"Right after you gave the speech there was a string of attacks that *really* got everybody's attention. What did you think about them?"

Mitch was dying to brag about his own accomplishments, and Tom was suddenly afraid of knowing too much. He tried to appear nonchalant. "At the time I didn't think they merited quite as big a reaction as they received, but people were on edge. Those attacks weren't the answer to the problem, any more than the food riots are now."

"Those attacks proved the OCSD's incompetence." Mitch looked smug. "You know, they never did finger the right guy."

I was implicated in those attacks. You and I both know they accused the wrong man, don't we? "Those attacks led to the implementation of more Restrictions, so tell me, is the end result what you anticipated?"

"It's not the end yet. I've been building up the Resistance for longer than it's taken to raise Jaycee. I guess you're gonna have to believe me when I say I've got it under control."

Tom felt as though he was being held prisoner all over again. In Mitch's mountain domain, Tom would never be in charge. How could he change the dangerous course Mitch had chosen for this revolution?

Chapter 15

4:37 AM
Saturday, December 2, 2034
Quadrant DC-001

The sounds of screaming and gunfire jolted Careen back to awareness. Her heart pounded, but her bruised and shackled body was otherwise unresponsive.

She opened her eyes, and in the flickering light she saw the familiar video footage of the food riots in OP-441, projected on the wall, larger than life. She tried to turn her face away, but her arms were numb after hours of being forced into the unnatural position behind her back, and without them she couldn't muster the strength to roll over. She closed her eyes to shut out the images. Soon she heard her own voice. It was her first video message, encouraging people to express their opposition to the OCSD's policies and refuse to take CSD. Her chin trembled, and a tear rolled out onto the floor as she looked at herself on the screen. She'd been so naïve to think she could change the world for the better with a short speech on an amateur video. The next clips showed people looting stores during the food riots. She began to sob.

"Poor little you." It was the first woman again. "Feeling bad about what you've done?"

She hiccupped as she fought to control her breathing. "I never meant to—"

"You and your ridiculous nonsense—Join the Resistance! Look at me! I'm so pretty! You led everyone to believe they could do whatever they wanted without consequences."

"It wasn't like that. I didn't—"

"Oh, but you did. And you've forced us to step in and undo all the damage you've caused. How many people did you *really* kill, Careen?"

She flinched at the sound of a single shot on the video.

"Where is Trina Jacobs?"

"I don't know."

Careen felt the video's staccato gunfire in her bones.

8:52 AM
Quadrant BG-098

"What do you think about evacuating?"

Lara stood at the bathroom sink, subduing her curly hair into a ponytail. Tom's image in the mirror went in and out of view as he paced in front of the bathroom door.

"I don't know. We've been okay here so far. You seem to have some thoughts on the matter, though."

"Mitch seems remarkably unconcerned about the OCSD questioning Careen." He stopped pacing, and their eyes met in the mirror. "But we know the kinds of things they'll do to her. How long can she be expected to withstand it?"

She nodded. "I was awake most of the night again, worrying about her."

"Regardless, I'm afraid we don't have much time left before the QM comes around looking for us."

"Where else can we go?"

"That's what we need to decide. With or without Mitch and the others, our family needs to leave."

It was up to her to smooth things out between Tom and Mitch. "He's just upset about Wes's death. He's not rational right now."

"We might not have enough time for him to get rational."

"Tread lightly. We're guests in his home. Let's try to manage it without creating any discord. We need to trust and help each other right now."

"I hope that's possible. People's secrets and ambitions have a way of revealing themselves at inconvenient times."

She smiled benignly, wondering if Tom was alluding to someone other than Mitch. "How about we worry about all this after we've had a cup of coffee?"

She and Tom were the first to arrive at the diner. Mitch, to her relief, appeared to be in good spirits. He'd made a huge breakfast and set it up buffet-style on the counter.

Mitch waved the television remote in greeting. "You gotta watch this." After they'd filled plates, he clicked Play.

Victor Martel, the director of Essential Services, ascended to the podium in front of the press corps in the ballroom of a capital quadrant hotel. One of the reporters stood up to be recognized.

"Do you view people buying and selling food on their own as a threat to Essential Services' system?"

Martel chuckled. "It's not so much a threat as it is a nuisance. The burgeoning private market has diverted the food from our regular suppliers to other sellers which, in turn, created shortages that compromise the Essential Services Department's ability to meet its obligation to the public."

Another reporter raised her hand. "So you still expect us to believe Essential Services is our best option? The former black market dealers and barter-friendly markets are *still* the only thing standing between some people and starvation."

"Using barter to deal with this emergency will not work past the short term. It's not like you can just designate a random thing valuable and use it for trade."

The reporter held her ground. "Of course you can. If people recognize and agree to the value of an item, it can be used as currency. If I had an apple, I could buy an apple's worth of something from anyone who wanted an apple."

"I suppose, but apples don't hold their value in the long term."

"I could spend my apple on anything I wanted. Or I could choose to eat it myself. I have a choice. But I can't choose *not* to pay for an Essential Services delivery that may or may not come."

Another reporter shouted, "Wasn't the bombing in OP-439 just another way to force people to accept the Essential Services system —even if they'd rather not?"

"I don't see how those two events could possibly be related. I have no information about the bombing. Please direct your inquiries to the OCSD's information office. From what I understand, everything is under control."

Several reporters clamored to be recognized.

"Nothing is under control! There are still food shortages and riots."

"People have been picketing in front of the White House, demanding action."

"Restriction-Free zones are popping up all over the country. People who prefer markets over ES want a choice."

Martel drew himself up to his full height. "Essential Services meal plan subscriptions are mandatory. The full delivery schedule will resume by the end of the week. There will be no more questions." He abruptly left the room.

Back in the studio, Pete Sheridan smothered a grin. "A group of protesters had an unmistakable message for Essential Services Director Victor Martel, who literally ended up with egg on his face as he left that press conference in the capital yesterday."

The accompanying video showed protesters, their shirts emblazoned with Careen's CXD symbol, blocking Martel's path as he exited the hotel. Someone threw an egg, which struck his cheek with a splat, and gooey yellow dribbled onto his suit coat.

Someone shouted, "We'll spend this food however we choose!" and the crowd pelted Martel with a barrage of eggs, fruit, and vegetables. He held up his hands to shield his face as he ran for the waiting limousine amid a chorus of "Enough for us! Enough for us!"

Sheila Roth looked wistful. "Oh my! Don't they know not to waste food? Especially the eggs. Egg whites make a wonderful facial masque. Quite a luxury these days, though."

Lara burst out laughing. "Why do they let that woman ad-lib? One of these days she's going to say something really stupid."

The rest of the adults had arrived and were in various stages of filling their plates. Lara made sure to address Mitch during a quiet moment. "The CXD rebellion is a bona fide grassroots movement, thanks to Careen and Danni. If it keeps on like this, it could soon be bigger than the Resistance. Wouldn't you say so?"

Mitch gave her a look that could have been an entreaty to shut up. "There have been a lot of peaceful protests. There's no such thing as bad press; that's for sure."

She nodded. "They're using Careen's symbol. And they seem to be following her suggestions—civil disobedience, nonviolence."

Tom cut in, but without as much diplomacy as Lara would have preferred. "Maybe the Resistance's goals can be accomplished without an all-out war."

Mitch shot him a suspicious glance. "Madalyn's not going to let us win without a war. Here's the other clip I was saving to show you." He cued the video.

Madalyn Davies smirked as she addressed the press corps. "In the two weeks since Lowell Stratford's death, we have been a nation in transition and in crisis. People have been disoriented and confused without their regular doses of CSD. We have experienced an unprecedented surge in civil unrest because of the incendiary actions of a group of dissidents. Food shortages have gone unresolved for much longer than anticipated, because people panicked rather than trusting in the Essential Services department to manage the situation.

"We have spent years reducing contact with other nations as a means of protecting our people. But now it is clear we face dangerous enemies inside our borders, too.

"Tighter security is needed to protect people against future food shortages and terror attacks. This is especially true now that we know terrorists walk among us and will stop at nothing to disrupt our way of life. These homegrown terrorists will make their rebellion sound glamorous. They will try to convince you that the OCSD does not make our nation's security its top priority. Do not be swayed by their lies.

"The suspect in the university bombing is awake and undergoing questioning. Know that the OCSD will not rest until it hunts down every last member of the rebel group responsible for this act of terrorism.

"If you know someone who claims to be sympathetic to the Resistance, it is your duty to report that individual to the quadrant marshals. The OCSD can only maintain the highest level of security when everyone monitors the actions of those around him or her."

Trina reached for another slice of toast. "I don't understand why she's not bragging about having captured Careen. Do you think they're really questioning her? What's the point of withholding her identity?"

"Most likely they don't want all those peaceful protesters storming the castle. But it's not going to matter in the end." Mitch clicked the remote to return to the live morning broadcast. "Careen isn't tough enough to last through a real interrogation. She'll spill the beans, and she'll get what she deserves. It's her fault Wes was killed."

Eduardo gave him a sharp look. "It's not fair to blame Carina. It wasn't her idea to set off the bomb."

Lara's horrified gasp cut off Mitch's reply. She pointed at the screen. "Oh no! No!" An artist's sketch of a young man filled the screen. News anchor Pete Sheridan announced:

"A nationwide manhunt is underway for eighteen-year-old Thomas Bailey, Junior, wanted in connection with the university bombing in OP-439."

Chapter 16

9:35 AM

Tommy rolled over and wrapped his arms around his pillow. It had been days since he'd wakened feeling refreshed. He yawned and opened his eyes, inhaling the breakfast smells that wafted up from downstairs.

Jaycee was curled up in Wes's bed across the room, staring at him. He tugged at his blankets self-consciously. "Jeez! What are you doing here?"

She snuggled in deeper. "Last night I couldn't sleep, so I came in to see if you were still awake. You snore."

"Do not." He threw a pillow at her. "Beat it so I can get dressed. I'm starving."

She giggled and threw it back before she skipped out of the room. He wasn't annoyed with her. Not really. It was kind of fun to treat her like the pesky kid sister he'd never had. If she'd slipped into the other bed in the middle of the night, she must be as rattled by what had happened as he was. Maybe more. She was waiting for him in the hall when he finished brushing his teeth, and as they headed downstairs, angry voices rose above the normal buzz of conversation and drowned out the television.

Jaycee halted and stared up at Tommy. "They're at it again. Our dads were arguing last night. I heard them while I was making your cheeseburger."

"What about?"

"Mostly how your dad isn't as important to the Resistance as mine, and everyone here has to depend on my dad to protect them."

"Ouch. I'm sure my dad loved that." Then he heard his mother's panicked cries, and his dad shouted, "Are you responsible for this?"

Mitch shouted back. "Hell no!"

"You liar! You snake! What is this, an eye for an eye? A son for a brother?"

Tommy ran the rest of the way downstairs, Jaycee at his heels, and burst into the diner just in time to see his dad take a swing at Mitch. Mitch ducked and grabbed Tom by the shirtfront. They grappled, ricocheted off the counter, and knocked over a table across the aisle.

Everyone else scrambled out of the way.

"Stop it! Both of you!" Lara cried.

Mitch hauled Tom off the floor and, still gripping Tom's shirt with his left hand, delivered two stinging punches to Tom's face. Tommy launched himself into the fray, tackling Mitch around the middle and breaking Mitch's hold on his dad. The force spun them around, and as they staggered in the aisle, Mitch's fists pounded Tommy's torso.

Everyone was yelling at once, and Tommy heard David shout, "Someone turn the hose on them!"

Tommy drove Mitch backward, which threw him off balance, and ended up with enough clearance to land punches to his stomach and solar plexus that left Mitch gasping. Before Mitch could rally, Tom and Trina forced their way between them. Tommy let his dad pull him away but fixed an intimidating gaze on Mitch.

He muttered, "Dad, are you nuts? What made you think you could take him? He's got, like, two inches and thirty pounds on you."

Tom turned his back to Mitch as he and Tommy continued their progress across the room. "You're all over the news; you're wanted in connection with the university bombing."

"And you attacked Mitch because … ?"

"I suspect it was he who turned you in. To even the score."

Tommy twisted his arm out of his dad's grip and started back across the room to where Trina stood with a restraining hand on Mitch's chest, but Tom stopped him. "Of course he denied it, but I was the one who lost control. It was my fault. Let's just all take a minute."

His mother joined them and laid her hand on Tommy's arm. He let her lead him to a chair on the far side of the room, where Jaycee appeared with ice wrapped in towels. Tom pressed his to his face; Tommy held his in his hand, not wanting to give Mitch the satisfaction of knowing he needed first aid. After a moment, he tossed the towel on the table and stood up to go. Jaycee edged closer and slipped her chilly hand into his.

From across the room, Mitch's gaze took in both of them, and his nostrils flared as he shouted at Tommy. "Oh, hell no! Don't even think about it."

"What?" Tommy was completely at a loss.

"That!" Mitch pointed an accusing finger. "Lay a hand on her and I'll finish you."

Jaycee dropped Tommy's hand and shrank away, her face flushed. Tommy's anger flared.

"Are you kidding? I wasn't … I wouldn't—she's just a kid!"

He'd only meant to defend her, but apparently Jaycee took it wrong. She burst into tears and ran upstairs.

Chapter 17

10:39 AM
Quadrant DC-001

The quadrant marshals' search of the BG quadrants had yielded nothing. Careen had also failed to yield any more information. The girl had resisted much longer than Madalyn had anticipated. The interrogation team needed to step up their efforts. Extracting the Resistance's location from Careen was essential if the OCSD were to clean up the pending loose ends and move forward.

The Cerberean Link would soon be ready, and Madalyn needed to focus all her attention on bringing the program to fruition. This would be her defining act and the real beginning of her tenure as director of the OCSD.

The idea for the Cerberean Link had first come about when Lowell Stratford was preparing to use CSD to build a civilian army. Conscripting everyone in the eighteen-to-thirty age range would leave most young children unattended. Even stepping up government run day-care programs and extending school days couldn't ensure the children were adequately cared for while their parents were actively engaged in the fight against terrorism.

Stratford had hired a developer to create a device that would serve the many functions needed to protect the children. First and foremost, it monitored health and vital signs, so children who were sick would receive prompt treatment. A GPS tracking system was included to make it easy to locate lost children. The system must also be able to access public records, such as Essential Services and health care plans, to make sure no child was denied anything to which they were entitled.

Soon, the Resistance would be finished, and the Cerberean Link would assure the health and safety of every child in the United States.

"Where is Trina Jacobs?"

The voice jolted Careen into consciousness. Her tangled hair hung in her face, obscuring her vision, and a bit of drool stuck her cracked lips to the floor as she mumbled, "I don't know. Please, can I just sleep?"

The voice was new. Harsh. Male. "No sleep. Where is Trina Jacobs?"

"I don't know."

"Who are the leaders of the Resistance?"

"I don't know."

"What other attacks is the Resistance planning?"

"I told you already; I don't know."

"Who was with you when you blew up the student center?"

"No one."

"Get up."

"I can't."

The interrogator grabbed a fistful of her hair and pulled. Careen whimpered as her neck bent back.

"You will if I tell you to." He slid one heavily muscled arm around her waist, and the other hand gripped her throat as he lifted her off the ground, bracing her against his body. Her pulse pounded in her head and her stomach churned as she struggled to breathe, hands still shackled behind her, feet kicking helplessly inches above the floor. His breath was hot against her cheek.

"You got some fight left in you, girl?" She squeezed her eyes shut. How many strangers had put their hands on her? Her humiliation never blunted; it threatened to crush her spirit each time she was slapped, or worse, groped through the flimsy hospital gown. *Oh, God, I wish I had a gun. Tommy was right all along. If I had a gun, I'd shoot whoever I had to and escape.*

The interrogator sniggered and abruptly released his hold; she lost her balance as her feet touched down. His meaty fist closed around her arm and yanked her upright while she gasped for breath.

"You ready to cooperate?" He slid his hand down her arm; she felt him fumbling between her lower back and her bound wrists, and then her arms fell limply to her sides. She breathed a silent prayer of thanks for the uncomfortable sensation of pins and needles in her hands. There was a long moment when nothing happened.

"Well?" His voice was close behind her.

She shook her head, lips pressed together. *Saying nothing is the only way I can protect everyone.*

He jerked her around to face him and imprisoned both her wrists in one hand, pulling her up on tiptoe. The stench of her own fear filled her nostrils. His mouth twisted into a triumphant smile. Then he laughed.

"Not so sleepy anymore, are you?" He tightened his grip on her wrists to emphasize her helplessness. "You're going to tell us everything we want to know."

Chapter 18

4:00 PM
Quadrant BG-098

Mitch spent most of the day holed up in his office, listening to his scanner for any QM dispatches in the quadrant. It wasn't prudent to give Tom so much time to turn the rest of the group against him, but he couldn't exactly say, 'you're all expendable and you're bound to get caught eventually. Good luck and Godspeed.' He hadn't turned in the kid; he hadn't needed to. He'd known Careen would crack. If she'd given up Tommy's name, she'd surely revealed their location, too.

He hadn't wanted to let the outside world into his haven, but it had been an emergency. Living with this many people was changing Jaycee, and he found it exhausting. Still, he supposed he'd better head off a full-scale mutiny. Everyone but the Baileys was in the sitting room at the boardinghouse, and when he entered the room, it felt like he'd walked into an ambush.

"Mitch!" David's eyes were huge behind his thick glasses. "The marshals are certain to show up here in the near future, so wouldn't it be prudent to evacuate?" He struggled up off the sofa and extended a hand to Grace. "We can't just sit around and wait. I'm not spending my golden years in prison."

Grace clasped his hand and rose to stand beside him. "What's the plan?"

They were testing him to see if he'd step up and lead. Well, let Tom do the heavy lifting for a while. As he walked back out the door without replying, he heard her reassure the group. He glanced over his shoulder as he strode back to the diner to find Grace and David following him down the path. For a couple that had divorced years ago, they had a close friendship. They were a good team. That kind of relationship was foreign to him.

He retreated into the kitchen, which was spotless except for one dirty frying pan on the range. Mitch waited until he heard them in the dining room and then picked it up and threw it into the sink. It landed with a resounding crash just as Grace appeared in the doorway. She cried out in alarm, and he unleashed his anger on the elderly couple.

"What? What are you looking at?"

She looked shaken by his outburst, but her voice was gentle. "Mitch, you have to give yourself time to grieve. No one blames you for being out of sorts. Have you decided what to do about the funeral?"

David cleared his throat as Grace pressed on.

"Your emotions are going to be all over the place. There's no right or wrong way to feel. But remember, what happened to Wes was an accident. It was nobody's fault."

"Wes and Tommy screwed up, and Careen made things even worse."

"Blaming any of those dear children won't change what happened."

"I'll blame whoever I damn well please. Get out and leave me alone."

4:05 PM
Quadrant DC-001

The looping video stopped, and Careen's ears rang in the silence, which seemed almost as loud as the screaming and the gunfire.

She was too exhausted to open her eyes or try to raise her head. Footsteps approached, and she braced herself for more brutal treatment, but the touch on her arm was gentle.

Whoever it was helped her sit up. She looked into the face of a young woman in a QM uniform, who regarded her with concern. "I brought you some water."

The marshal grasped her arm, and Careen winced as she got to her feet; pain shot through her arms and legs as her blood began to circulate more freely. Trembling with fear and fatigue, she didn't resist as the marshal guided her out of the circle of light to a table flanked by two folding chairs. She slumped into a seat, strength sapped by that short walk across the room. The marshal held a cup of water for her to sip, draped a blanket over her shoulders, and sat across from her.

"Careen, Madam Director is very disappointed that you haven't held up your end of the bargain."

The marshal's voice was unexpectedly kind, and Careen's lip began to tremble. She looked down at her bandaged hands lying in her lap. She still didn't know how badly they'd been hurt in the explosion. Why had she survived? "You're going to kill me eventually, so why don't you get it over with? It's not like anyone will ever find out what really happened to me."

"We've been ordered not to kill you. The OCSD directed us to keep you here and question you for as long as it takes. This isn't going to end unless you end it by telling us what we want to know.

"You have the opportunity to help yourself! Why do you keep lying to us? We're going to eliminate the Resistance one way or another, so you might as well tell us where to find them. If you don't help us, you'll face harsher punishment for your own crimes."

A tear slipped from Careen's eye and she let it fall. "But … then everything I've worked for—all the things I believe in, the sacrifices we've already made—will be for nothing."

The young marshal shook her head. "The elite squads that are on their way to the BG quadrants have orders to enter and search every building. It's not the best option, because lots of innocent people could be hurt or killed. If you tell us where to find the Resistance, we can do the job efficiently, with little or no collateral damage. Help us. If the Resistance continues its activities unchecked, many innocent people will suffer. I know you don't want that."

More tears fell with tiny plops onto the bandages. "I can't. I won't. Do whatever." She looked away. *Resistance makes me free. This is the only way I can keep fighting. It's my choice.*

The marshal leaned forward and spoke just above a whisper. "Listen. I'm trying to help you. You don't seem to understand that we've been taking it easy on you so far. You say, 'do whatever,' but there are guys on the interrogation team who are hoping I'll fail so they can have a try at whatevering the information out of you."

The marshal's eyes locked on hers for a long moment. She pulled a small, amber bottle from her pocket and set it on the table between them.

Careen stared at the bottle. She'd never taken Phase Two, but she knew how it affected Tommy and Lara. *If she doses me, I won't be able to control what I say. What can I tell her that won't destroy the entire Resistance?*

The interrogator touched the dropper with her index finger. "Do we need to use this?"

She shook her head. "I didn't realize."

"Didn't realize what?"

"I didn't realize what it would mean to be a part of the Resistance. I didn't know the power my words could have. The CSD riots and the food riots were my fault."

"Everyone in the Resistance is guilty of treason. You didn't act alone."

"If I tell you where to look, promise me they won't be hurt."

"Of course, Careen. I promise. Where will we find them?"

"At a boardinghouse near a diner. In BG ... 098."

"Good, Careen. That's very good. Who will be there? Tell me names."

Bile rose in her throat, and she willed herself not to vomit. *Give her names they already know.* "Trina Jacobs. Tom Bailey. Lara Bailey. David Honerlaw. Grace Hughes ... and," she drew a sobbing breath, "Tommy Bailey."

The interrogator pulled out her phone. Careen watched her key in a number. *Strange that I'm not more upset. I'm just sleepy. Really sleepy.* The black snow clouded her vision and closed over her.

Chapter 19

4:10 PM
Quadrant BG-098

As soon as Grace and David were out the door, Tom hurried into the room and spoke to Jaycee. "We need to evacuate to someplace safer. Will you help us?"

"Daddy doesn't want to leave his land. We should just go to the bunker."

"Bunker? Mitch has a bunker?"

"Well, yeah. Doesn't everybody?"

Eduardo nodded. "Why doesn't that surprise me?"

"Well, it's not just his. It's our family's, and it's been there forever—at least since the Cuban Missile Crisis."

Lara broke in. "Where is it?"

"Over on the other side of the ridge. Takes about an hour to get there."

"Is there room for all of us?"

She glanced around. "Yeah. No problem."

"Then it's settled. Pack up everything you brought with you. Meet back here as soon as possible." Tom laid a hand on Jaycee's shoulder. "We'll count on you to get us there."

Lara and Trina headed to their rooms. David and Grace came back, and Tom drew David aside. Jaycee cocked an ear to listen.

"Can you hang onto something for me?"

"Of course."

Tom handed him a chip drive. "Keep it safe. We might need it in a few days."

David pocketed it, and he and Grace followed Tom upstairs, leaving Jaycee alone with Eduardo.

"Thank you for bringing Tommy back. Now that Wes is dead," she said, swallowing hard to clear the lump in her throat, "I ... we need him." She hurried from the room before her tears began again. She checked upstairs in the boardinghouse and dashed out to the target range, but there was no sign of Tommy. She headed back to the diner to pack a change of clothes and found him seated at her desk reading one of Careen's notebooks. "What are you doing?" She slipped into the room and closed the door.

"I dunno." He looked down at the scribbled handwriting on the page. "She liked writing on paper, not on a computer or tablet."

"Use the present tense when you talk about her, for crying out loud! She's not the one who's dead. Why are you wasting time mooning over her notebook? Everyone's evacuating to our bunker before the QM comes back." She slapped his shoulder to get his full attention. "Let's get out of here right now. You broke into the OCSD once. You can do it again. Take me with you to rescue Careen."

Tommy looked up at her, and she saw none of the energy or sense of humor that had made him so appealing—and so different from the brooding men in her family. He sighed. "Your dad totally flipped out. Don't you think we ought to steer clear of each other for a while?"

"So you're hiding in my room? Great plan."

"I wanted to take a look at some of these books. Careen *cares*," he said, pausing for emphasis, "so much more about this stuff than I did. Now I get it. I could be arrested for being part of the Resistance; how can I be sure I'm doing the right thing unless I know more about ..."

He examined each book before he separated them into two stacks. As he worked, he spied the bracelet with the lock and key that had been his mother's, marking the place in one of the books. He'd given it to Careen on the day they'd fled the OCSD. Now, he let the green stones slip through his fingers before he put it in his pocket.

Jaycee's redheaded temper flared. "Listen, if I have to make the decisions for both of us, then we're doing what I want for a change. Forget about the books and let's go to the capital." She ran out of the room and returned with his packed duffel bag and his gun. With a sigh of resignation, he crammed Careen's notes and a couple of books into the bag and shoved the gun in the back of his waistband.

She grabbed her rifle off its pegs on the wall, stuffed boxes of shells into the pocket of her hoodie, and dragged him out of the room.

She led the way as they hurried downstairs and rounded the

corner into the diner's main room, heading for Wes's black pickup in the parking lot, but stopped short when she heard Trina's pleading voice.

"Mitch, come with us."

"You go. I've got to stay and protect what's mine."

"I'd think you'd be concerned about protecting your daughter. She's coming with us. But fine—stay here if this is what's most important to you." Trina hurried out of the kitchen and paused, startled, at the sight of them. There was an awkward pause before she recovered her poise.

"Oh good! You're here. Let's go meet the others." As Trina shepherded them out the back door, Jaycee caught Tommy's eye, trying to make sure he understood she hadn't changed her mind about leaving.

Chapter 20

5:07 PM

Everyone but Mitch departed from the boardinghouse, each carrying a few extra items of clothing they'd claimed from Mitch's wardrobe during their weeks at Resistance headquarters. Jaycee, who'd never been in charge of anything before, led the way up the wooded path to the ridge while Tommy brought up the rear. They passed the rock where he and Careen had talked and looked up at the stars a week ago, and he half expected to see her sitting there. Under the pretense of tying his shoelace, he lingered long enough that he didn't notice his parents had fallen behind the rest of the group until he heard his mother exclaim, "Tom, no! You can't!"

Tommy strained to see in the fading daylight. His parents stood alone on the trail; his mother was gripping his dad's arm with both hands.

"Lara, I've got to try. Maybe I can convince Madalyn to work out some kind of compromise that will satisfy both the OCSD and the Resistance. While I'm there, I'll do my best to convince her to release Careen."

"But what if she won't listen? What if she arrests you? You've been accused of terrorist activities, too!"

Tommy's stomach clenched with dread as he ran toward them.

"This way, maybe you and Tommy won't have to hide forever. I couldn't stand it if they locked you up again, sweetheart. I'm sorry." She leaned her forehead against his chest, and he stroked her curly hair. "Trust me."

Her laugh was choked with tears. "I always do."

Jaycee came scrambling back down the hill. "What's the matter? We're not even halfway there yet, and it's getting dark." Eduardo and Trina were close behind her, and Grace and David hovered farther up the trail.

Tom addressed the group. "I'm turning myself in to the QM."

"Are you crazy?" Eduardo said. "Do you know what we went through trying to rescue you the last time?"

"I'm perfectly sane. This has gone on long enough. I don't want any of us forced to live in hiding." Tom put one arm around Lara's waist and the other on Tommy's shoulder.

David and Grace stumbled into the circle that had formed around the Baileys, and David harrumphed. "What if they don't let you come back?"

"David, you have the files. If I don't make contact with you by Saturday, make sure it all goes public."

"That's too long. Plenty of time for Madalyn to lock you up someplace where we'll never find you—or worse."

"Dad, let me come with you."

His father's grip tightened on Tommy's shoulder. "Absolutely not. You're a wanted fugitive!"

"So are you!"

"There's nothing to be gained by—"

"You need backup!"

"—putting you at risk. I'll return. I promise. It won't be like last time. This is a summit, not an abduction."

Tom kissed Lara on the forehead and pulled her and Tommy close. He released them abruptly, and headed down the path without looking back.

Tommy took a few steps after his dad and stopped, watching until he disappeared into the shadows. "Seriously? Someone has to go with him."

Jaycee gripped his arm with the same fervor his mom had shown when she pleaded with his dad. "We need to get everyone else to safety." She lowered her voice to a whisper. "Once they're all in the bunker, we'll sneak out and go after him."

Tommy hesitated a moment, and when he nodded, Jaycee dashed back to the head of the group. His mother was waiting for him farther up the path. He took her arm and together they followed the others, but inside he was seething, sure his dad was only making things worse.

He marveled at the way Jaycee kept everyone moving, staying in the cover of the pine trees as they worked their way to the top of the ridge. Once they'd crossed to the other side, she turned on a flashlight before she left the trail and started downhill through the underbrush. Everyone followed her, slipping and skidding on the leaves and pine needles until they could brace themselves against an outcropping of limestone that nestled against the side of the hill. When they'd skirted the rocks to reach the valley floor, she slipped between two boulders, where a metal door was set into thick concrete. She punched a series of numbers into the keypad on the door, and it clicked open.

Inside, it was chilly and damp, as if they'd entered a cave. The party moved single file to descend a short flight of stairs illuminated by dim emergency bulbs, and emerged into a room large enough to accommodate them all comfortably. Jaycee turned on the lights. Shelves stocked with canned goods, MREs, and bottled water rose against the walls, and camping supplies were piled on and around several pieces of mismatched furniture. Eduardo inspected the computer set up on a desk against the wall.

David stood in the center of the room, hands on hips, as he surveyed their surroundings. "There was a bomb shelter in our neighborhood when I was a teenager. Never used for its intended purpose, of course, but I seem to recall hearing of romantic liaisons that took place ..." He stopped and glanced around. Jaycee had a confused look on her face. Grace shook her head in exasperation. Tommy laughed out loud for the first time since he'd returned to BG-098.

"But indeed, that could have been exaggeration." David hastily changed the subject. "So, how thick are these walls, Jaycee?"

Tommy looked at each of them in turn. Trina. Grace. David. Eduardo. Jaycee. His mom. He wasn't willing to put any of them in more danger. Jaycee would be mad enough to shoot him once she realized he was gone, but he'd deal with that next time he saw her. If he hurried, he might be able to catch up to his dad and convince him to change his mind. He made sure no one was watching, set his duffel bag on the floor, and slipped back up the stairs.

Chapter 21

5:15 PM
Quadrant BG-098

Mitch watched everyone head up the path through the trees and then ran to the barn to secure the Resistance's records and contraband communications equipment. There hadn't been any QM dispatched out this way today, but it was prudent to stay a couple steps ahead of the law. He tugged at the rough wooden shelf unit that stood beside his office door until it concealed the entrance and then sank several screws to attach it to the wall. He swept away the drag marks on the floor and scattered some straw that had collected in an unused stall. As an added deterrent, he moved his truck so close to the shelves that even Jaycee, thin as she was, would have trouble squeezing between them.

He headed back into the diner and poured a mug of coffee just to have something to do with his hands. He was adding sugar and cream when the ancient pay phone on the wall rang twice and then was still.

Perfect timing. Mitch carried his coffee onto the front porch. The sight of Wes's black pickup in the parking lot gave him a momentary jolt, and he glanced around, half expecting to see his brother. *You stupid kid. Why didn't you listen to me? If you were here right now, I'd . . .* His eyes stung, and he blinked the unexpected tears away. *If you were here, I swear I'd hug you.*

He leaned against the porch railing and took a sip. It was late for coffee, but he probably wasn't going to sleep again tonight anyway. Soon he heard the hum of approaching vehicles and tossed the rest of his coffee into the bushes as four Jeeps turned into the parking lot, their headlights slicing through the darkness. He looked out over the group as they approached. The marshals who'd had breakfast at the diner were back with reinforcements from the local post.

"I haven't seen a dinner rush like this in years."

Paul McComas stepped forward and cleared his throat. Paul had been his most trusted ally since the fourth grade, when Mitch had made a bomb out of a matchbox and gunpowder and blown up their teacher's desk during recess. Paul had witnessed the whole thing but didn't rat him out. Instead, he'd provided Mitch with an alibi. The crime had been the stuff of schoolyard legend. To this day, it remained unsolved. "Mitch, we're all real sorry about Wes. And we hate to do this while you're mourning your brother, but we got orders to search your place for fugitives."

"There isn't anyone here but me."

"Like I said, I'm real sorry."

Mitch led the way inside, where the sergeant who'd questioned him that morning took over. "We get a bounty on every member of the Resistance we bring in."

"I told you—I just run the diner."

"You ever hear of Tom Bailey? Or David Honerlaw?" The sergeant squinted at the screen on his phone as he read the names.

"I'm Tom Bailey." Everyone turned toward the voice as Tom came out of the kitchen carrying a mug of coffee and a slice of pie on a plate. "Hello. I hope you don't mind that I served myself. No one appeared to be on duty behind the counter."

The four out-of-town marshals scurried past Mitch and drew their weapons. Tom set his coffee and pie on the counter and raised his hands. Their sergeant snarled at Mitch. "No one here but you, huh?" Then he turned back to Tom. "Where's the rest of 'em?"

Tom looked insulted. "I don't know what you're talking about. However, I do have business with OCSD Director Davies, and if you'll contact her, I'm sure she'll confirm that she's anxious to meet with me."

"Not until we make sure there's no one else here. Besides you, we've got warrants for Trina Jacobs, Lara Bailey, David Honerlaw, Grace Hughes, and Thomas Bailey, Junior." The sergeant paused and licked his lips, wolf-like.

Tom's expression remained blank. "I'm alone. You have my word."

"Your word don't mean squat to me, mister. Everyone knows the Resistance is a bunch of liars and terrorists." The sergeant turned a scrutinizing gaze on Mitch.

Paul McComas jumped in. "Mitch? Resistance? Nah. I've known him since we were kids. He's the kind of feller who likes to be left alone. Never known him to care what's going on outside this quadrant. His brother was QM. Killed in the line of duty last week."

The sergeant looked unconvinced. "Search this place."

His marshals swarmed through the diner, into the kitchen, and upstairs to the living quarters, while the locals stood soberly by. Mitch winced at the sounds of breaking glass and china in the kitchen. Heavy footsteps pounded back and forth overhead. Before long, the youngest marshal ran into the dining room, waving what looked like a white flag.

"Look! She was here!" He held up a white T-shirt bearing the letters CXD written in permanent marker. "She was wearing this in that video! Just wait! When we catch 'em we'll be all over PeopleCam!"

Mitch chuckled. "Don't count on it. What you see on the news is hardly ever what really happened."

The sergeant stared at Mitch. "You think you're funny, don't you? I've got a few more questions for you. Where do you get your supplies?"

"Through all the usual channels."

"Let me see your license and paperwork."

Tom took a seat at the counter and pulled his pie closer, while Mitch brought a sheaf of papers and a debit card reader out from under the counter.

The sergeant barely glanced at them. "I'm shutting you down."

"What? Why? My paperwork's all there."

The marshal pointed at Tom. "You served food to a member of the Resistance. That's aiding and abetting."

"Hell, this one wandered in on his own and stole that coffee and pie. Besides, I don't run background checks on people before I serve them food."

"You should."

Mitch muttered, "Son of a . . ." He'd detected a hint of a smile on Tom's face as he raised his mug to his lips.

The sergeant's tone was triumphant. "You had it coming. I've known there was something going on since the first time I ate here. Your food is far too good to be legal."

6:24 PM

Eduardo flipped the power switch on the ancient computer, and it whirred and whined without doing anything. He held up a square of hard plastic. "Why did they call this thing a floppy disk?" He was about to insert it into the drive when Jaycee's cries startled him.

"Where's Tommy?" She stuck her head into the tiny bedroom off the main room and then ran up the stairs. She was back in seconds. "He's not anywhere!"

Eduardo looked around. Sure enough, the kid had vanished. "He must've gone back down to the diner."

"No! How could he do that?" She looked as though she were going to cry.

Lara didn't look surprised. "How could he not?"

David Honerlaw shook his head. "Impetuous youth."

"Now what?" Trina sat on the arm of the sagging sofa.

Eduardo spoke up. "Looks like we're stuck here for a while. I was hoping this computer equipment was operational, but it's older than I am. I can't get a signal to send a text from in here, either. These walls must be lined with lead or something. I didn't know I was going to be stuck out here indefinitely. I've got stuff to do. I've got to get in touch with the president again."

"Again?" Grace regarded him with interest for the first time since he'd arrived. "When did you last communicate with the president?"

"I got an appointment to see him at the White House about three weeks ago. The Postmaster General helped me." He turned to Trina. "I tried to tell him. You and *mi carina* ... you're not terrorists. You didn't kill Stratford. But he gave me the brush-off."

Trina nodded. "It's not going to be any easier to convince him now, what with—"

"*Claro.*" Eduardo nodded. "We can't do this alone. The president has the power to help us. There might be others who will help us, too, but how are we going to accomplish anything if we can't communicate with the outside world?"

An uncomfortable silence settled over them. Without Mitch and Tom to act as leaders, Eduardo took over. "Well, at least we can make a plan while we wait, *no?*"

"Rescue Careen." Jaycee's expression dared anyone to question her.

"Rescue Tom, too, more than likely." David shrugged and sat on the sofa.

Eduardo refused to joke. "Our mission is much bigger than rescuing Carina. We know Madalyn accused her and Trina of murder to cover up her own crimes. If we find someone willing to challenge Madalyn's authority and expose the truth, we can bring Stratford's real killer to justice."

Chapter 22

7:40 PM
Quadrant BG-098

Tommy heard car doors slam as he emerged from the woods behind the diner. He worked his way deep into the underbrush near the side of the building, where he could see the Jeeps lined up in the parking lot.

He crouched in the shadows, listening as the marshals fanned out on the property and searched the barn and the boardinghouse. Flashlight beams played through the trees, reminding him of the night he and Careen escaped from the capital. He'd hoped he'd never have to go back there again. Now it looked like his return was inevitable.

When the marshals wrapped up their search of the area and prepared to depart, Tommy saw his dad, in handcuffs, walking among them. The marshals helped him into the back of a Jeep and, one by one, they roared away. As soon as the last one was out of sight around the bend, he headed for the back door.

Mitch jumped to his feet as Tommy burst into the dining room and then slumped back onto his stool at the counter. "What the hell was that all about? Your dad's lost his marbles. He's messing everything up."

He ignored Mitch and began rummaging beneath the counter. "Where are the keys to the truck? I'm going after him."

"Hold on. You can't do that."

Tommy faced him across the faded Formica, index finger inches from his nose. "No! Just shut up for once! I've had enough of you, my dad, and even Wes telling me what to do. I can't let my dad go to the OCSD alone, and while I'm in the capital, I'm going to find Careen. I don't really care what you think." He almost wished Mitch would take another swing at him. "Where are the keys?"

"Fine. Go. Keys are on the hook by the walk-in." Mitch pointed into the kitchen.

Tommy stepped over the shattered plates, broken glasses, and pots and pans that littered the floor and grabbed the keys off the hook. He heard the bell on the diner's front door jingle, and assuming Mitch was mounting one more attempt to block him from taking the truck, he dashed back out of the kitchen and froze. Mitch stood behind the counter, hands in the air, as a lone quadrant marshal advanced on him with gun drawn.

The marshal turned his gaze on Tommy and slowly smiled. "You look a lot like your pa, don't you, boy?"

Tommy stepped up beside Mitch and raised his hands.

"He lied when he said you weren't here. Bet your mama's around, too. By God, I'll turn this place upside down until we find every last one of you rebels. Tom Bailey ain't as smart as he thinks he is."

His eyes narrowed as he regarded Mitch. "He was protecting you, too, I'll wager. I thought the local marshals bought that story too easily. Friends of yours, ain't they? I know how things work down here in the hills. Well, they're not here to protect you now, so you'd best cooperate. Things'll go easier for you. Come on, out with it!"

Tommy held his breath while he waited for Mitch to answer. His glance darted around the room, looking for some escape route, some kind of hope. Then he saw a flicker of movement outside, over the marshal's shoulder.

The marshal chuckled at Mitch's hesitation and turned his attention to Tommy. "Why don't you toss me those keys, boy? You're not going anywhere." Tommy underhanded the keys across the counter and intentionally threw wide. The marshal lunged and caught them just as Danni shouldered open the diner's front door, carrying a cardboard box loaded with food.

Startled and off balance, the marshal whirled on her. Two shots rang out. Danni dropped the box and food rained down around the marshal's body as he hit the floor. Mitch looked at Tommy in amazement.

"Nice shooting, kid."

Only then did Tommy look down at the gun in his hand and realize he'd drawn and fired on instinct. He stumbled out from behind the counter and recoiled at the sight of the sprawling body, the two bullet wounds, and the spreading blood that tainted the spilled food.

"Oh shit. Oh God. Oh shit." He laid his gun on the counter and turned his back on the scene, fighting the urge to puke.

As Danni locked the door and shut the blinds, Mitch knelt and felt for a pulse, then shook his head. Nothing. He hurried into the kitchen and came back with latex gloves, a roll of plastic wrap, and a stack of towels. He tossed a pair of gloves to each of them.

"Come on. Lift him up so I can contain the mess. We can stash him in the freezer."

Tommy's stomach lurched but he obeyed, pushing the body to a sitting position while Mitch wrapped several layers of plastic around the marshal's torso and pinned his arms to his sides. Mitch grabbed the feet, and they hefted him up and carried him to the walk-in while Danni soaked up the blood with the towels. Tommy's heart thudded as he back stepped, crunching through broken dishes and stumbling over a stockpot while trying not to look at the burden he carried. *How could Mitch and Danni be so calm?*

They concealed the body behind some crates in a corner of the walk-in, and on the way back, Mitch grabbed a mop and a bottle of bleach.

Danni dropped her bloody gloves on the mound of blood-soaked towels, and Tommy gladly did the same.

She grabbed the gun off the counter and caught Tommy by the arm. "Mitch, I'll send you a message when we get there."

She guided him out the door to her truck, shoved him into the passenger seat, and climbed aboard. "We'll take the back road off the mountain. We're less likely to see anyone that way."

He nodded, crossed his arms on his chest, and tried to stop shaking.

Chapter 23

8:15 PM
Quadrant DC-001

Garrick phoned Madalyn to share the latest development in the hunt for the members of the Resistance. "There's a squad of QM on their way up from BG-098 with Tom Bailey."

"Really? Wait … you mean Tom Bailey, Junior, right?"

"No, it's the not-so-dead guy." He couldn't resist the dig. "He turned himself in when the QM showed up at that diner."

"Why would he do that? What about the rest of them?"

"Your guess is as good as mine. And he denies knowing the whereabouts of anyone else in the Resistance."

"What? That's ridiculous. There are so many people hiding in that quadrant; it's a wonder your marshals aren't tripping over them. Tell them not to rest until they've apprehended Trina Jacobs!"

"I can dispatch another squad to look around, but it'd be better to wait until tomorrow."

"These delays are unacceptable!"

"Why are you so afraid of this guy? Is he really that dangerous?"

"Of course he's dangerous. He's one of the leaders of the Resistance. Their seditious acts pose enough danger to keep the national terrorist threat level at Elevated. The Resistance's aim is the same as that of any other terrorist group—they are trying to destroy our way of life."

"But if Bailey faked his own death, why is he resurfacing now? Why turn himself in?"

"I have no idea. But apprehending the members of the Resistance —both the live ones and the ones who are pretending to be dead— should be your top priority."

"What about the investigation into Stratford's death?"

"That's old news. Tracking down Trina Jacobs is the key to everything. Once we have her in custody, we can close Lowell's murder investigation and eliminate the threat posed by the Resistance."

"The Resistance isn't just going to go away, even if you arrest every man, woman, and child in the BG quadrants. You do realize that, don't you? I've been getting reports of increased Resistance activity, and that CXD group has been in the news. Their Restriction-Free Zones are cropping up on college campuses all over the country."

Madalyn huffed out an exasperated breath. "Then I'll order PeopleCam to stop coverage of anything that has to do with CXD or the Resistance—unless it's to report that they've all been apprehended and put in jail. Now might be a good time to announce that Careen Catecher is in custody, and let all those dissidents know that in exchange for her cooperation and her willingness to share information about the Resistance, we're going to let her work for us."

9:56 PM
Quadrant OP-439

Henry Nelson's grandmother used to say that if you want to make friends with a new neighbor, go to the back door. He wasn't interested in making friends, but it was still good advice. He approached the vacant store from the alley this time.

He'd inked CXD on his hand with a Sharpie before he left his house, and now he pulled off a glove and flashed the symbol to the young man standing in the doorway.

"What's the password?"

"Careen." It had been on the slip of paper.

"That was last meeting's password."

"Aw, come on. I heard about it, but I couldn't make it last night."

"Yeah?" He motioned another boy over and muttered something to him about a new guy. Nelson tried not to look too eager.

"Yeah, all right. No phones in the meeting. You get it back when you leave."

Nelson shrugged, shut off his phone, and handed it over. He chose a seat off to the side, where he'd be inconspicuous but could still see everyone in the room. He recognized half of them. It was a marshal's duty to know all the families in his assigned quadrant by sight and by name, but college kids from other quadrants could exist unnoticed as long as they stayed out of trouble.

He eyed the group of teenagers that was breaking curfew to attend the meeting. He had to put a stop to this before their minds became poisoned against the OCSD.

He kept his expression neutral when that loudmouthed kid Jude spoke up. "Okay, it's too dangerous to try to re-establish the Restriction-Free Zone in the same location now that the QM is cracking down. We've got to be proactive. From now on, we'll operate the Restriction-Free Zone as a pop-up. We can establish a Zone anywhere and move on if the QM hassles us. We'll reach more people that way, anyhow."

He'd bust that kid for something—anything. He was enjoying his role as organizer too much. Unchecked, it wouldn't be long before he was just like Careen and Tommy Bailey—setting off bombs.

8:56 PM
Quadrant BG-098

As soon as Mitch finished cleaning up the mess in the diner, he showered and changed. Out in the barn, he unscrewed the shelves from the wall and shoved them aside to expose his office door, where he stowed trash bags full of his clothes, boots, and the bloody towels. He grabbed his satellite phone from the cabinet and when Atari answered, he spoke without preamble. "I've got two birds flying the coop, on the way to you."

"Hope one of them is Danni. How I've missed that sweet little piece of—"

"Jeez, Atari. This is an emergency. Could you be serious for once? And could you avoid referring to my cousin that way, at least to me?" Mitch squeezed his eyes closed and pinched the bridge of his nose.

"Since it bothers you so much, I'll save my sentiments for when I see her. Wanna know about your candy man?"

"Yeah. Seen him?"

"He's under lock and key, but he's all right. For now."

"Okay. That's something, anyway. Bailey's on the way there, courtesy of the QM. What's the word on Careen?"

"Ah yes, the sweetheart of the Resistance and another sweet .... Does it bother you if I objectify *her*? She's not a relative, is she? Never mind. Nope. Haven't seen her."

"Well, keep looking. How long before the Link is ready to go?"

"It's ready now."

"Well, for Pete's sake, you're gonna need to stall! It's too soon for Madalyn to find out it's a dud."

"Oh, it's not a dud. The Cerberean Link works. It *really* works. I'm beyond brilliant, if you want to know the truth."

"What the hell, Atari! It wasn't supposed to work!"

"How am I supposed to cultivate my reputation as one of the world's greatest criminal masterminds if my gadgets don't work? I have to consider my future. I might want contracts with other desperate, inept world leaders after we topple the OCSD."

Mitch disconnected the call and fumed as he shoved the shelf in front of his office door. Atari had agreed to the plan. This was no time to change things. He stomped back into the diner, where the smell of bleach was overpowering. He was going to have to mop the floor again before he called the QM back out. He turned on the television and went into the back for a fresh bucket of soapy water.

Splat. He worked the mop across the floor. The water in the bucket grew cloudy the first time he dunked the mop. He wrung it out, and as he looked up, he swore at the sight of Careen's picture on the television screen. He dropped the mop and turned up the volume.

"We come to you live with breaking news. The suspect being held in connection with the university bombing is none other than Resistance leader Careen Catecher."

"She's certainly racking up the criminal charges, isn't she?"

"I should say so. But reports from the OCSD confirm that she has agreed to turn state's evidence against members of the Resistance in exchange for immunity from her own crimes."

Chapter 24

8:50 PM

En route to Quadrant DC-005

"Hey, you all right?" Danni had turned up the heat in the truck, but Tommy was still shivering. "Reach behind you. There's a blanket on the floor." She pulled off her black knit cap. "Put this on. And get the bottle out of the glove box."

Tommy dragged the wool blanket over his lap and put on the hat but hesitated before opening the glove box. "What kind of bottle?"

"Relax. It's not CSD this time. It's whiskey. Just do it."

He obeyed and raised the bottle to his lips. The first swallow burned on the way down. He took another, then a third.

She glanced sideways. "That's enough for now."

He capped the bottle. Her cultivated air of boredom was gone, and she spoke in a way that was as close to gentle as he figured she'd ever get. "Wanna talk about it?"

"Not really. My dad insisted we should evacuate to the bunker. Mitch wouldn't come with us. When we were about halfway there, Dad decided to go back and turn himself in, because it was the best way to protect the rest of us. I didn't think he should go without backup, so I followed him. The QM took him away, and I was going to follow in the truck, but one of them—the one who was there when you came in—must've been suspicious and doubled back."

"Why did you kill him?"

Did she have to put it that way? "I just told you."

"No. Say it. Tell me why you shot him."

"He was going to turn us all in—including the marshals who are Mitch's friends. He was going to hunt down my mom, Trina, everyone. I couldn't let him do that. When you came in, you startled him. He might've shot you."

She nodded. "Shooting people is never the recommended first course of action. But it happens on occasion. You protected everyone."

"Maybe I could've—"

"No. Try not to dwell on it or wonder what-if. It'll make you crazy."

Tommy took another drink.

"Why are you in the Resistance?"

"I don't know."

"You'd better know. And you'd better have a damn good reason or you don't belong with us. This isn't a game."

He considered it for a moment before he spoke. "Last July, the OCSD's thugs ran our car off the road. When I woke up in the hospital, the doctors told me my parents were dead. But it was a lie—they'd been kidnapped to keep my dad from going public with the fact that the OCSD was staging terror attacks so they could justify passing more Restrictions.

"When Wes told me the Resistance had found my parents and they were still alive, I went along on the rescue, but I had no idea what I was getting into. I just wanted my parents back. Then, a few hours later, Careen was accused of Stratford's murder, and it became about protecting her, too."

"What about Wes's brilliant plan to blow up the university?"

"That plan was simple enough. I was supposed to flush out the security guard and then pull the fire alarm to signal Wes, but somehow the alarm went off before I was ready. I guess Wes thought that was the all-clear and lit the fuse. I barely got out before the place blew up, and I never saw him again. Now I need to get Careen and my dad back safely."

Danni chuckled. "Your reasons never involve more than two or three people."

"So? Does that mean I should forget about helping them?"

"You wouldn't be in this mess at all if it weren't for them."

His anger flared. "No, I'm pretty sure I wouldn't be in this mess if it weren't for *you*. I only went along with Wes's plan because ..." He stopped and turned his face to the window.

"That's a valuable and costly lesson."

He was starting to wish she'd just shut up. "What?"

"I said you learned a valuable and costly lesson. Not the lesson I was planning to teach you, but oh well." She grinned, flirting for a minute, but it didn't make him feel any better. "Your loss. Maybe next time you'll think twice before you do something dangerous and stupid to keep your girlfriend from finding out you cheated on her with me."

"Nothing against you, Danni, but I don't plan to cheat on Careen with anyone."

She turned to him, and again he caught a glimpse behind her carefully built facade. "This isn't a game to me. I was raised to do this job. I make sure people have food and other necessities. It's dangerous, but I'm not afraid. I can handle it. I'm realistic about what I can change and what I can't. I don't know why you'd risk your neck to rescue your dad or Careen. Your dad's going to do what he wants, regardless, and as for Careen, she was pretty easy to manipulate. You can't trust her. She's not worth it."

"Who manipulated her?"

"Mitch. Duh. He was using her and her videos as a diversion, a decoy. He was glad when she attracted so much attention because it threw Madalyn Davies off the trail of what he's really up to. I bet it'll be easy for the OCSD to make Careen do or say whatever they want."

"If Careen's cooperating with them, it's to try and save herself."

"Exactly. Someone who can't stick to their convictions isn't someone worth saving."

Tommy took another swig from the bottle. "I wish I could make sure my dad doesn't end up a prisoner at the OCSD again. And I don't care what any of you say about Careen. I want to help her. Hell, I love her. I also want to help change things so the OCSD doesn't have so much power over everyone. But I don't know how I'm going to do any of it." He tipped the bottle up and took one more gulp. "And I can't believe I just told you I love her. I want to tell *her* that I love her—not you."

Danni took the bottle and stowed it under her seat. "Yeah. How about you get some sleep, okay? You can start on your list when you get to the capital."

"Oh Lord, Mitch! What happened?" Paul McComas scratched his head and gave Mitch a sidelong glance.

"Your guess is as good as mine. I just found him in here." Mitch nudged the frosty corpse with his boot. They leaned in closer.

"Looks like someone shot him."

"Yep. Sure does."

"They wrapped him in plastic. Who do you think did it?"

"Couldn't tell ya."

"Mitch, even though you called this in, I gotta take you down to the station. Check for powder residue. Prove it wasn't you. You understand."

"Yeah. I get it."

"Where's the rest of his squad?"

"They're taking Tom Bailey to the capital. Apparently this guy decided to double back for something."

"And you've got no idea—"

"Nope. You know we never lock our doors around here. I was out in the barn. Didn't hear a thing."

"Where's Jaycee? She hear anything?"

"Nah. She was with me. I sent her over to the boardinghouse. She doesn't need to see this. She's pretty upset as it is. I'll just leave her a note." He scribbled something on the back of an order ticket.

Chapter 25

10:55 PM
Quadrant MV-287

Tommy jerked back to consciousness and looked around. He must've fallen asleep. They'd stopped at a gas station. There were no other buildings in sight.

"Where are we?"

"Somewhere in the MV quadrants. We're still hours away. "

"In that case, I'll be back in a minute."

He stumbled on his way out of the truck and staggered sideways, ricocheting off the gas pump before he righted himself. *So this is what too much whiskey on an empty stomach feels like.* It was different from CSD but no better. The cold air helped clear his head, and he walked a fairly straight line around the side of the cinderblock gas station. The restroom door was locked, so he relieved himself against the rear of the building, and even though it was childish, he smiled as the steam rose. He was nearly done when he heard the truck's engine roar. Danni pulled around the back of the building and slammed on the brakes in a swirl of gravel. He zipped up in a hurry. Danni jumped out, and he joined her at the corner of the building to peer over her shoulder.

She whispered, "Hear that?"

He held his breath, and as he listened the rumble of approaching vehicles grew louder.

"I saw an awful lot of headlights."

The cold air, so bracing at first, was creeping in through his layers of clothes. He shoved his hands in his sweatshirt pocket and hunched his shoulders.

Oversized armored vehicles lumbered into sight and streamed past the gas station. Danni pushed him farther behind her and hovered in the shadows at the corner of the building, keeping watch with one eye.

"It's a QM convoy. Armored vehicles mean riot patrol. They must be bringing them in as reinforcements for some local post."

Tommy's heart thudded in his guts and his chest. He closed his eyes and leaned back against the cinderblock wall, listening to them rumble by. As the minutes passed, the monotonous droning lulled him into a more relaxed state; that is, until Danni gasped and grabbed his arm. His heart jump-started and began to pound again.

"Some of them are turning in here." She flattened herself against the wall beside him.

Doors slammed. Voices rose. Footsteps crunched in the gravel. Someone lifted the nozzle off the gas pump.

Three or four sets of footsteps grew closer. Danni's grip on his arm tightened. There was no place else to hide. She turned her head toward the approaching footsteps and Tommy couldn't help it—he looked, too.

But the footsteps stopped, and a few seconds later he heard the metal-on-metal of utility belts being unbuckled and then the familiar splash against the side of the building. One of the men mumbled something he couldn't make out, and the others laughed.

"So then I said, 'If you have nothing to hide, you've got no reason to clam up.' He started talking, but he wouldn't shut up about probable cause and his rights as a citizen and a bunch of other shit." There was another burst of raucous laughter.

"Hope you set him straight."

"Yeah, you gotta nip that in the bud."

"He's probably still yelling about his rights, but where he's going, no one's listening."

"Can't wait to put down those rebels up in OP-439. They're infecting the rest of the country."

"All in a day's work, right?"

Tommy and Danni both exhaled slowly as they listened to the men's footsteps grow fainter.

He strained to hear, imagining the scene as the marshals got back in the vehicles. Engines roared to life with menacing growls. Danni held up a hand in warning, and they waited until the sounds had faded away before she crept around the side of the building.

When she returned, she motioned for him to get in the truck. When she turned the key in the ignition, he worried the convoy of marshals would hear them a quarter mile away. He was glad they were going in the opposite direction. They traveled several miles into the mountains before he spoke. Even then, his voice sounded too loud.

"Do you think they were serious about going to OP-439?" At this rate, there was bound to be nothing left of his home quadrant.

Danni nodded. "For a bunch of spoiled rich kids, they're pretty well organized. They've tapped into the former black market network to help get food to people who need it. They basically launched the CXD network, and that Restriction-Free Zone thing was inspired. They only thing wrong with them is they're so pro-Careen. They're devoted to her because she did, like, a month or two of classes at the university. Woo-hoo. Big deal. She's not even from there."

"I think it makes sense that they're ticked and reacting—with or without Careen in the equation. OP had the worst food riot of all in 441, and then there was the university bombing in 439, practically next door, a week later."

"Yeah, maybe."

"The Resistance is responsible for that. We pushed those people to riot."

Danni shrugged. "There's unrest everywhere. But you won't have to worry about that for long."

"You never said exactly where we're going."

She grinned but didn't take her eyes off the road. "I could tell you, but then I'd have to—"

"Seriously? Fine. Never mind. Want me to drive for a while?"

"No. I got it."

Chapter 26

11:45 PM
Quadrant BG-098

"Where's Tommy? Why hasn't he come back?" Jaycee paced the bunker's main room. "How long have we been in here, anyway?"

Trina shrugged. "It's late. Maybe they decided to wait till morning to come back for us."

Jaycee doubted Tommy would stay at the diner with her dad unless he had no alternative. More likely, he'd cut her out of her own plan and gone to the capital alone. She had to get out of there and find out. "What if something happened? They could be hurt with no one to help them. I don't care what time it is. I'm going back."

A babble of protest arose, but she shushed it. "I'm the only one who can go without attracting attention. I live here. I'll come back for you when it's safe."

Lara looked like she wanted to forbid it, but instead she pulled Jaycee into a hug and then walked her to the door. "If the marshals are still there, you turn around, but don't come back here unless you can do it without being followed. Promise?"

Jaycee nodded and slipped out into the night.

Snow flurries swirled around her, and she blew out her breath in frozen puffs. The air smelled fresh, especially after being cooped up in the underground bunker. She held her rifle in the crook of her arm as she climbed uphill through the underbrush. She wasn't afraid. She knew how to take care of herself. It was change that frightened her; what frightened her most was that she longed for it so much.

Just before she reached the top of the ridge, she heard the crunch of footsteps in the fallen leaves and stopped, alert and wary. She parted two pine branches, and a startled doe broke into a gallop. She breathed a sigh of relief and watched until it was out of sight.

The trail was mostly downhill this time, and she moved faster alone. By the time she reached the flat rock near the boathouse, she no longer noticed the cold, and she'd unzipped her jacket long before she emerged from the woods behind the barn. She slipped in the diner's back door and wrinkled her nose at the unexpected smell of bleach. There was a note on the counter, weighed down with a set of keys.

Jaycee—I went down to the station with Paul. One of the marshals got shot, and they need my help with the investigation. Be back as soon as I can. Dad

Wait—what? He never goes to town. Never. There was no sign of Tommy or Mr. Bailey, and of course her dad hadn't mentioned them in the note. She dashed upstairs and cried out in dismay. Her clothes, stuffed animals, and books had been dumped on the floor, the quilts and sheets pulled off the beds. The other two bedrooms looked much the same.

She dashed over to the boardinghouse, where every room in the place had been ransacked. It was going to take forever to straighten up the mess, but it could wait.

She ran back to the diner and snatched the keys off the counter. She didn't need anyone's help to put her plan into action; she'd been driving since she could reach the pedals. Soon she was guiding the truck down the mountain road. All she had to do was find her way to the capital, locate the OCSD building, gain access, and rescue Careen.

After a few moments' reflection, her enthusiasm for her sketchy plan began to fizzle. The truck's gas tank was half empty. She hadn't thought to fill the tank with the ethanol Mitch kept stored in the barn, and she lacked a debit card to buy more. She was out way after curfew without a travel pass. And she didn't even know for sure that Careen was at the OCSD.

When she came off the mountain, she paused at the crossroads. Turn right, and she'd soon be on the highway; instead, she sighed and turned the wheel to the left.

The redbrick quadrant marshal station was the only building with its lights on in the deserted town square. She parked on the street and headed up the wide concrete stairs.

She'd never been inside the station before, and, with a vague sense that she shouldn't be there, she tiptoed down the checkered marble hall, wondering where to find her father.

"Josephine!" She jumped and whirled around. The young quadrant marshal who'd been at the diner hurried to her side and fell into step with her. "It's me—Seamus. Remember? How did you know to come in tonight? He just got here about an hour ago. I'll get your paperwork, and then you can see him if you want to."

Confused, she followed Seamus into an office, where he handed her a sealed envelope. Then he led her to a set of double doors at the end of the hall.

"He's in the chapel. Do you want me to go in with you?"

She shook her head.

"All right. If you need anything, let me know."

She hesitated outside the door until Seamus was out of sight and then slit the envelope. She flipped through pages. Most of it made no sense, but she read every word of the death benefit form. *So that's what a death benefit is—money! Wes left me money.* She skimmed the rest of the pages until she found a form authorizing the transfer of Wes's death benefit to another registered debit account. It required a parent's signature for anyone underage. She nearly cried in frustration. *Well, how else did you think they'd give it to you?* She thought for a moment. *There's more than one way around that.* She shoved the papers into her jacket pocket. She tiptoed inside and hesitated behind the last row of pews. She'd never seen a dead person before. Especially not someone who was family.

Her father stood in front of an open black casket, head bowed, and spoke to his brother more kindly than she could remember him doing when Wes was alive.

"Sometimes I forgot you were a kid. I put a lot of pressure on you. Maybe I relied on you too much." A harsh sob, almost like a laugh, escaped his throat. "I guess we're out of chances to get it right, little brother."

Suddenly she wanted to see him, too, and went to stand beside her father. He did a double take, put his arm around her shoulders, and pulled her into a tight hug. She stared at Wes over her father's shoulder. He looked peaceful, but wherever he was, she bet he was angry. He'd missed his chances. She vowed that she'd figure out a way to complete the job he'd left undone.

Chapter 27

2:15 AM
Wednesday, December 6, 2034
Quadrant OP-439

Henry Nelson pulled on his riot gear—the bulletproof breastplate and the helmet with the face guard. He'd never worn it for anything but practice drills before. He grabbed his shield and fell into line with the Special Forces group who'd been rushed in from the MV quadrants. He didn't see any of the marshals from his command post. He climbed into a Jeep with three other marshals he didn't recognize. There were so many tanks in the convoy that he felt like part of an invading army.

The vehicles fell in line, and the ominous rumble echoed in the otherwise quiet streets. Lights went out in some of the houses as they passed, but here and there he saw movement behind curtains and blinds.

The driver followed an armored transport vehicle onto the front lawn of a two-story brick house. Marshals piled out of both vehicles, and two of them rushed the front door, splintering it on the second swing of their battering ram. As Nelson and the rest of his team ran across the lawn, a stun grenade's flash pierced the darkness inside the house. He stopped in his tracks; someone jostled him as they ran by.

Before he got inside, some of the marshals reappeared, dragging out the family of five who lived there. All were in their pajamas, their hands cinched behind them with plastic zip ties. One of the marshals shoved the woman as they herded the family onto the front lawn, and Nelson stepped forward and caught her by the elbow to keep her from falling. The man struggled against the marshal who gripped him by the arm, panic and bewilderment on his face. "We've done nothing wrong!"

"Your children took part in the protests on campus. They are in direct violation of Restrictions. And what about this?" The marshal wrenched the teenaged daughter's arms up in an unnatural position to show the back of her hand, which bore the CXD symbol.

"Daddy!" The girl screamed as she squirmed, trying to escape the painful contortion. She burst into tears as the marshal dragged her toward a waiting van. The son, silent but visibly trembling, put up less of a fight. The two marshals who manhandled him across the lawn laughed when he staggered and fell, and then hauled him up and shoved him into the van after his sister.

"Where are you taking my children?"

The squad leader snarled. "Your children, sir, have engaged in treasonous activities. It's none of your business where they're going."

The wife's knees buckled, and Nelson tightened his grip. Their younger boy, maybe ten years old, stood barefoot on the lawn, nervously hopping from foot to foot, his blue pajamas too thin to protect him from the December night.

The squad leader stepped up until his face was just inches away from the man's nose. "You've endangered this child by allowing him to be exposed to your older children's seditious activities. We'll be taking him as well, to make sure his mind doesn't get too polluted."

The boy looked over his shoulder, panting like an animal caught in a trap, and called out to his mother as he was led away to a different van.

"Jason! Don't worry! It's going to be all right, sweetie." The van door closed, and the woman's voice choked off into sobs.

Nelson looked around. The scene was the same at a house across the street and two doors down.

A third van screeched to a stop in the driveway, and one of the marshals slid open the side door. It was half-full of adults, all still in their nightclothes. Nelson guided the faltering woman toward the van. He was about to help her step inside when an earth-shattering boom made them both jump and cower.

Another marshal stepped up and shoved the woman inside, sliding the door closed after her.

He pounded a gloved fist into his other palm. "That'll teach 'em! Guess we won't have much trouble in this quadrant after tonight."

Nelson felt a swell of satisfaction. The dissidents had brought this chaos on themselves.

Chapter 28

5:30 AM
Quadrant YP-145

Tommy stirred as the truck rolled to a stop, tires crunching in the gravel along the side of the road; he came fully awake at the sight of the QM patrol car's flashing lights as they danced and reflected off the windshield and mirrors.

Danni glanced at the rearview and spoke through gritted teeth. "Turn your face toward the window. Pretend you're asleep. Let me handle this." Two marshals approached the truck on the driver's side, and she rolled down the window.

"Travel pass and identification."

Danni took the travel pass off the dashboard and handed it out the window, along with an ID card.

One of the marshals scrutinized them in the beam from his flashlight. "You're out way past curfew. That your boyfriend?"

"Not really."

"Wake him up so we can check his ID."

"How about I don't? What if it's just us and …" She fumbled around on the floor for a second and came up with the bottle "Jack?"

One of them made an approving sound. "Have it your way, darlin'. You and Jack step out of the vehicle."

Tommy heard someone open the tailgate and lift the tarp. There was some rummaging around, and then the gate slammed closed. Danni said something he couldn't make out, her voice low and throaty. One of the marshals laughed. He heard their footsteps recede, and then the patrol car door opened and closed. He lost track of the minutes. The door slammed again, and then the patrol car's engine revved as it sped off.

Danni climbed back into the driver's seat and took a swig from the bottle of whiskey, spat it out the window, and wiped her mouth with the back of her hand. The dread that washed over him was for her safety, not his own.

"What happened?"

As she pushed back her tousled hair, the memory of making out with her rose unbidden to his mind. "Sometimes they only want a share of the food." She shrugged and handed him the bottle.

The full meaning of her inference hit him; he was horror-struck and ashamed for not intervening. "But they've got no right to harass you! You've got a travel pass. You're a legitimate food supplier."

"Doesn't matter whether I'm legit or not." She put the truck in gear. "Black market dealers sometimes had to charm marshals with bribes and other favors. My charm, if you wanna call it that, kept me out of jail more than once. To some of our fine law enforcement officers, nothing's changed." She paused. "Like I said, before you get in any deeper, you'd better know exactly why you chose this fight." Tears sparkled in her eyes, and he felt his own well up in sympathy. "It's okay. Really. I give in without a fuss, they take what they want, and we all move on."

"You didn't have to do that for me."

"I didn't do it for you."

Her words stung, and he took another drink.

Chapter 29

7:30 AM
Quadrant DC-001

Madalyn answered the early-morning summons to the Oval Office with no idea how to explain Tom Bailey's impending arrival in the capital; everyone believed he and Lara had died in an auto accident last July.

She'd had nothing to do with it. She hadn't been part of the power struggle between Tom and Lowell or Lowell's decision about how to resolve it. Her own worry centered around the fact that the rest of the Resistance had somehow disappeared into the wilderness. The president's personal secretary had to tap her on the shoulder to get her attention before she ushered her in to where President Wright and another man rose to greet her.

"Madam Director, this is Senator Brandon Renald, soon to be the new assistant director of the OCSD."

"Oh?"

"Yes. I'll be making his appointment official this afternoon. You'll remember he's been a senator for six terms, chaired the Subcommittee on Crime and Terrorism, and has also been a member of the Select Committee on Intelligence. He has experience in matters related to security and terrorism."

"But, sir—"

"I realize things have been extremely disorganized since Lowell's death. You need someone to help you share responsibility. I'm sure you'll find his expertise most welcome."

Someone with experience? That's the last thing I need. "I've already selected a new assistant director," she blurted in desperation. "I didn't have time to tell you; we've been so awfully busy. The QM just apprehended one of the leaders of the Resistance. They're en route, and I will personally take charge of the interrogation when he arrives."

"But whom did you appoint? Surely you can agree Senator Renald's experience would make him a valuable asset to the OCSD."

The president appeared completely disinterested in the news of the arrest, and that left her wrong-footed. *I guess we're not through talking about Renald. I don't want him spying on me. I need someone who won't make me look bad. But who?* "Of course, sir, but my new assistant director has already been quite helpful. Indispensable. Perhaps there's a place for Senator Renald in another agency if he's tired of being a senator."

"I'll expect you and the new assistant director here at noon. Senator, I'd be pleased if you're able to attend."

She smiled to mask her panic. "We'll look forward to seeing you then."

On the drive back to the OCSD building, Madalyn mentally compiled a short list of potential assistant directors. But who could she produce with a mere four hours' notice? Her only option was Kevin. He'd worked at the OCSD for years without showing any signs of the ambition and guile that made one successful. On the contrary, he'd been pleasant, open and friendly.

She could boss him around; she'd been doing it for years. His intellect was unlikely to make her look bad. She fished out her phone. It was going to take an army to get her new assistant ready for a presidential inspection.

9:00 AM

Tom Bailey, flanked by the three marshals who'd transported him to the capital, strode into the lobby at the Office of Civilian Safety and Defense. His jeans, borrowed from Mitch, were belted tight at the waist and hung off his lanky frame, but they would've done so even if he'd regained all the weight he'd lost while he was imprisoned. As he endured a security pat down, he caught sight of himself in the mirrored elevator door. He hadn't had a black eye in thirty years, but this one made up for it. Purple bruising spread from his left brow to his cheekbone, and his lip was cut and swollen. When had he last had a haircut? In his camouflage jacket, he looked more like the leader of a rebellion than an attorney.

Two security guards escorted him upstairs to a sitting room and took up positions on either side of the door. He paced the plush carpet as he reviewed what he intended to say to Madalyn, but forgot everything when his ex-best friend, Art Severson, stepped into the room. He accepted the proffered hand, smiling until Art dismissed the security guards who hovered at his elbow. As soon as they were alone, he caught Art off guard with a right hook to the jaw.

Art staggered back, shock registering on his face before he composed himself. "Your kid hits harder than you do."

"Then you ought to be glad he's not here."

"You should be, as well. Did you know there's a warrant out for his arrest?"

"Was it you who pressed charges?"

"I didn't have to. A witness identified him at the bombing in OP-439. Apparently they've got a good description of him—plus his DNA on a gun. Add that to whatever Careen Catecher might have said about him during questioning, and there was more than enough to issue a warrant. Of course, when the time comes, I'll be glad to make a list of all the laws he was breaking that day he assaulted me at the lake house."

"I might have known you'd find plenty of kindred spirits at the OCSD. But honestly, I'm disappointed."

"Hey, it was you who drew me into this web of lies and deceit, my friend."

"Where's Madalyn? I assumed I'd be meeting with her."

"She couldn't fit you into her schedule on such short notice."

"Oh, I'm confident she'll make time to see me. Perhaps it would speed things up if you intervened on my behalf." Art bristled at the sarcasm.

"Look, I tried to help you last summer when you were in hot water, and nothing good came of it. You and your problems wrecked my marriage. Now I'm salvaging what I can. Just think—you could be looking at the next assistant director of the OCSD. But don't make the mistake of considering me an ally." Art sneered as he stepped into the hall. "Good luck planning your revolution—or whatever it is you tell yourself you're doing. Coming here was a stupid move."

Tom heard the click of the lock and resumed his pacing.

9:15 AM

As Madalyn came into his room, Kevin caught sight of two massive guards lurking in the hall. She looked at him, puzzled, and he glanced down. He'd been wearing the guard uniform for the last four days, and compared to the real thing, he looked like a kid dressed up for Halloween. She was too wild-eyed and frantic to be interested in the details, and he didn't volunteer an explanation.

"You've got to shower and shave right away. The tailor's on his way up."

"Why?"

"The president tried to appoint some senator as my new assistant director; he wants someone looking over my shoulder. I told him I'd already appointed you. We have a meeting in three hours. I've brought in a team to make sure you look the part. Hurry! We're wasting time."

"Wait—what?"

She looked annoyed that he hadn't comprehended. "After the problems with CSD and the food riots … can you even begin to imagine the pressure I've been under? It isn't easy to run things the way Lowell did. The president doesn't trust me. Garrick thinks I'm a joke." She paused. "I can't believe I just told you all that. You *do* want the job, don't you?"

"Yeah." Actually, he did. Once he'd have given his right arm for a chance like this. Now, he could only hope that he'd be up to the task of sabotaging Madalyn while working right under her nose.

She was halfway out the door when she called over her shoulder, "Come upstairs when they're finished with you."

Chapter 30

10:45 AM

Tom felt his pulse quicken, ready for battle, as the two guards escorted him to the director's office. Madalyn rose from her chair as he stepped inside. He shook his head. "Maddie, hasn't this gone on long enough?"

Her face contorted, and she snapped at the guards, who made a hasty exit, closing the door behind them. "You're looking a little rough around the edges."

"I think I look pretty good for someone who's been dead for five months."

"Yes, that is quite a while. Long enough that no one cares about you or your opinions anymore. No one would notice if you disappeared for good this time."

"That's not going to happen. Plenty of people know I'm here, and I've got an insurance policy. If I don't walk out of here unscathed, I'll become a voice from the grave, divulging all the carefully hidden scandals of your past. You can't stop the truth, Maddie. It always comes out." More kindly, he asked, "In over your head again, aren't you?"

"No." She folded her arms on her chest and glared at him. "But I certainly don't have time to worry about you spreading rumors about things that happened ages ago."

"Oh, I won't tell unless you force me to. And some of them are definitely worse than others. Personally, I think the reason you were thrown out of law school is the least of your worries now."

"Then how about we discuss current events, like the warrant for your son's arrest? Seems he was part of a Resistance-led terrorist attack. Like father, like son?"

"I have no comment, other than to say I'm sure the charges are completely without merit."

"Careen Catecher gave us more than enough information to build a case against him—and the rest of you, too. Before long, every member of the Resistance will be joining you here under lock and key."

"I highly doubt it, though the OCSD does make a practice of kidnapping and detaining people without regard for the law."

"Our laws don't protect terrorists."

He snorted. "You know damn well Careen's no terrorist. She's just a convenient scapegoat. Her participation in any alleged Resistance activity was auxiliary, at best. You've attempted to vilify that young woman, and yet the public has united behind her. The best thing you could do to gain the public's approval is release her."

"Release that poor, confused creature when she's obviously been brainwashed by your cult?" She gave him a sly smile. "Are you trying to get your son's toy back for him? Or maybe you want her for yourself?"

"The only one taking advantage of that girl is you. A real investigation and a fair trial will prove that she wasn't responsible for either Stratford's death or the university bombing. I'll be happy to represent her if it comes to that."

"If she's innocent of the university bombing, does that mean your son is guilty?"

"Absolutely not. Surely the OCSD has more important things to do than conduct a witch hunt against two teenagers. Aren't you concerned about how things have eluded your control since you took over? Lowell must be spinning in his grave."

She looked uncomfortable, almost contrite, for a moment. "CSD was Lowell's project, and I agree it's time to let it go. My new security program addresses the needs of our country's children and promotes personal responsibility."

"Interesting."

"Your son is eighteen?"

"He's not part of this discussion. Period."

"You don't get to control the room anymore, Professor."

"If you're serious about doing something worthwhile during your tenure as director, I can offer you something that will be far more effective than your flagrant manipulation of Careen. Bring me on as a consultant."

"Why?"

He found her incredulous look insulting, but chose to ignore it. "Don't you see how unrealistic it is to force people to live under the Restrictions, now that the Essential Services debacle proved they can do more harm than good? Re-evaluate and make some changes or I'm afraid you'll face a full-out revolution. You don't want that, Maddie. I know, at base level, you honestly do want people to live happy lives."

"Of course I do."

"Then let me ask you: what does it mean to be happy?"

"I don't understand the question."

"You just agreed you want people to be happy. So, what makes a person happy?"

"Well, I don't know!"

"Precisely. How about bungee jumping?"

She shuddered. "Goodness, no!"

"Point made. For someone else, though, bungee jumping might be the thing that brings them the most happiness. How would you like it if the world's most enthusiastic bungee jumper got to make decisions on your behalf? What if they mandated that everyone over the age of eighteen had to bungee jump at least twice a week?"

"That's crazy. It could never happen."

"Think. Don't you see where I'm going with this?" He leaned his elbows on the back of the chair. "Let me help you before the current situation escalates further. There is a happy medium. We won't always agree, but we don't have to be adversaries. You have the opportunity—and the potential—to do more good than Lowell ever did."

Madalyn was silent for a long time. Then she glanced at the clock on her desk. "Well, this has been very interesting, but I have another appointment waiting."

"I beg your pardon?"

"I'm very busy these days. Besides, I'll need time to think about your offer to, as you say, consult. We'll talk again tomorrow. Or the next day."

"What, exactly, am I supposed to do until then?"

"You'll stay here, of course. In our guest quarters."

"I've seen what passes for your guest quarters, and I respectfully decline."

"All guests are subject to our security protocols. Even you." She pushed a button on her desk to summon the guards. "Take him away."

As she watched him leave, she wondered how soon she could push Careen back into the public spotlight.

Chapter 31

10:30 AM
Quadrant DC-005

Tommy yawned as Danni guided the truck past blocks of abandoned warehouses and office buildings. Morning sunlight glittered through shattered windowpanes. The litter-strewn streets alluded to something that had once been vitally alive but was now useless and broken.

She turned into the driveway behind a dilapidated-looking brick warehouse with boarded-up windows, and though Tommy expected to hear the screech of rusty, unused metal parts as the security gate slid open, it ran almost silently. They crossed the weed-choked surface lot, passed a loading bay, and headed into an underground parking garage. The switchback ramp wound down to the bottom level, where she concealed the truck behind a pile of construction materials and orange barrels. When she turned off the headlights, the darkness in the subterranean garage was absolute. Her flashlight beam cut through the gloom; rusty rebar sprouted from chunks of concrete and cast eerie shadows on the wall. Tommy shivered as he followed her past the debris to an elevator. She inserted a key in the panel, and he blinked in the bright light as they stepped inside. The elevator was modern, clean, and warm, completely out of place based on what he'd seen so far. A security camera was mounted in a corner, its red light flashing.

Danni punched him on the arm. "Welcome home."

He pulled her into a hug and held her until they came to a stop, hoping the embrace would convey his respect and his thanks.

They emerged in a gallery with sleek, black-leather-and-chrome furniture and a rainwater-style fountain illuminated by changing colored lights. Hulking vintage arcade games were spread throughout the room, where they twinkled, pulsed, and made chirpy "game over" noises. An antique pinball machine stood in a corner, lights flashing red and yellow. Spotlights accentuated framed pop-art renderings of video game logos.

Tommy turned in a slow circle, so caught up in the contrast between the building's shabby exterior and the opulence inside he didn't realize Danni had left him behind. A blast of gunfire brought him back from his reverie. His first instinct was to hit the button to summon the elevator, but he heard Danni laughing, so he followed the sound of her voice to a room where giant televisions covered three walls, and computer equipment ranged along a semicircular desk. Danni stood beside someone in a black leather office chair, watching the avatars on the center screen blast each other with AK-47s.

She noticed Tommy standing in the doorway and motioned him inside. The person in the chair paused the game and spun around, and Tommy nearly burst out laughing at the sight of a slight, dark-haired man wearing red-tinted virtual reality goggles; the overall effect reminded him of a praying mantis that had once been part of an elementary school science lesson. The man peered up at him.

"Ahh! Tom Bailey the younger! Welcome to Command Central. Sit down and grab a pair."

"Umm … what? No thanks."

He looked at Danni for clarification, but she ignored him and settled on the bug-like man's lap.

"Atari's Resistance. Like us."

He's nothing like me. I'm nothing like Danni. Do I belong here?

Atari pulled off his goggles. "I remember you from the day Stratford bought the farm. You were with Wes and that pretty little what's-her-name. Right?"

He winked and growled and Tommy bristled. He'd only been there five minutes, and already he wanted to punch the guy's lights out. He looked down at Danni and muttered, "What the hell?"

She shrugged and grinned at him; she was back to acting the way she had the day they'd met—carefree, dangerous, and up for anything. "I need to let Mitch know we made it. Then I'm going to crash for a while. Coming?" She slid off Atari's lap and trailed her fingers across his shoulders. He responded with an exaggerated shiver.

Tommy's stunned reaction must have shown on his face, because Danni purred as she sauntered past. "Don't judge. Freedom to use my downtime the way I choose is what keeps me from getting as batty as Mitch."

As soon as she was out of the room, Atari seemed to forget about her. He kicked a rolling chair in Tommy's direction. "Have a seat. Let's play!"

"Seriously, no thanks. I'm not into video games."

"If you'd rather, the gym's one floor down."

"I didn't come here to work out, either."

Atari laid down his game controller and gave Tommy his full attention. "Then how may I serve you, young master?"

Screw you. "I don't need anything from you. I'm here to get my dad and Careen away from the OCSD."

"Oh, really?" He restarted the game and blasted away. "Because Confucius say, 'rittle boys who shoot quadrant marshals shar remain grounded. Indefinitery.'"

"You know about that?"

"I know about everything."

Tommy rolled his eyes behind Atari's back and muttered, "Bet you don't know if my dad's all right."

"*Au contraire, mon frère.* They brought your dad in three hours and … fourteen minutes ago." He paused the game, grabbed a keyboard, and began pecking at the keys. The main screen's display changed to a grid of black-and-white surveillance video footage, time stamps rolling in the upper corners.

Atari clicked to bring one feed up on a screen by itself, and Tommy recognized the main lobby of the OCSD. Atari rewound the footage three hours and fourteen minutes, and Tommy watched his dad enter the building.

"He met with some guy—no idea who *he* was—and then with Madalyn. Of course, there are no surveillance cameras in her office, so I couldn't follow him in there. He's recently been installed in plush accommodations on the fourth floor. No skyline view but better digs than the secure ward in the basement."

Though he could tell Atari was kind of a jerk about everything, Tommy took offense to that last remark. His mom had been held and tortured in that basement because of his dad's misguided devotion to his convictions.

"How long do you think they'll keep him there?"

Atari shrugged. "No way to know."

"Dad said before he left that if he isn't released by Saturday, something is going to go public. Information of some sort. One of the professors has the file."

"That could turn out to be interesting. Guess we'll have to mark our calendars. Come on, kid. Have a seat." Atari tossed him a pair of goggles.

"What about Kevin? Did he make it to the OCSD?"

"Yeppers. They had him on lockdown, but as of this afternoon, he's out and about in what looks like a five-thousand-dollar suit. I don't get audio on the security feed, so I'm not sure what's up with that."

"And Careen?"

"Nah, bro. I wouldn't mind keeping an eye on her, but she hasn't surfaced yet." A few seconds later, he was engrossed in his video game again.

Tommy stood in silence, watching, until he couldn't stand it anymore. "There's no way I'm waiting around for days. Let's go get my dad out of there!"

Atari shrugged and stood up, leaving his goggles on the desk. "No can do. Mitch says no rescue mission, so we are forced to chill. And chill you must." He pointed his thumb over his shoulder. "Kitchen's to the right of the elevator. You can't miss it. Guest suite's out that door, around the corner, third door on the left. It's yours as long as you need it. My rooms are that way." He pointed with the first two fingers on both hands, like a flight attendant giving safety instructions. "But I'm hanging out the Do Not Disturb sign for a while, if you know what I mean. You really should check out the gym downstairs. Take the self-guided tour and get to know your way around. This place is pretty bomb. I should know; I designed it myself." He fake-punched Tommy on the shoulder as he headed for the door. "We're roomies now. And you're gonna be here a while."

Chapter 32

11:05 AM
Quadrant BG-098

Mitch breathed an audible sigh of relief as he guided the black pickup into the barn and cut the engine.

They'd spent the morning at the funeral home, making Wes's final arrangements. It was a new experience for Jaycee, and she'd been unusually quiet on the way back up the mountain. Though it had been a while since he'd had to deal with death, he'd found himself able to detach and go through the process almost by rote.

They had two days until the funeral. There was so much to do in that short time. He was halfway out of the cab when she spoke.

"Where's Tommy?"

"Gone after his dad." He slammed the door. The less she knew, the better—at least until he had word from Danni.

She hurried after him. "What happened last night? How did the marshal get shot? Now that we're home, you can tell me. Is Tommy really all right?"

"Go straighten up the mess at the boardinghouse."

She brightened for a second. "Is everyone coming back? Can I go get them from—"

He glanced around and shushed her.

"What?"

The mutinous look on Jaycee's face could have belonged to her mother. How could she so faithfully recreate her mannerisms when she had no memories from which to draw? He kept his tone low. "The QM could be watching us, so it's gotta be just us for a while, understand?"

She put her hands on her hips. "Then why do I have to bother cleaning up the mess at the boardinghouse?"

"It has to get done sometime. Might as well be now."

She turned on her heel and stomped out of the barn, muttering under her breath. As soon as she was gone, he hurried over and unbolted the shelves from the wall, shoving them aside to reveal the door to his office. Inside, he retrieved his satellite phone from its locked cabinet. The encrypted message from Danni was brief. She'd made it to the safe house, and Tommy would be out of the way.

With the phone stowed safely back in the cabinet, he collected the trash bags full of bloodied items he'd stashed there the night before. He paused in the doorway and watched Jaycee emerge from the boardinghouse, shake out a throw rug, and hang it over the back porch railing.

As soon as she disappeared back inside, he hauled the trash bags out to the clearing to burn. He piled brush and logs on top of the bags and used lighter fluid to get the fire going. He had to make sure everything that could connect him to the marshal's death was destroyed.

Focused on the task at hand, he nearly missed the first sign of life in the two-way transmitter he'd been wearing in his ear ever since Kevin left for the capital.

11:15 AM

Kevin surveyed himself in the full-length mirror in his room. The tailor had transformed him into a man who looked like the assistant director of the OCSD. He adjusted the knot in his tie and thanked the tailor and his assistants, who all bowed their way out the door. The guards were no longer stationed in the hall, and he walked upstairs alone. Nicole's eyebrows shot up when he entered the director's suite. He couldn't help grinning as he let himself into Madalyn's office.

The desk that had been the right size and scale for Lowell Stratford dwarfed her and reinforced the other indicators that she was in over her head, but Kevin didn't have a second to waste feeling sorry for her. Her perfectly manicured nails tore a neat spiral of foil from a familiar-looking candy wrapper, and she popped a piece of chocolate into her mouth. He all but ran forward, plucked the rest of the roll out of her hand, and blurted out the first thing that came to mind. "The camera adds ten pounds, you know."

She glared at him for a second and then nodded. "You're right. Take it. You need it more than I do."

He could feel his heart pounding as he slid the candy into his breast pocket; he'd reclaimed it in time to keep the two-way transmitter Mitch had hidden inside a secret.

Madalyn quickly recovered her imperious tone. "Sit down. You need to be able to answer questions about the new security program. Otherwise the president won't believe you're really the assistant director."

He took a seat. "But I really *am* the assistant director, right?"

Madalyn made an impatient face. "Of course you are. Now pay attention. It's clear that a number of our recent problems have resulted from disorganization, miscommunication, and lack of compliance. The people need us to be ready to take care of them when disaster strikes. It's only a matter of time before we face another crisis. How many people fell through the cracks during the food riots? How many children will be left hungry and uncared-for if the system breaks down again?"

Kevin recalled Mitch's reaction when this scenario had been discussed during a Resistance meeting. His stomach lurched with dread.

"The Link is going to fix everything. No child will ever be denied access to food or government services that are rightfully theirs."

Then her focus seemed to drift. She glanced at her phone. "I have one more thing I need to take care of before we leave for the White House. Meet me downstairs in half an hour."

Kevin headed for the elevator. He breathed a sigh of relief as he opened the door of his old basement office. His assistant director ID badge granted him access to any room in the building, just like the one Atari had given him the day Stratford died. But this one was the real deal, not a forgery.

The familiar office was the size of a shoebox compared to the assistant director's suite upstairs. He sat in his creaky chair, laid the roll of candy on the desk, and pulled the pieces out until he found a tiny ear transmitter wrapped in foil. His fingers trembled as he turned it on and inserted it. "Can you hear me?"

Nothing happened. "Am I doing this right?" Still no response. His body sagged, and he dropped his head to the desk. "Are you kidding me?"

Then he heard a voice, and for a moment he imagined a two-inch-tall Mitch perched on his shoulder, like a cartoon incarnation of his conscience. But would he be dressed as an angel or devil? It was hard to know for sure.

"Hey! Yeah, I can hear you. Everything all right?" Mitch was breathing hard, like he'd been running.

"What's going on? Are you okay?"

There was a rustling sound and something that could've been the crackling of logs in a fireplace. "Yeah, sure."

"Okay, if you say so. You're never gonna believe what happened today. Long story short—I've got a meeting with the president in half an hour."

"Great! I'll be right there with you. Looking forward to it."

11:20 AM
Quadrant DC-001

Careen woke, disoriented, to complete darkness. She winced as she curled into a ball and wrapped her arms around her middle. She took slow, measured breaths, hoping it would help her overcome the panic that gripped her. *Where am I?* She wasn't at home, where she always left a light burning to allay her fears of the dark. It took a minute for her brain to clear enough to remember what had happened. She counted to one hundred while she waited for her eyes to adjust to the inky darkness, but still she could see nothing. Finally, curiosity outweighed her fear, and she tried to get a sense of her surroundings.

She was so achy and sore that any movement brought protests from her muscles. She let her brain flash quickly through everything that had happened since she went into the student center in search of Tommy and Wes; lingering too long on any one memory would upset her tenuous grip on her emotions. She still had no idea where she was and reached out with one arm until she touched the edge of the bed. There were no rails, so it wasn't a hospital bed. Her heart leaped

when she realized her wrists were bare; the crazy-person restraints
and the bandages on her hands were gone. Her fingers eagerly sought
more clues. The bed linens were soft and warm and felt expensive.
She was wearing pajamas made of some kind of slippery fabric.
Satin? The bandage was gone from her head, but one remained on
her cheek.

Her fingers brushed the edge of the nightstand and found a lamp.
She switched it on and gasped as the light revealed a bedroom
decorated like something she'd expect to see in a movie about a
queen. Now she really had no clue where she was. After the privation
and abuse at the hands of her interrogators, how had she ended up in
this place? How long since she'd made the bargain with Madalyn?
It could be a day or a week, for all she knew. Curiosity eventually
outweighed her soreness. Just sitting up caused her to whimper in
pain, and she steeled herself before taking the first step.

Thick carpeting cushioned her feet as she limped across the room
to peek through the floor-to-ceiling velvet drapes, but they masked a
solid wall. She made the long trip back across the room to where
a door stood ajar and stepped into an oversized bathroom tiled in
marble. The shower was large enough for two, with a touch pad
that controlled several different jets and nozzles. She'd never seen
anything like it in real life and wondered which of the settings would
be gentle enough to soothe her bruises. The long countertop held
stacks of fluffy towels and a range of expensive-looking beauty care
products with unfamiliar brand names.

She peered at herself in the full-length mirror, glad to see the
minor cuts and scratches on her face were healing, but when she
peeled back the gauze on her right cheek, her stomach lurched; the
black stitches that had closed the deep gash across her cheekbone
were ripped loose. The half-knit wound was ragged, and dried blood
crusted around the edges. As she replaced the bandage, she forced
herself not to think about how it would look when it healed. She'd lost
count of how many times she'd been slapped there. Her blackened
left eye was as bad as Tommy's had been, and her right temple was
swollen and tender to the touch.

She unbuttoned her pajama top and slipped it off, shuddering at
the sight of the bruises that had blossomed on her arms, shoulders,

and torso. One was shaped like a handprint. She prodded her side. *You can't see cracked ribs, can you? I'm pretty sure I can feel them.* She looked over her shoulder into the mirror. Her back was almost as battered as Tommy's had been after combat training.

Next she dropped the pajama pants and inspected the abrasions on her knees and hip. *I look thinner … and not in a good way.* It would be a while before she recovered physically. How much longer would it be before she'd be able to forget and forgive herself?

Everything hurt as she stooped to pick up her pajamas and pulled them back on. Who had dressed her in them? She shook off the cringing feeling of embarrassment, determined not to dwell on the many things she couldn't control, and returned to the main room, where there were two doors yet to be examined. She pressed her ear to one, then the other, but heard nothing. She grasped a doorknob and gently tried it, not wanting to attract attention if someone were on the other side. It was locked.

The remaining door opened easily, and a light came on as she stepped into a walk-in closet the size of the bedroom at her old apartment. It was stocked with clothes, shoes, and accessories that still had the tags on, and as she glanced at the prices, she became more bewildered than ever. Business suits, dresses, jeans, and blouses, more than she'd ever seen outside a store, hung in neat rows. Stacks of sweaters were folded on shelves. The drawers held underwear, and she scrabbled through the bras and panties, all new, all in her size.

What day is it? Is it sunny outside or the middle of the night? She was a prisoner; that was the only thing of which she was certain. But her cell was more like an opulent hotel room, and her prison garb rivaled the wardrobes of the wealthiest of her former classmates at the university.

Back in the main room, she spied an envelope addressed to her lying on the desk. She opened it to read a handwritten note on official OCSD letterhead:

This has been waiting for you since you arrived. It's a small thank you for facilitating our elimination of the Resistance. You've made the right choice. Madalyn Davies, Director, Office of Civilian Safety and Defense

Careen's knees buckled and she sank to the floor, her body convulsed with sobs of grief and pain. She'd meant to take the responsibility and the punishment upon herself; instead, had she doomed everyone to suffer an even worse fate than her own? How stupidly optimistic to think she could protect certain people simply by withholding their names! Of course Mitch and Jaycee would be captured, too, if the occupants of the Resistance headquarters were surprised by the QM's arrival. She couldn't save anyone. Then she remembered.

There was one name that hadn't come up. It could never, ever, cross her lips, even if the interrogations started all over again. Not if she were drugged or beaten or … whatevered. She vowed to die rather than betray the last member of the Resistance's inner circle. Kevin.

11:25 AM

As soon as Kevin was gone, Madalyn signed on to her computer. There was a message from Garrick waiting, and she scrolled quickly through his update. It was ridiculous that the intel they'd gained from interrogating Careen had ultimately yielded nothing more than a T-shirt and Tom Bailey. The shirt was useless, and Tom's arrival had only whetted her desire to apprehend them all. Especially Trina. Knowing she was out there, combined with Tom's threats … Well, it would be best to eliminate anything that could distract people's attention from the benefits of the Link.

Her attempt to log in produced an error message. She impatiently started over, but the error message came up again. She shouted at Nicole through the closed door.

Her assistant replied over the intercom on the desk. "Yes, Madam Director?"

"I keep getting an error message when I try to access surveillance."

"I'll try from out here, ma'am."

Madalyn drummed her fingers while she waited. There was no time for error messages or delays. She and Kevin were due at the

White House in half an hour, and she was dying to see if Careen was awake.

"There's no signal from the video feed, Madam Director. I'll submit another repair ticket to IT."

"This is unacceptable! How am I supposed to optimize my time without surveillance cameras?" *I can't go over there and peek in on her every time I want an update.* "Of all the places in the whole country, you'd think PeopleCam could keep their video equipment in working order."

11:35 AM

Kevin, his new earpiece transmitter in place, arrived in the lobby before Madalyn. A man with a neatly clipped gray mustache waited near the elevators. Kevin didn't recognize him, but as soon as Madalyn appeared, they both started toward her.

"Let's go. Can't keep the president waiting." Madalyn held out her coat to Kevin, and he dutifully helped her into it.

The other man regarded Kevin with curiosity. "Is he your new driver?"

"What? No." Madalyn flipped her hair free of the coat collar and peered at him. "What happened to your face?"

"Bailey. Never mind that." He gestured toward Kevin.

"This is Kevin McGraw, the new assistant director. Kevin, this is Art Severson."

Art stepped between them and spoke through gritted teeth. "I assumed *I'd* be the new assistant director."

"We never discussed any such thing."

Madalyn stalked past him before he had time to reply. As Kevin followed, he glanced back over his shoulder. Art Severson glared at him. *Great. Just great. Looks like my first unofficial act as assistant director was to make an enemy.*

Chapter 33

12:09 PM

"It's a pleasure to meet you, Mr. President. Sir." They shook hands, and Kevin gulped. All of a sudden, the expensive new necktie seemed to be cutting off his airway.

President Wright gestured Madalyn and Kevin to the sofa across from him and Senator Renald. Kevin wondered if the casual seating was supposed to relax them or catch them off guard. *Renald wants my job; so does that guy Severson. But it's mine. I've got to prove I deserve it.*

Mitch's voice came over the earpiece. "You can't measure the success of any program by its intent alone. You also have to consider the unintended results."

He paused periodically to allow Kevin to deliver the message at an unhurried pace.

"For example, take the Travel Restriction. Keeping people close to home was intended to make it easier for the QM to monitor the residents of their quadrants and recognize strangers, thereby preventing more terrorist attacks. But what about the unintended consequences?"

Madalyn was slowly shaking her head. He swallowed hard and pressed on. It was too late to stop now.

"How much did that Restriction cost the nation? How many tourism dollars were lost? How many auto workers lost jobs when the number of people allowed to own cars suddenly dropped by seventy-five percent?

"All but two of the major airlines and all the midsize carriers went bankrupt. Only one foreign airline has regular flights in and out of the United States. That's got to be a direct result of the Restriction that bans air travel by civilians for pleasure."

The president looked at him like he had two heads. Kevin shrugged.

"It seems like no one considered what the travel Restriction would do to our economy. I don't know why it didn't get attention from the national press."

"*Daddy!*" Jaycee's shrill voice blasted through Kevin's earpiece and he winced before he could stop himself. Renald didn't even try to conceal his curiosity as he stared at Kevin.

"*You don't get to ignore me just because I've decided to leave.*"

"*Hush!*" Mitch's voice boomed in his ear. "*I'm with Kevin.*"

Kevin's eyes bugged out in his efforts to ignore the voices inside his head. *What if the others can hear them, too?* With effort, he focused on Madalyn, the president, and Renald, who were all staring at him.

"The what? I'm sorry …"

Madalyn gave him a straighten-up-right-now look. "I said just think of all the terrorist attacks that were prevented!"

Kevin heard Mitch chuckle, but he kept his own expression earnest. "None. Not a single one. I've checked with Analysis and Integration, the Chief QM's reports, and the airport screening reports. There is no evidence that forbidding people to travel out of their home quadrant by car or take pleasure trips by air has prevented a single terrorist attack."

"But that's because the air passenger screening program is highly effective." Madalyn's voice was tight.

"No. Again, the airport screening isn't monitored as closely as it was fifteen or twenty years ago, because so few people take domestic flights these days. Even so, statistics show airport security fails to detect and confiscate about eighty percent of disallowed items in the screened baggage."

"*Bye, Kevin!*" Jaycee's sarcasm-laden voice pulled him back into the space between the two conversations. Mitch stopped feeding lines to Kevin and began hollering at her. There was no way to turn anything off, and he caught himself turning his head from side to side, like a spectator at a tennis match.

The words garbled in his earpiece. Was it his turn to speak to the room? There was a lull in Mitch and Jaycee's shouting match, and when Mitch barked, "No debit card!" it popped out of Kevin's mouth before he could stop himself.

The president's tone was dismissive. "Mr. McGraw, how does the elimination of debit cards fit in? Why would you suggest such a thing?"

Trina's words came to him, as though it was she who was whispering in his ear. *"You know more about the inner workings of the OCSD than you think you do."*

"Umm, what I meant to say was … actually, getting rid of debit cards wouldn't fix the issue. If I wanted to make a real difference in how people live, I'd adjust the protocols for reports submitted to Analysis and Integration. That office is deluged with reports of terrorist activity that are simply unfounded."

He glanced Madalyn's way. She was making no attempt to disguise the surprise on her face. Was it because he was suggesting changes to the status quo or because he spoke with authority? Either way, her reaction gave him confidence.

"We waste so much time and manpower checking out leads that always—yes, always—come to nothing. Some of the claims are nothing more than ways to bully people. Sometimes they're family feuds or disagreements with neighbors. In fifteen years, the OCSD has never prevented a terrorist attack because of a report submitted by a Watcher.

"I recommend we dial it back and raise the standards regarding evidence that must be presented before we investigate a claim. We might even penalize a person who makes a claim that's determined to be malicious."

Madalyn nudged him with her elbow, and he took that as his cue to shut up. She smiled at him, a smile that made his blood run cold, before turning to the president. "You see why Mr. McGraw is the man for the job. He's an expert on Analysis and Integration."

She settled into her seat and turned on the authority. "I'm more focused on implementing my new security system, which is nearly ready to go."

The president nodded. "So you've been saying. Are you able to clue us in a little? Or is it going to be a big surprise, like CSD?"

Her gaze narrowed a little. "I'll be glad to give you a quick overview of what it will mean for the future of this country. Imagine a security system that marries individual responsibility with complete and irrevocable access to help and protection, 24 hours a day, 365 days a year. Imagine a society in which children are never lost, never in danger, never denied food, medical care, or other resources that are rightfully theirs. Imagine a justice system that works swiftly and efficiently, punishing the wrongdoer and championing the victim."

Renald cleared his throat. "Sounds like a wonderful thing. How do you propose to achieve this, um, utopia?"

"It's simple, really. I don't know why no one ever thought of it before. Well, maybe people thought of it in the past, but now our advanced technology makes this kind of security possible for every American."

2:03 PM
Quadrant BG-098

David Honerlaw's own snores woke him up. He sat up on the sofa and looked around at everyone in the bunker, bemused. "How long was I asleep? More importantly, how soon can I open those files Tom left behind? I feel like a child waiting for Santa Claus."

Grace wagged a finger at him. "Time's not up yet. You agreed to his plan."

"But surely a little peek wouldn't hurt. This inquiring mind wants to know—even if I never get to expose all of Madalyn's deep, dark secrets." He stood up and wandered over to the computer equipment, his ex-wife at his heels. "Useless! This machine is far too old to be compatible with a chip drive."

Lara fidgeted in her seat. "Do you think I should've let Jaycee leave? I feel responsible."

Trina tried to reassure her. Again. "Surely she spent the night down at the diner or the boardinghouse. It would have been far too late to come back here last night."

Grace came back to her chair. "Sometimes I think that child's been raised by wolves. A girl that age needs a mother. Look at the way she clings to you, Lara."

"She's just lonely. I'm sure she misses Careen and Wes."

"Now Tommy's probably gone, too. That leaves no young people for company."

"Danni's around from time to time."

"She doesn't seem like a very good influence on a girl Jaycee's age. Mitch ought to pay more attention to her upbringing."

Trina quickly grew weary of the conversation. "You all sound like a bunch of gossipy church ladies after service on Sunday. Mitch is doing the best he knows how. And Jaycee's fine." She wasn't sure why she felt the need to defend Mitch now, when she'd accused him of the same thing just yesterday. She wished Kevin was there to rein her in. Her lack of diplomacy and discretion had gotten her in trouble before. She needed to get along with everyone, for God only knew how long they'd be packed into the bunker together like sardines. She cast about for another topic and blurted out something that was sure to command their attention. "Mitch is buying the CSD formulas from Madalyn."

"What?" Lara leaned forward in her chair.

"Why?" Eduardo looked wary.

Trina shrugged. "He's got a plan to use them against her. Expose her as corrupt and get her removed from the director's post."

That increased Eduardo's frown. "If he buys those formulas, he should make sure they're destroyed."

Lara asked, "Do you know any more about his plan?"

David sat back down in his place on the sofa. "Mitch appears to be doing the wrong thing for the right reason. No great surprise, really."

Grace nodded. "Buying the formulas from Madalyn is an interesting move."

Trina relaxed a little. *Okay, good. Now everyone's on the same page.* "He said he was pretending to be the leader of a terrorist organization."

"Then it's a sting operation." David looked gleeful. "Nothing like fighting tyranny with subterfuge—and a healthy dose of the truth. If I could just get to what's on this chip drive ..."

"David, Tom trusted you with his secrets." Grace tried not to smile. "Although I must admit, since it's about Madalyn, I hope it's something truly awful."

Eduardo said, "We're all part of the Resistance. We should work out our plans together, *no?*"

Trina nodded. "I agree we'll be more effective if we all have the same information. I also overheard him speaking with Victor Martel. He said Martel's part of the Resistance."

David rubbed his palms together as though contemplating evil deeds. "The head of Essential Services? He's one of us?"

"Martel's definitely in the Resistance. Essential Services didn't plan the food riots, but Mitch and Martel took advantage of what happened to make the point that depending on the government for food wasn't such a good idea. Remember, Mitch said that the best way to expose Madalyn's incompetence was to pile problems on top of problems and let her crash and burn."

Grace chuckled. "Crash and burn indeed. How will we ever know what's going on in Mitch's head?"

"Why don't you just ask?" They all turned toward Mitch's voice as he strode into the room, Jaycee at his heels.

Lara looked past them. "Where's Tommy? Why isn't he with you?"

Mitch hesitated. "Yeah. About that …"

"What? What's happened?"

"The QM showed up, pretty much on cue, and took Tom to the capital. Tommy arrived after they'd left, and he and Danni followed the convoy to the capital. They sent a message to say they made it to our safe house there." Lara nodded, and Mitch congratulated himself; the minimalist spin on what had happened sounded pretty good, even to his own ears.

"Tom insisted he was the only member of the Resistance here, and the QM bought it, for the most part. But …" He paused as though this were the worst thing that had happened that evening. "The QM shut down the diner."

Jaycee gasped. "Daddy, why didn't you tell me?"

"What does that mean, exactly?" Trina asked. "Will they force you to leave?"

"I'm not sure. As far as shutting down, you know it's not the diner itself as much as what else goes on there. If people occasionally come and go, it doesn't look suspicious when members of the Resistance or people transporting black market goods are among them. But we'll be watched from now on, and that could affect some of Danni's business dealings. On the other hand, we live at the diner, so unless they force us out entirely, we should be able to keep working in a limited capacity."

Lara spoke up. "I'm afraid Tom going back to confront Madalyn is going to put us in greater jeopardy. We can't all stay in this bunker forever, either. It's time to relocate to another quadrant."

"The QM will be watching the roads, searching vehicles for members of the Resistance. They had a list of names. Everyone was on it but Eduardo, Jaycee, and me."

Eduardo nodded. "If we go, it should be in small groups anyway, *no*?"

Mitch reached into his coat pocket. "Yeah. You and Lara could leave first." He produced an authentic-looking government ID card for Lara and a travel pass. "I had this made for you weeks ago, as soon as we found out you and Tom were alive. Eduardo, you're safe using your real ID. As far as we know, you're not on their radar."

"What about me, Daddy?"

"I told you. You're not going anywhere."

"It's just as dangerous here as anywhere. This isn't a secret hideout anymore."

"No. You're too young."

"Eduardo and Lara need me! Neither of them can handle a gun like I can. You won't go because you're afraid. But I'm not. Wes would totally understand. He wanted to go, too. Now it's my turn. I'm not going to be stuck at the diner my whole life."

She buried her face in Lara's shoulder and sniffled as though trying not to cry. Lara stroked the girl's unruly, rust-colored hair and gave Mitch a helpless look over her head.

Mitch shook his head. "You don't even know where they're going. *They* don't even know where they're going!"

"OP-439." Lara and Eduardo spoke at the same time.

Eduardo grinned. "We can use my apartment for now. If Tom joins us it might be too crowded, though."

"Eventually, we'll *all* need to go to the capital, right, Mitch?" Trina's look left no room for argument, and he threw up his hands.

"Maybe. Yeah. Looks like it."

Jaycee released Lara and turned to her father, no tears in sight.

"So, we'll meet you there really soon! Please, Daddy?"

Mitch sighed, and the delight on her face told Trina that Jaycee had taken his failure to answer as a yes.

Chapter 34

1:09 PM
Quadrant DC-001

Back in the car, Kevin slumped against the seat and resolved to leave Mitch's secret transmitter behind next time he had a meeting with the president. Why had he repeated the wrong thing? He'd sounded like he couldn't keep his train of thought. At the crucial moment, Mitch's presence had been so distracting that it had hurt more than it helped. He felt like he'd run a marathon. "I'm looking forward to sleeping in my own bed tonight."

As Madalyn keyed rapidly on her phone, the chipped polish on her right index finger drew his eye. She didn't look up. "Your suite of rooms on the third floor is ready. They're right next to your office."

"I was thinking I'd go home—to my apartment."

"Oh, that won't be possible. When the security threat is at Elevated or above, the director and the assistant director stay on-site. It's the best way to assure our safety."

"But all my stuff ... my clothes—"

"I had the tailor bring you a complete wardrobe and put everything away in your closet. You can't possibly need a thing from your old apartment. Pick up your keys from Nicole when we get back."

The car had slowed to a crawl. "Driver, can't you hurry up? I've got appointments and things to do."

"I'm sorry, Madam Director. Road's closed up ahead, but I didn't get any indication of an accident on the GPS."

Kevin peered out the tinted windows.

Madalyn was engrossed in sending a text. "Find another road."

"I can't, ma'am; we're gridlocked. This is as fast as we can go until we get past whatever's blocking the intersection."

Nearly everyone who still had driving privileges was a government worker; traffic snarls were common in the capital and surrounding quadrants. Madalyn, whose eyes were still glued to her phone, hadn't noticed what Kevin had seen as he watched the crowds on the sidewalk. The CXD symbol was everywhere—inked on people's clothing and spray-painted on the walls of buildings.

They'd been idling in the same spot for five minutes when she looked up again. "Well? What's the matter?"

"Looks like there's a big crowd of people in the intersection."

"Honk the horn and make them move! Don't they know who I am?"

The driver leaned on the horn. As if on cue, people spilled off the sidewalk and into traffic, swarming the cars on the road.

Madalyn shrieked and shrank away from the window as the crowd enveloped the car. Fingers shaking, she dialed 911. "The middle of the road cannot be a Restriction-Free Zone!"

2:30 PM

As soon as the car pulled up in front of the OCSD, Madalyn shouted orders to the driver. "Don't go anywhere! I'll need to leave again shortly. Stay right here!" She threw open the car door and hurried inside. Kevin went straight for the restroom and dug the tiny transmitter out of his ear.

The outer door opened with a bang, and he jumped. He lost his grip on the transmitter, and it ricocheted off the edge of the sink. "Shit!" He trapped it under his palm as it bounced toward the drain. He was so intent on what he was doing that he was startled to see a tall, thin man reflected in the mirror beside him.

"You the new assistant director?"

Kevin shoved his hand into his pants pocket as he turned around. "Yeah. I mean yes."

The other man extended his hand. "I'm Hoyt Garrick, Chief QM." Kevin dropped the transmitter into his pocket before he shook hands, but his composure was shot.

Garrick inclined his head toward the door. "There are some things we need to discuss right away. Come with me."

"Umm, all right." Kevin followed him into the lobby.

"How about we talk in your office?"

Kevin pushed the Down elevator button out of habit and then hastily punched Up before Garrick noticed.

As soon as they were safely inside the assistant director's office, Garrick locked the door, strode over to the computer, and loaded a chip drive. Kevin glanced around for an escape route, but he didn't even know which of the other doors led to his suite of rooms. This space had only been his for a few hours.

Garrick folded his arms. "Madalyn has no idea, does she? You're a Resistance spy."

Kevin gulped, and before he had time to respond, Garrick started playback of a video file. Cold fear spread to his fingertips as he watched himself follow Trina and Tommy into her lab. *I'm gonna be locked in the secure ward before my first day as assistant director is over.*

But as he and Garrick watched the surveillance tape, worries about his current situation took a back seat. Tommy had stayed behind in the lab to wait for some of Stratford's files to download, and Kevin had never wondered what happened while they were apart. Now he watched as a security guard entered the lab. He'd been no match for Tommy, who'd knocked him out and dragged him out of sight behind the desk as if it was no big deal.

"If circumstances were different, I'd want that kid in the QM. But that's not likely to happen, is it?"

Kevin didn't answer.

Garrick shut off the video. "Look, I won't say anything to Madalyn. I want you to help me."

"Help you how?"

"Why were you and Trina Jacobs with Tommy Bailey? What does he have to do with Stratford's death?"

"Nothing. He and Careen were there to rescue his parents. Trina didn't have anything to do with it, either. I won't help you frame her." Double agent he could handle. But would this make him a triple agent? He wasn't sure he could keep track of the lies it would take to pull that off.

"Relax. I'm certain Trina didn't do it. But what's Tommy Bailey's connection to all this? His parents faked their own deaths last July, and now he's wanted for taking part in the university bombing."

"No, they didn't. Their disappearance was an OCSD plan to silence Tom's opposition to the Restrictions. After the accident, they were brought here and held down in the secure ward for months. I know because I saw them. So did Trina—and so did Madalyn. Stratford had them moved on the day of the press conference, but Tommy and Careen tracked them down and helped them escape. We all met up at Resistance headquarters. Tom's a good guy. They're all good guys." He glossed over the part about the university bombing. Triple agent or no, he wasn't helping Garrick build a case against Tommy.

"So why did Bailey turn himself in to the QM this afternoon?"

"I don't know. Can we talk to him without Madalyn?"

Chapter 35

3:26 PM
Quadrant DC-005

Danni wandered into the kitchen in an oversized sweatshirt and a pair of boxers while Tommy was pouring himself a bowl of cereal. She grabbed an orange out of the fridge and favored him with a sultry grin as she left the room.

Yesterday, after Atari joined Danni, Tommy had gone downstairs and checked out the gym, but he'd been too tired to be interested in working out. He'd crashed in his room, slept the clock around, and wakened wishing his meals were prepared for him, like at Resistance headquarters.

He took his cereal into Command Central. Atari was already there, and Tommy shot a sideways glance at him as he settled into the other chair. "Could you show me how to work the surveillance camera thing so I can keep tabs on what's happening at the OCSD?"

Atari propped his elbow on the arm of the chair and drummed his fingers against his own cheek as if he were studying Tommy. "Did you seriously—please correct me, because I hope I'm wrong— *seriously* turn down a literal roll in the hay with Danni?"

Tommy dropped his head against the back of the chair and closed his eyes. *I can't take three more days of this guy.* "You know about that, too, huh?"

"This is a communications hub. Nothing is secret. Nothing is sacred."

"Maybe to you. I disagree."

"Oh?"

"Yeah." He looked Atari in the eyes. "I love Careen. Turning down Danni was a no-brainer."

"Oh, so you listened to your brainer instead of your ... gotcha."

Change the subject. "So, you handle explosions and fireworks for the Resistance?"

"Why? You after my job?"

"No." He'd had enough of bombs to last him a lifetime. "Just wondered."

"I serve a myriad of functions in the organization; that is to say, I wear many hats. My role requires extraordinary technical and people skills, formidable intellect, and, of course, an abundance of charisma. I don't mind saying that I excel at everything I do for the Resistance."

Danni walked past the doorway, and Atari called out, "Don't I, baby?"

"Don't call me that," she replied without missing a beat.

Tommy choked his laugh into a cough. "But what exactly do you do?"

"Okay. I'm not sure I can get it down to words of one syllable for you, so try and keep up. My job in the Resistance is, first and foremost, to create shiny objects to distract Madalyn."

Tommy shrugged.

"But that's not all. I use my unsurpassed hacking skills to behave like a slowly creeping virus, taking over her world bit by bit. For example, Stratford was totally addicted to his surveillance system, but I've been messing with the cameras ever since the day he kicked the bucket. None of their experts have been able to properly diagnose the problem, let alone fix it. Thus, I have trained Madalyn not to rely on it. She doesn't even use it anymore. I can see her, but she can't see me. And so we keep tabs on what's going on over there. Behold."

He pecked at one of the keyboards, and Tommy watched closely once he realized Atari wasn't actually going to explain it to him. Atari pushed back his chair and stood up.

"Oh, and I blow stuff up. Actually, there was this one time I was hanging upside down under a bridge trying to wire—"

He left the room, and his voice faded as he wandered down the hall. Puzzled, Tommy waited for him to return and finish the story. He never did.

Chapter 36

4:30 PM
Quadrant DC-001

A bleating alarm filled the darkness and jerked Careen out of a deep sleep. She groped for the lamp, knocking it over in her haste to turn it on. She swung her legs out of bed and righted the lamp, but its soft glow had barely penetrated the inky blackness of the windowless room when the overhead sprinklers activated, showering her with cold water.

There's a fire! She raced around the bed to the door, heedless of the pain that shot through her body. Her fingers slipped as she tried to grip the unyielding doorknob. Water ran down her face as she pounded on the heavy door, screaming to be heard over the alarm. *What if no one comes for me? Will they remember I'm locked in?*

She pushed her wet hair off her face, dropped to her knees and sniffed near the bottom of the door. Smoke. She jumped up and ran into the bathroom, skidding on the marble floor, and grabbed a towel off the rack, the memory of a school fire-safety lesson in mind as she turned on the tub faucet.

She was lifting the soaked, heavy towel out of the tub when the alarm went silent. She hurried back into the bedroom, so intent on preserving her air supply that she bumped into the guard before she saw him.

Careen shrieked and clutched the wet towel to her chest, rivulets of water pooling on the carpet around her feet. The door to the hallway stood open; there was no smoke, no fire. She began to shiver uncontrollably.

She dropped the towel as the guard slipped the hated black hood over her head. He took her by the arm and led her from the room.

The sound of her chattering teeth filled the space inside the hood. Her bare feet felt the thick carpet in the hallway as she stumbled along beside the guard, tugging at her wet pajama top with her free hand so it wouldn't cling to her in the wrong places.

She prayed there really was a fire. If she could just get outside, maybe she could escape. It wouldn't matter that it was December, and she was already freezing cold.

The guard jerked her around a corner and through a doorway. The floor was smooth here. Not tile. Cement.

The guard removed the hood and retreated, leaving her in the spotlight. She crossed her arms over her chest and clenched her jaw to stop her teeth from chattering. Her hair, hanging in wet strands around her face, only emphasized her trembling. She recognized the voice that came from behind her, outside the circle of light. *Madalyn.*

"You've lied to us again. The members of the Resistance were not at the diner in BG-098."

She felt a surge of energy and bit her lip, silently giving thanks that she'd been strong enough to give them time to escape.

"The QM is proceeding with the planned house-to-house search. When the fugitives are found, we'll make sure their accommodations and treatment are nowhere near as nice as yours." There was a long pause. "You look like a drowned rat. Take off those wet things."

"What? No." Her voice was barely above a whisper. She bowed her head and her cheeks flushed hot, despite the cold and the bone-chilling fear.

"This is an important lesson for you, Careen. Do as you're told."

She pressed her lips together and closed her eyes.

Madalyn's voice was harsh. "Your lies are wasting time and resources, and that will not be tolerated. Next time, maybe you'll think before you lie to me. Now do as you're told."

She gulped and kept her eyes shut tight. Her fingers shook as she felt for the buttons on her pajama top.

Chapter 37

4:30 PM
Quadrant BG-098

The meeting of the remaining members of the Resistance had gone smoothly. Mitch liked it better without Tom's tacit disapproval and Tommy's glowering presence. Plus, he'd saved the best item on the agenda for last. "Madalyn's prepared to sell me the CSD formulas." He took a flourishing bow and was disappointed when no one applauded. "You guys know already?"

"Trina mentioned it." Grace raised an eyebrow. "Why did Madalyn decide to do that? Does she know who you are?"

"My contact reported that she's checked out the fake me, and she knows who she *thinks* I am. I suspect she's anxious to complete the transaction and collect the money I promised her."

"She's not content with her director's salary?" Lara shook her head. "All these scandals would hurt her credibility if anyone was paying attention. She has no qualms about committing treason against her own country."

Mitch nodded. "We've got her right where we want her. Victor Martel is on the verge of pushing the Essential Services system off the proverbial cliff, and Atari is deep undercover at the OCSD, engineering and preparing for the launch of that new security device thing. It's based on an idea Stratford had years ago. Atari says the technology is kind of out-of-date, but Madalyn's in love with the idea, so Atari's telling her it's a state-of-the-art solution to individual security.

"She's set to spend billions of taxpayer dollars on this program, and Atari's been directed to make sure it doesn't work. Two huge, expensive failures right on the heels of the CSD debacle should generate enough public outcry from our newly awakened populace to convince the three legitimate branches of government to correct the OCSD's overreach."

Eduardo spoke up. "When I met with the president, he insisted that Madalyn was doing a good job and had everything under control. Might be hard to convince him to act if he really believes what he said."

"Oh, we'll convince him. It's time to put together the next part of my plan." Mitch was ready to rally the troops. "David, Grace, we need a step-by-step on how to disband the OCSD without completely undermining national security and leaving us vulnerable to real terrorists. Can you put together a practical and doable blueprint for how to proceed? Keep it simple. The stuff in your textbooks is too academic. We need easily digestible bits of information—something even politicians can get their heads around and repeat without botching it too much."

5:19 PM
Quadrant DC-001

"So you're telling me Essential Services has bottomed out again?"

Victor Martel watched Madalyn finger-comb her hair and press her fingers to the bags under her eyes, pleased to see the constant strain was wearing her down.

"Yes, Madam Director, because you insisted we not deliver any food until we can meet the federal nutrition standards for ES meals. We can provide incomplete meals to most of the population, or we can provide approved meals to about a third of the population."

"Then people will just have to wait a little longer."

Martel was ready to stop his deferential treatment of Madalyn and move on to the next phase of the Resistance's plan to rebuild the country's private food distribution networks. "Don't you think starving people would be grateful for *any* food—even if you can't give them balanced meals yet? You're foolish to insist on following some arbitrary rule."

"People aren't starving."

"And it's a good thing! Lifting the Restriction on nongovernment food vendors may seem chaotic but it's working."

"So what's your recommendation?"

"Let private vendors sell food. Give people the option to receive fewer meals through ES. I would go so far as to allow people to cancel their ES service entirely if they wish. We definitely need to offer people the option to keep the money that's deducted from their monthly pay rather than subscribe to ES."

"What? No! We can't do that. The program's running at a huge deficit as it is. We need all that money coming in."

"It will cost less if ES serves fewer people. It's possible that some people will want to continue receiving all their meals through Essential Services. From now on, we're going to let them decide. I'm scheduled to make the announcement on the six o'clock news. "

"That's unacceptable! If we let people drop out of the ES system, how will we monitor what they're getting to eat? How will we protect them? Ensure their safety?"

Martel stared at her. "Are you listening to yourself? Do you honestly believe what you're saying?"

"Yes." She sank into her chair. Then she rallied, pointing her finger at him as she spoke. "If you announce that full participation is no longer mandatory, your tenure is over. Over! Do you understand?"

"I understand. It will be my pleasure to let my television appearance serve as my resignation."

Martel was smiling as he left her office.

6:51 PM
Quadrant DC-005

Tommy watched the surveillance camera footage while he waited for Atari to come back, but as time passed, his return seemed less and less likely. He wandered out into the foyer. The vintage video games, with their hulking cabinets and simple graphics, appealed to him more than whatever Atari had been playing the day before. He tried one until he got the hang of it and then moved on to another, and played until dinnertime. Even though he was confined to the safe house, he couldn't help feeling his time could be better spent. When Atari ambled through on his way back to Command Central, Tommy hurried after him.

"Danni still sleeping?"

"No, she's gone."

"Gone? She didn't say good-bye."

"Man, she never does."

So much awkward. "Back in BG-098, I had a bunch of books I was going to read, but I had to leave them behind. Thought you might have some of the same ones here."

"Books? With words? Really?"

Jerk. "Yeah. Until just recently, reading and studying was more Careen's thing. But now that I've been in the Resistance for a while, I want the big picture."

For once, Atari didn't make a snarky comment. He pecked at the keyboard, and soon a black-and-white video came up on one of the screens. "Then how about we start with a history lesson. Back in the 1950s, they showed stuff like this to school kids."

The opening cartoon featured a turtle in an air-raid helmet. The narrator's voice sent a chill up Tommy's spine.

"We all know the atomic bomb is dangerous, and as it may be used against us, we must get ready for it, just as we are ready for many other dangers that are around us all the time."

Atari cringed, wiggling his fingers. "Ooh! I'm so scared. No, I'm not. I've seen this one before."

On the screen, a classroom full of elementary school children listened, eagerly attentive, as their teacher warned about the impending threat of a nuclear strike.

"First, you have to know what happens when an atomic bomb explodes. When it comes—and we hope it never comes, but we must get ready—it looks something like this ... "

Tommy flinched at the bright flash of light on the screen.

"... duck and cover beneath a table or desk." The children scrambled beneath their school desks.

"Can you hide from a nuke under a desk?"

"What do you think?" They watched in silence for a time.

The narrator's voice was surprisingly upbeat, considering he was telling little kids they could survive a nuclear attack by covering themselves with newspaper or huddling in a doorway. Was this supposed to be comforting? Empowering? It was having the opposite effect on Tommy, who marveled at the futility of the instructions. *"The man helping Tony is a Civil Defense Worker. His job is to help us when there is danger of the atomic bomb. We must obey the Civil Defense Worker ... "*

Tommy pointed at the screen, and Atari paused the video. "That's what they told us—that we needed to take CSD for our protection. They wanted us to obey without thinking too much about it. Has it always been this way?"

"What do you think?"

"We didn't need to take CSD. So how can we believe anything the OCSD tells us?"

Atari shook his head. "Don't think in absolutes. Domestic security is a real concern. It's not a joke."

"Neither is lying to everyone about a fake terrorist threat."

"Consider the lengths to which people like Stratford and Madalyn will go to gain control. Because when you understand that it's all about control, you can see that, yes, it's nothing new." Atari shut off the video. "You can download and watch anything in our film database on any computer in the building. Start with the ones labeled Propaganda and Dystopia. They're banned from the government-run networks, so you probably haven't seen them. You should also check out the library one level up. We have lots of print books.

"If you're serious about your education, try to absorb a little of everything—history, politics, economics, sociology, even music, film, and pop culture. The stuff about the fall of the Soviet Union in the late 80s is pretty interesting."

Tommy took the stairs up one level to the library, which occupied the entire floor and was the largest collections of print books he'd ever seen. He pulled a few off the shelves—some he recognized from his dad's home office, others from the stack Careen had been keeping in her room. He wandered over to a computer terminal and pulled up the film database. There were dozens of unfamiliar titles. This would definitely keep him busy. He hoped he wasn't stuck here long enough to view them all.

He headed back downstairs with a stack of books and set them on the desk in Command Central. "Atari, why did you get involved in the Resistance?"

"I wanted to do something to change the world. The real world, I mean. I'd conquered the virtual world when I was younger than you. But when I joined the Resistance, it was like the moment of my real birth—the moment I found my passion.

"You remember when they shut down our access to the Internet in 2028, right?"

"Yeah. Sort of. I was like, twelve years old. I wasn't allowed much screen time when I was a kid, so it really didn't affect me. We needed PeopleNet for our school research, but I didn't use it for anything else."

"Exactly. Of course, the plan was to keep terrorists from learning anything about us online, so they assembled a team of experts to block the flow of information and create a kind of virtual shield, or dome, over our country that would keep us insulated. Or isolated, if you prefer. But PeopleNet's startling lack of information keeps any terrorists who may be on American soil from learning much, either.

"Once the work was done and access to the global information network was cut off, some of the great minds on the team reconsidered what they'd done. They tried to get the OCSD to rescind the Restriction. Most of them aren't with us anymore."

"Seriously? You mean they were killed?"

"Most were forcibly expatriated—you know, kicked out of the country. But yes, some of them were permanently silenced. Stratford loved the Shield. Thought it was one of the greatest things ever. Until he came up with his plan for Phase Four, that is."

"That's the new, innovative security system that's so wonderful they won't tell us what it does?"

"Yeah." Atari snorted. "Although it's not new or innovative; in fact, it's a blatant recycle, but with a twist. It's really intent that makes it different—and much more worrisome."

It bugged Tommy how much Atari reminded him of Mitch when he said stuff like that.

"Madalyn's claiming the Link is the cure for all the world's ills, but it's nothing new. Our cellphones have had GPS trackers in them since the early 2000s. We're tracked everywhere we go, spied on every time we send an email on PeopleNet. But you can turn off a phone, or leave it at home, or lose it, right?"

"I accidentally left my phone in a marshal's van. Haven't seen it in six weeks. Never got a new one."

"Exactly my point. The Link's wonderful innovation is that it's permanently affixed to our children. They can't lose it, forget it, or take it off. Its battery runs off their body's energy."

"And you invented it?"

"I can't take credit for conceiving it. Stratford forwarded me a list of must-haves, and I merely made it a reality."

"But why did you build the Link when you know it's going to be used for something bad?"

"Because to deploy a system as large as the Link, I'd get to pierce the Shield and open up the flow of information again. But that's top secret. Only Stratford knew that, and I'd bet the farm he never mentioned it to Madalyn.

"Mitch wants the Link to fail. I was supposed to deliver it, deploy it, and watch it crash and burn. Then I'd disappear forever rather than suffer Stratford's wrath when it didn't work. But a lot of things changed after Stratford died, and during the food riots, I realized the Link was even more useful as a screen play." He nudged Tommy with his elbow. "See? I included a football reference for you. I'm trying to help you keep up. Anyhoo, if we can get the OCSD to concentrate on the Link, I can piggyback some other programs I want to get out there. Things we used to have. Things that can really help. But I've got to be careful not to let the OCSD realize what I've done until people start using the good stuff and no one wants to give it up."

"Can't you do all that and still have the Link not work?"

"That's what Mitch keeps asking, but he doesn't understand. If the Link doesn't work, at least for a while, someone might notice the leak in the Shield and plug it up again."

He settled back in his chair, fingers still for the moment. "The unobstructed flow of information is the key to freedom."

Tommy sighed as he settled in and opened a book, glancing up at the surveillance camera monitor every few paragraphs, keeping an eye out for his dad. He'd been at it for a while when a familiar face on one of the monitors made him forget everything he'd just read. He stood up, pointing. "What's he doing there?"

"He who?"

"Art. Art Severson. I mean, I didn't think he was going to be stuck out at the lake house forever, but how did he end up at the OCSD?"

Chapter 38

6:20 PM
Quadrant DC-001

Victor Martel had carried out his threat and dealt the Essential Services department a crippling blow. Madalyn turned off the television and beat the remote against her desk to vent her anger. *Apparently we're just going to turn everyone loose to manage his or her nutritional needs without help. Will anyone prefer to stay with the program, or will they opt out because of one hitch in the system? If I've lost the Essential Services battle, I must make sure the Link is a success.*

She swore and threw the remote across the room. Connecting individuals to their Essential Services accounts had been one of the greatest benefits of the Link. Now that Martel had given everyone permission to drop out of food delivery, Essential Services would have to herd them all back in again once they were Linked.

Well, she could play Martel's game. She'd order the public relations campaign for the Link to commence right away. She sent Kevin a message, and less than a minute later, he hurried through her door.

"What's up?"

"Come on. We're going over to PeopleCam. Now."

6:35 PM

Kevin waited while Madalyn unlocked a control room at People-Cam studios and then followed her inside. On the other side of the glass, Careen stood in the spotlight on an empty soundstage. He averted his eyes.

Madalyn pressed a switch to open the microphone. "Get dressed." Careen jumped, startled out of her stupor, and grabbed her shed pajama top.

"What the ... why is she—" He'd always suspected Madalyn was heartless, but it sickened him that she could torture and humiliate Careen, seemingly without a shred of remorse.

"She's a liar. I hope she's learned her lesson and is ready to do as she's told. We're going to start recording videos for the Link tonight."

"You're going to use her on camera? With that black eye? Don't you think it would be better to wait until she's completely healed?" She looked like someone had been using her as a punching bag.

"I realize she's an absolute mess. Makeup can hide some of it, but if she looks a little ragged in her first few appearances, it's just proof that actions have consequences." She looked at him sharply. "Don't you dare feel sorry for that girl. You're going to have to learn to be less squeamish if you're going to do your job properly. She does not deserve to feel comfortable."

Madalyn activated the microphone and spoke as though giving orders to someone else, so Careen would assume she'd overheard by accident.

"... begin again immediately. Have her taken—" She cut the microphone and punched a number on her phone.

"Security? Take her back up to her room. Someone from hair and makeup will meet you there."

Kevin silently promised Careen he'd help her escape, no matter the cost, and with or without Mitch's assistance. She wouldn't be here, in this battered and broken state, if he'd been brave enough to follow her into the student center.

6:35 PM

Careen had been standing in the light for so long that she believed she was dead to any embarrassment; her earlier worry about how she'd ended up in those expensive pajamas in the first place had been silly and prudish. But the moment she was given permission, she covered herself with her arms and dropped to the floor, dressing as quickly as she could.

Madalyn's voice came over the speaker, then cut off abruptly, but Careen had heard enough. *Oh, God, they're going to question me again.* She drew a sobbing breath and began to shake violently from the feel of the cold fabric against her skin and the surging adrenaline response. Neither flight nor fight was an option.

The now-familiar guard appeared in the circle of light, expression unreadable. He slipped the hood over her head and took her by the arm. She could learn to believe her body no longer belonged to her and tell herself it didn't matter what she ate, what she wore, or who shamed and humiliated her. Her heart was the only part of her that still protested. Stumbled. Rebelled.

They came to a halt sooner than she expected. It had been the first time since her arrival here—wherever *here* was—that she hadn't tried to figure out where she was being taken.

The guard removed the hood, and she was surprised to find herself back in her own room. It was spotless. The bed was made, the lamp righted. She curled her toes in the thick carpet. A slight dampness was the only evidence that she hadn't dreamed the whole fire alarm thing.

The guard held the door open to admit a woman dressed in a plain black top and pants, her blonde hair pulled into a severe ponytail. She carried a large fishing tackle box into the suite. The guard pulled the door closed behind him.

The woman set the box down on the table with a thump and moved closer, peering at Careen's face, and she trembled at the thought of the interrogations starting all over again. The woman's hand snapped out, quick as a snake striking, and caught her by the chin.

She tossed her head and tried to turn away, but the woman held her in a tight grip. "What's in the box?" The shaky whisper communicated Careen's fear, and she regretted speaking at all.

"Has no one been attending to the cut on your cheek? You're going to have a scar." She clicked her tongue regretfully. "I'll do what I can, but I'm not a miracle worker."

She turned Careen loose and opened the tackle box. It was full of makeup. Careen let out an involuntary whimper of relief.

"What color will you be wearing?"

"For what? Who are you?"

"There are only two and a half hours until your call. I'm Fawn. I'll be doing your hair and makeup. No offense, but it's a big job.

It'll take a while to cover up your bruises, and we have to get rid of those highlights, too. Get in the shower and I'll choose an outfit."

Careen hesitated. Was this some kind of joke? "You're serious?"

"Of course. Now move it."

7:55 PM

Fawn hurried Careen onto a soundstage with five minutes to spare, and a man wearing a headset told her to sit at a familiar-looking desk. The lights powered up and realization dawned. *I'm at PeopleCam. I've been at PeopleCam all along. It's like some crazy make-believe game. Except it's not a game.*

There was no security guard in sight, and none of the stage crew treated her like a prisoner who might bolt at any second. She wished she could get up the nerve to try, but she was caught in the spotlight again. There was nowhere to run.

She picked nervously at the cuff of her sweater. Orange was not a color she usually chose for herself. Fawn had insisted, saying it was stunning with her dark hair, which was now glossy and radiant after a quick color job, a deep condition, and Fawn's skillful styling. But the sweater reminded Careen of the CSD antidote. She'd have preferred to wear pink.

The floor manager called for quiet and then addressed Careen. "Ready?"

"What am I supposed to say?"

He pointed to a small screen beneath the camera lens. "Your script's been loaded in here. Just read from the prompter, all right? Good. In three ... two ..." He pointed at her.

"I'm Careen Catecher. I was responsible for the university bombing and ... the death of quadrant marshal Wesley Carraway. Though I can't undo what I've done, I feel compelled to atone for my mistakes, so I am offering my assistance to the OCSD."

Tears sprang up in her eyes. "I am no longer part of the Resistance or CXD. I urge you to avoid participating in unlawful activities of any kind, even acts of civil disobedience that seem as though they hurt no one. Lawbreakers will be punished. Even though I'm helping the OCSD, I am not guaranteed immunity."

She took a deep breath and plunged into the final lines. "I am a criminal, not a hero. I didn't understand that the things I did on behalf of the Resistance would have such far-reaching consequences. I wish I had done nothing wrong. Then I'd have nothing to fear."

When the taping was over, the guard was there to escort her back to her room, but this time she was allowed to see where she was going. She breathed more easily now that she understood cooperation would buy her privileges.

Once she was alone her room, she waited for over a minute, ear pressed to the door, before she tried the knob. It was locked, but she wasn't disappointed. Not really. Freedom and trust had to be earned bit by bit.

She had little interest in the dinner tray that waited on the table but forced down a few bites before she crawled into bed. She turned out the lamp on the nightstand and fell almost immediately into a deep and restorative sleep.

Chapter 39

7:59 PM
Quadrant OP-439

After Victor Martel's surprise announcement that evening, people all over the country took to the streets to celebrate, and all available marshals were dispatched to keep the revelers from becoming too unruly. Henry Nelson had been assigned to the square in front of the old courthouse near the university campus. Rule breaking was no longer confined to those infernal Restriction-Free Zones. People set up food stalls right on the square. He'd heard on his walkie-talkie that a market was in full swing in front of the ES food distribution warehouse in OP-441. He couldn't get over how brash the citizens had become.

PeopleCam had announced a live address from Careen Catecher would be broadcast at eight p.m.. As the designated hour approached, a crowd gathered beneath the huge television screen mounted to the wall above the news ticker.

At first Henry had kept his eyes on the crowd as they watched the video, on guard for any troublemakers. But then he started paying attention to what Careen was saying, and his anger flared.

"Hang on. So all this time they've been blaming her for Stratford's murder and the university bombing, and now all of a sudden she's on television working as a spokesmodel for the OCSD? What kind of justice is that?"

He got a few sideways glances. No one was willing to take the bait and argue with a quadrant marshal, but he would've welcomed a fight. This whole situation was ticking him off more and more. The OCSD had just handed a *de facto* pardon to Wes's murderer.

The gathered crowd watched her speech in silence. When it was over, someone began to boo, and others in the crowd joined in. The news ticker below the screen ran the text of her speech, and the crowd's ranks swelled as other passersby stopped to see what all the fuss was about.

It wasn't just teenagers and college students wearing the CXD symbol anymore. Plenty of adults were there, too, raising their Sharpie-scrawled fists and booing as lustily as if they'd just watched an ill-advised attempt at a squeeze play or a critical missed field goal. The crowd had grown so large he couldn't fix position on any other marshals. He decided not to act and held his position, fearing the crowd would turn from vocal to violent.

The walkie-talkie at his belt crackled to life. "Need backup at the former student center on campus. Group of protesters numbering around three hundred. Repeat. Send backup immediately."

9:07 PM
Quadrant DC-001

Mitch's voice boomed in Kevin's ear. "Where've you been? I was about to send Atari in to find you. I thought Madalyn got wise during the meeting at the White House and had you carted off to the secure ward."

"I'm fine. I can do the job on my own. I'll use the transmitter for emergencies. Then I won't, um, rely on you too much." *I gotta make sure I don't tick him off so he'll help me. But I can't have him in my ear all the time. He'd drive me nuts.* "I'm sorry. I should have checked in with you before. We've got a huge problem. Madalyn's furious that the QM hasn't succeeded in rounding up the Resistance, and she's taking it out on Careen."

"Well, what do you want me to do? Turn everyone in?"

"God, no! I want you to help me get Careen out. She's being tortured worse than anything Stratford did to the Baileys or David and Grace. She looks like hell. You should see the bruises." Kevin paced. "I don't know if I can handle this."

"You gotta be less squeamish."

Yeah, so I've heard. "Did you see Careen's announcement at eight?"

"Yeah."

"Madalyn's not going to stop until she destroys Careen. We need an extraction plan before it's too late."

9:00 AM
Friday, December 8, 2034
PeopleCam Studios
Quadrant DC-001

Pete Sheridan led off the morning news over video footage of people carrying signs that read OCSD=LIES and FREE CAREEN.

"Yesterday's message from Careen Catecher sparked outrage nationwide. Seems like we've barely settled the unrest over the food shortages, and now protesters are back in front of public buildings, blocking access and refusing to disperse in direct violation of the Restrictions."

Sheila Roth slapped the news desk with the palm of her hand. "It just shocks me, Pete. I know we're not supposed to share our own opinions when we report the news, but I can't keep quiet any longer. Why do people sympathize with Careen Catecher? It seems to me she's been given a great deal more consideration than she deserves. Why, just think about all the bad things that have happened since she and Trina Jacobs murdered Lowell Stratford, and now, instead of blaming her—"

Pete cut her off. "People numbering in the tens of thousands have taken to the streets in quadrants all over the country. You can see footage here of the Quadrant Marshal Special Forces moving in to occupy troubled quadrant IN-654. Hundreds were arrested as marshals worked to quell the violence and re-establish order."

Restoring order looked like a military invasion with scores of marshals in gas masks and riot gear moving in ahead of tanks and armored vehicles. The broadcast cut away to commercial just as the marshals released tear gas into the crowd.

12:45 PM
Quadrant DC-001

Careen was finishing lunch when Fawn arrived to do her hair and makeup. She was dressed in a fuchsia blouse and black jeans and boots, but Fawn shook her head. "No pink."

"Why?"

"You really have to ask?"

"Oh. Yeah. I guess not."

Fawn retrieved more choices from the closet. "Here. Blue? Yellow?"

Blue as the lake. Blue like Tommy's eyes. "Yellow, please."

All too soon, it was time to take her place in the studio. She read from the teleprompter with just enough energy to avoid comment from Madalyn. "The Resistance's attempts to undermine the authority of the OCSD came to a head when I interrupted a press conference last month. The Resistance ordered me to distract the witnesses in the room while Trina Jacobs poisoned then-OCSD Director Lowell Stratford. Dr. Stratford's death caused people to fear taking the antidote that was meant to keep them safe."

Careen's mind whirled as she read from the teleprompter. *Seriously? She's still clinging to this when everyone knows the terrorist attack was a setup? We never needed to take that …. Oh hell, it wasn't even an antidote.* She took a calming breath and went on.

"The Resistance's propaganda videos were overly simplistic and poorly researched, because we knew it would take no more than a rallying point to get people's attention."

Anger fueled a tiny flame of rebellion in her heart. She forced herself to keep reading. "The Resistance is directly responsible for the food shortage and everything bad that's happened since then. As I explained to the quadrant marshals while I was in custody, I didn't realize just how much my actions would affect others.

"How could a bunch of outlaws know more about what's good for our country than the experts at the OCSD? If you listened to me before, I hope you'll listen to me now, because I'm telling you the truth for the first time."

2:00 PM

"Could we take the stairs? I'd really love to stretch my legs."

Though Careen had just been granted the privilege of using the regular elevator, she felt like pushing for more.

The guard remained expressionless as he opened the stairwell door. *He's never said a word to me. He's never treated me like a person.*

"I haven't seen daylight in I don't know how long. Could we please go down to the lobby? And maybe I could look out a window before I go back to my room?"

She kept up a determined pace as they descended, and he let her keep going until they emerged on the ground level. The guard closed his fingers around her upper arm once they were in the hall. One whole wall was window, and Careen stared out at the sunlight that glittered on the surrounding buildings. A courtyard with trees, now bare, ran along the outside of the building. Benches lined the brick walkway. Maybe by spring she'd be allowed to sit outside. She drew closer to the window and pressed her nose to the glass, moving on reluctantly when the guard tugged at her arm.

They rounded a corner into the main lobby, and she looked eagerly toward the glass entrance doors, where a throng of people obstructed her view of the street. They were blocking the entrance. Guards stood between them and the doors. Careen stopped to stare. She'd never seen a real protest, even though she'd encouraged them in her Resistance videos. She made eye contact with a woman at the front of the crowd. The woman's mouth flew open as she pointed toward Careen, and everyone began to push against the guards.

She stood, uncomprehending, gaping at the advancing mob. Garbled shouts erupted in her guard's earpiece, and though she couldn't tell what was being said, the tone was clear. The guard broke into a run, dragging her with him. Heavy pounding and a muffled roar echoed in the cavernous lobby and doubled in volume as the wave of people exploded through the doors.

Careen looked over her shoulder; someone at the front of the group pointed at her, and they surged forward, shouting her name.

The guard caught her at the waist, dragged her around a corner, and shoved her onto the service elevator. She sprawled on the floor as he seized the doors and slammed them shut, pushing the hasp into place.

As they rumbled upward, she scrambled to her feet, breathing hard. "What's happening?"

"They know you're here."

Again she heard the faint voice barking orders in his earpiece.

As soon as the elevator slowed, he muscled open the doors and dragged her out before it came to a stop. He ran with her down a side hallway and up a half-flight of stairs. This wasn't her floor—hers was carpeted.

At the end of the hall, he pushed her through a plain wooden door and slammed it shut, leaving her alone in the dark. She was so stunned that it took a moment before she began to panic. She seized the doorknob and twisted it, even though no doorknob had yielded for her since she'd arrived. Sobbing, she groped around the perimeter for a light switch but found none. The room was so small she could touch opposite walls without straightening her elbows.

She pressed her palms against the cinderblock and squeezed her eyes shut, breathing slowly to calm her racing heart. Once composed, she opened her eyes, steeling herself to face the isolation for however long she might need to. A narrow strip of light showed through the gap at the bottom of the door, illuminating the toes of her boots. She dropped to the floor, pressed her face against the cold cement, and breathed in the light.

Chapter 40

9:48 AM
Saturday, December 9, 2034
Quadrant DC-005

Tommy balanced his plate in one hand and his book in the other as he came out of the kitchen into what had once been an employee dining room so large that he could've eaten at a different table every day for a month. He returned to the kitchen for his glass of orange juice and was on his way back to the table when the elevator door in the foyer slid open, and a man in an OCSD security uniform stepped out. *What the hell? I thought this place was supposed to be secret. How did he get in here?* The guard removed his cap and ran his hand over his brown buzz-cut and then surveyed the room, hands on hips. Tommy ducked back to avoid being seen and banged his elbow on the refrigerator. Juice spattered in a wide arc as his glass shattered against the tile floor.

The guard strode into the kitchen, boots pulverizing the broken glass as though he couldn't be bothered to avoid it. He gave Tommy an appraising glance and shook his head.

"Wazzup, Butterfingers?" he said as he poured himself a cup of coffee.

Tommy took a closer look. "Atari?"

The guard opened the fridge in search of milk. "Natch. Who else would I be? There's a broom and dustpan in the pantry."

Tommy cleaned up the mess and poured himself another glass of juice. He found Atari at his table in the dining room, eating the breakfast Tommy had made for himself.

He sat down and pulled his plate away from Atari's fork.

"You get a part-time job as a security guard?"

"I prefer to stay in character until I get home."

"Did you really go to the OCSD like that?"

"Sure. Sometimes I go in as the janitor. You remember him, right? Depends on what intel I'm after. When I'm the janitor, no one looks at me twice. I fade into the woodwork. People talk in front of me like I'm stupid. When I'm a security guard, I can interact with people. Get totally different kinds of info with my two alter egos."

"So you just come and go from the OCSD whenever you want? What happened to your hair? Is your greasy mop up under a wig?"

"The greasy mop, as you call it, isn't as greasy as this bacon." He grabbed the last slice and spoke with his mouth full. "Didn't you blot this? Paper towels, man." He wiped his mouth on his sleeve. "When I meet with Madam Director, I am Atari, visionary designer of her new security device. Atari bears no resemblance to any of my other personas." He pushed back from the table. "Come with me to Wardrobe. Prepare to be amazed."

Tommy followed him down the hall past his bedroom. Atari opened a door with a flourish and led the way into a huge walk-in closet with a lighted makeup mirror, like those in a theater dressing room. Tommy stared at a shelf of wigs and imagined Atari in everything from dreadlocks to a bald cap.

"Wow!"

"Yeah. Please tell me you weren't impressed by Mitch's little operation down in the sticks. This is where all the magic happens."

Atari tossed his ID badge and elevator key onto the dressing table, hung up the uniform jacket and pants, and wriggled out of a padded undershirt that made him appear more muscular and broad-shouldered. He slipped into an Asian-style silk dressing gown, peeled off the brown wig, and pulled his dark hair out of its ponytail. Then he popped out a false bridge with crooked front teeth. "Come down to Command Central with me."

Tommy followed, but he was already considering the infinite possibilities presented by Wardrobe. In disguise, he could come and go as he pleased. The safe house suddenly seemed less like a prison.

10:14 AM
Quadrant DC-001

Kevin decided living at the OCSD had its good and bad points. Though his work never seemed to cease, he didn't need to sneak around to set up the plan to extract Careen.

He brought his tablet into Madalyn's office and pointed to it with feigned puzzlement. "The videos aren't working."

Madalyn's confusion was genuine. "Not working how?"

"According to the polls, Careen's approval rating—and yours, unfortunately—is plummeting. People don't think she's trustworthy. The only thing her videos seem to do is make people angry."

She stared at him for a moment before he realized she was waiting for him to present a solution to the problem. He floundered a bit to make it seem authentic. "Umm … why don't we … ? It's an old ploy, but it might work."

"What? Tell me."

"Do the cute kids and animals thing."

"I don't know the cute kids and animals thing."

"People like cute kids and animals. They associate good feelings with things they like. Maybe if there was a photo opportunity? Careen with some puppies?"

"That's ridiculous."

"No, wait—I've got it! How about the Inaugural Link ceremony? We're going to have the group of Linked kids at the press conference, so how about we include Careen? She is the spokesperson for the Link."

The smile that played across her lips signaled trouble. "Now that you mention it, I think it's a wonderful idea to include Careen. Have Garrick see to the extra security."

Kevin consulted his tablet. "Garrick will be out of town. The Link Ceremony is scheduled for the same day as the memorial for the victims of the OP-441 food riots."

"Those events can't be on the same day. How will I be in two quadrants at once?"

"I can represent you at OP-441. Assistant directors do that kind of thing, right?"

"I suppose, but it's pointless to have a memorial now. The food riots are over. The Link is the future of our administration, Kevin—and the future of our country. You take care of the details. I have an appointment waiting."

10:45 AM

"I thought you'd be Asian."

"I get that all the time." Atari pushed black-framed glasses up on the bridge of his nose and peered at Madalyn. "I was always a huge fan, you know? As soon as I was eighteen I had my name legally changed."

"Fan of what?"

"Vintage video games. The Atari Corporation completely defined the electronic entertainment industry in the 1970s." He sighed and put on a rapturous look. "That was the golden age of arcade video games. Sure, the interactive technology is far superior now, but back in the 80s, a pizza and a handful of quarters to play Pac-Man was, like, the perfect evening."

"Really? I can't imagine." He noticed her shift in her chair.

"Their video game Pong was the start of it all. I mean, I was born almost thirty years after it was released, but I still try to model my own life after the beauty and the simplicity of Pong."

"Excuse me, but could we stay focused on the Link?"

Atari raked his lank, greasy hair off his forehead and pushed up his glasses again. "Oh, sure. Of course, Madam Director. So glad you asked. When we implement the Cerberean Link program in the capital and surrounding quadrants, we can piggyback on license-plate scanners that are already in operation. Of course we'll still need to install scanners in every home and place of business, but that can be done piecemeal. The Link could be up and running in a limited capacity within days, but again, the scanners currently in place won't be a reliable way to track subjects inside buildings.

"When we extend the program to rural quadrants, we can put more scanners on existing communication towers. Of course, we will need to supplement with hundreds of millions of additional sensors to get complete, nationwide coverage. That will take time."

"Of course."

He flipped open his tablet and opened a file. "This is just a simulation, but imagine how, in times past, rescue parties could comb a remote area for days and still not locate a missing child. That child would be alone and frightened or—worst-case scenario—could even die of exposure before being found. Now, an active Cerberean Link means a missing child's exact location can be pinpointed within seconds and rescue efforts made much more efficient."

Madelyn looked pleased. "It will be so much easier to find missing children once we start the program. We've been microchipping animals for fifty years. I don't know why it never caught on to do the same for the most vulnerable members of our society."

He nodded. "Admirable sentiments, Madam Director. Allow me to demonstrate."

He pulled a strip of red plastic out of his messenger bag and activated a toggle switch on the inside of the band with a flick of his thumb. "It snaps on like this." He secured it around her left wrist. "Give it a second to read your pulse and body temperature."

She made a face. "Is it supposed to be this tight?"

"Yes, it has to be snug so it can learn your body's rhythms and signals. Basically, it becomes a part of you."

"Ow!" Madalyn winced and tugged at the band.

"Oh, I should have told you to expect a tiny bee sting. It takes a one-time blood sample so it can store your DNA code. If the system were online, we would then complete your login process, and your new Link would download your Essential Services information, your debit account, and your health care benefits. Entitled to food? Here's your proof of your delivery schedule. Once you're in the Cerberan Link database, all you have to do is ..." He gave an affected, beauty-pageant wave. "... as you pass by any scanner and you will be recognized."

"Everything? It will know *everything*?"

"The short answer is yes, as I'm sure you know since you read the specifications. Cerberean Link has access to all public records— birth, marital status, arrest record. As long as you're someplace where the scanners are installed, the GPS can locate you within seconds. It takes a little longer for a satellite to pick up the signal.

"Too hot? Too cold? Use the Link to adjust your inner temperature so you'll be more comfortable. If you have a heart attack, epileptic seizure, or even a fever, it'll know. This band has everything you need, even the 'I've fallen and I can't get up' motion detection feature that automatically summons an ambulance or the police."

"Okay, great. Now take it off."

"It's not possible to remove it. I made a point of saying so in the product specifications. Once it's snapped into place, the clasp lock is permanent. Otherwise, how can we guarantee people's cooperation?"

She tugged at the band. "I don't care. Take. It. Off."

Got her. He maintained a businesslike attitude. "I didn't realize you weren't participating."

"What makes you think I'd be participating? This is a program designed to hold people accountable for their actions—I mean, to assure that children have access to public services and care. Can't you get some scissors or wire cutters or something?"

"That's fine gauge reinforced steel inside the plastic. You can't cut through it. I'm not exaggerating when I say it would be easier to chop off your hand and slide the Link off the stump." He lowered his voice. "I actually had to do that during one of the early prototype tests. It was messy, but I can do it again, if you insist. I'm not squeamish."

Madalyn clutched her wrist with her right hand. "No. Never mind. When will you bring the system online?"

"I'm still coordinating the scanners and cameras. But we could run a test, oh, within a week."

Stratford had envisioned Phase Four as a program for children. But Madalyn had just realized it could be so much more. She wouldn't be the only one caught in its snare.

11:30 AM

Tom glanced at his watch; most people kept track of the time on their phones these days, and wearing a regular wristwatch, like the one he'd been given by his father, was considered hopelessly old-fashioned. He was glad he hadn't abandoned the practice. There were no clocks or televisions in his suite of rooms, and he hadn't had a phone since July. The simple features on his watch, which none of the guards had thought important enough to confiscate, had enabled him to keep track of both time and date during his confinements at the OCSD.

In the absence of a watch, he might have tallied the days by counting his meals. They were feeding him regularly. The privations associated with the food shortage did not touch the OCSD.

Nearly all the allotted time had passed; there was just one more day until David would release the information in the files he'd left behind. Would he be able to sway Madalyn's convictions before then? He'd bargained on her vanity overruling her common sense. Could she truly be so unconcerned about having her dirty laundry made public?

Once, long ago, she had been eager to listen to him. If he could get her to listen now, he might be able to help her change course before it was too late.

When the security guards came for him, he left Mitch's hunting jacket lying on the bed. Maybe he'd make a different impression in the white button-down.

When he arrived, Madalyn walked behind her desk and gestured Tom toward the wing chair across from her.

He sat. "How've you been?"

"Busy. You?"

"Not busy at all. Shall we continue our discussion from the other day?"

She shrugged. "Why not? Though I don't see how you can help."

"You need help. You got caught lying to the entire country; that destroyed your credibility and cost you the trust of the populace. Rebuild that trust by using the OCSD to protect the rights of the people, rather than to hobble and control their every move. The public sentiment is moving toward a revolt against you. The Resistance has the ability to destroy the OCSD."

"The Resistance? You mean you? Are you that important, Tom?"

"Maddie, I'm not here to threaten you. I'm trying to help you.

I don't want to see you destroyed any more than I want to see our country torn apart. Take steps now to find a middle ground, and you'll avert disaster. If you give the Resistance a reason to keep pushing against the OCSD, it won't end well."

"People rely on the OCSD; they need the Restrictions to feel safe. They might complain, but there's no way they'd turn on us. Who would feed them and see to their safety?"

"I'm sure Louis the Sixteenth felt the same way, but I think you're making a mistake by viewing adults as helpless children."

Madalyn bristled. "You're wrong. Victor Martel's decision to destroy Essential Services is going to cause people to panic! They need to know there's someone strong enough to take care of them."

"It's dangerous to build a society in which people rely on the government rather than themselves, and the food shortages should have proved that beyond a shadow of a doubt. Look beyond the safety and security thing for a moment. People are more successful and tend to live longer when they have more control over their circumstances. Plainly put, people are happier when they get to make decisions for themselves. Bungee jumping, remember?"

"But the OCSD has shouldered the responsibility of stopping people from making bad choices—exactly like bungee jumping. We save people from themselves." She shuffled a stack of papers on her desk.

He was losing her attention so he raised his voice a bit. "What determines whether someone's making a bad choice? How can you presume to know, when what's right for me might not be right for you? Besides, one could argue that bad decisions are made on our behalf all the time. The Restrictions and Essential Services are prime examples. And don't forget CSD. That was a huge mistake!"

"But it isn't your fault if someone else makes bad decisions on your behalf. Wouldn't people prefer to go through life blameless?"

"Then they're merely victims! And besides, blaming someone else doesn't make living with the consequences any easier. The younger generations haven't progressed beyond a level of personal responsibility you'd expect a young teenager to shoulder. Liberty and responsibility are inseparable."

Madalyn shook her head. "But if we have another crisis, they'll panic."

"Like I said, it's not a quick fix. For instance, people will need a chance to get used to shopping for their own food. But the changes will take hold, and everything will start to turn around for the better. People under twenty-five are too young to remember life without the Restrictions. But teenagers and young adults are naturally rebellious and independent. You'll see. It won't be long before they'll enjoy having some autonomy."

"That's too much change."

"It's needed change if you want to avoid trouble. The OCSD's security measures assume people are incapable of managing their own lives; unfortunately, many people have started to believe it, too. But it's harmful to take that much responsibility away from individuals. It's in everyone's best interest to know what true responsibility feels like."

She smirked. "You say you favor personal responsibility, yet you say you're also here to intervene on behalf of Careen. Don't you want her to know what true responsibility for her actions feels like?"

"Careen was never really part of the Resistance." He had to mask how much he wanted her released. "Kids can be idealistic and read into things. She's not important enough to bother with."

Madalyn smiled and nodded. "That's very interesting."

Chapter 41

4:00 PM
Quadrant BG-098

Jaycee stood alone beside the open grave, watching her father, Paul McComas, and a detail of QM carry Wes's casket through the gate of the family cemetery. Three sharpshooters who comprised the honor guard followed behind.

She'd never been to a funeral before. She'd expected to feel the weight of finality and the permanence of death, but it was impossible. Everything she'd thought was permanent was changing.

She was leaving. She wasn't planning on coming back in a box, either.

She cast her eyes down as the pallbearers positioned the casket on the winch that would soon lower it into the earth.

Mitch took his place beside her as the funeral director read from a tattered hymnal. Every face around the coffin was solemn, but there were no tears.

As the funeral director's voice droned—"Help us to live as those who are prepared to die … "—she closed her eyes, the phrase playing over and over inside her head until she was startled by the men's voices blending together in the final Amen.

The honor guard stepped back and raised their rifles with the muzzles pointing over the casket and fired a volley of three shots into the air. Beside her, her father murmured, "Now the battle resumes."

The pallbearers shook hands with Mitch and nodded to Jaycee as they filed out after the honor guard. Paul paused to place a hand on Mitch's shoulder for a moment before following them down the hill.

"Josephine?" She whirled around. Seamus Owens, in his dress uniform, approached through the crooked gravestones. "I know my timing stinks, and it's not really right of me to ask at a funeral, but … " He ducked his head shyly. "Could I see you sometime? I mean, some other time when we're not going to have to talk about things like funerals. I'm kind of lonely here. You don't come to town much, and I don't know when I'll get another chance to tell you I'd like to get to know you better."

The only decent smile at a burial was a sad one, so she did her best not to appear too pleased by his attention. "Seamus, I'd, well . . . " She glanced at her father, who was staring at her like he was watching her walk the edge of a cliff blindfolded. "I'd like to, but no. I'm sorry. I can't."

"Good-bye." She touched his jacket sleeve, wondering what might have happened between them if she weren't leaving for OP-439 right away. She returned to her father's side, and Seamus left the cemetery without looking back.

"What was that all about?"

"Nothing, Daddy. He's just a boy."

She could tell he wanted to ask more questions, but instead he turned his attention to the funeral director who had come to stand at his elbow. "Go ahead. Let him down and fill it in."

"Are you sure, Mitch? We can wait till after you've gone."

"No, I'd rather you did it now."

Mitch stooped and picked up a clump of the freshly turned earth, and Jaycee did the same. They stood poised at the edge of the grave until the whirring of the winch ceased. He tossed the dirt into the hole; again, she copied his movements.

The ritual complete, Mitch threaded his way through the generations of departed members of the Carraway clan. Jaycee trailed behind, pausing to read names and dates. She felt much less connected to the family that lay here under the ground than she did to the members of the Resistance. Mitch stopped by one of the oldest graves and waited for her to catch up. "We gotta change into work clothes before we come back."

"Back? To do what?"

"To dig, of course."

"But Daddy, I'm leaving this afternoon, remember? Eduardo and Lara are waiting for me."

"Not so fast you're not. I need your help."

"That's not fair! You said—"

Someone cleared his throat behind them.

She whirled around and recognized one of the pallbearers.

"Is there a family gathering afterward?"

"No." Mitch spoke abruptly, and Jaycee couldn't tell if the anger in his voice was directed at her or the interloper.

"I'm sorry to intrude, but I came to the funeral partly because I wanted to meet Wes's family. I'm Henry Nelson." The marshal extended his hand. When neither of them made a move to shake it, he hesitated for a moment and then exclaimed, "Look, I don't know how much you know about what's going on …"

Mitch raised his eyebrows.

"My post commander's not doing a thing to bring Wes's killer to justice. He's too worried it'll look bad to acknowledge there was a terrorist cell in OP-439. Careen Catecher is getting off scot-free, with a cushy new job at the OCSD to boot. But I don't think she acted alone when she blew up the student center.

"I was Wes's closest friend in the marshals. I wouldn't feel right if I didn't do my utmost to arrest Tommy Bailey myself."

4:30 PM
Quadrant DC-001

"I have an exclusive for you."

Sheila Roth, who was having her makeup done for the evening broadcast, caught Madalyn's eye in the mirror and smiled. "Madam Director! What a lovely surprise." She glanced around. "Pete's not here right now. Naturally, I'd include him if he were, but since he's not …" She stood up and took Madalyn's arm, leading her away from the hair and makeup staff.

Madalyn pulled a chip drive from her handbag. "Do you happen to remember Tom Bailey?"

"Killed in a car accident last summer; the wife died, too. Left a son …" Sheila's eyes lit up as recognition dawned. "Tommy Bailey. Why didn't I make that connection myself? I must be slipping."

Madalyn lowered her voice. "You'll never guess who's back from the grave. And you get the exclusive on the story." She handed her the chip drive and a sealed envelope. "Here's your list of questions and answers. Pick a producer who can help you—one who will keep his mouth shut. This is going to have a huge impact in the fight against the Resistance. Can I count on you to take on more assignments like this in the future?"

4:50 PM

Madalyn smiled to herself as she took the elevator up to the top floor. Sheila had salivated at the thought of breaking such a huge story.

Outside one of the small soundstages, she summoned Careen's security guard.

"Bring her here."

He nodded and disappeared down the hall. She let herself in, powered up one spotlight, and waited in the darkness until the guard returned with Careen and steered her into the center of the room.

She was snarly-haired and doe-eyed after spending twenty-four hours huddled on the floor in a broom closet, but she stood with her chin lifted. So her spirit wasn't broken yet? Madalyn felt a thrill of triumph run through her body. She was finally going to snuff out the hope that fed the girl's inner strength.

She walked up to the edge of the circle of light. "Careen, you've achieved true celebrity status. The death threats you've been receiving were obviously real. We had to take emergency measures and keep you sequestered overnight. For your safety. I hope you weren't too uncomfortable." She paused for effect. "Tom Bailey was here."

Madalyn's anger flared as the girl's eyes darted about, obviously hoping to see him. "He is?"

"He *was*. He and his son organized that lynch mob that broke in looking for you. But you don't have to worry about them anymore. They're in custody."

Careen dropped her gaze to the floor.

"You're safe now, of course. But they were here to kill you. Listen to what Tom Bailey said during his interrogation."

She held out a digital recorder and pushed Play. Tom's voice came through loud and clear. "It's ridiculous to assume Careen was ever important to the Resistance. Kids can be idealistic and read into things. The Resistance has the power to destroy … her. She's a liability that needs to be eliminated."

The girl's shoulders began to shake.

Madalyn turned off the recording. "I've been telling you all along, Careen; the Resistance never cared about you. Now that you've ceased to be useful to them, they'll stop at nothing to eliminate you. The safest place for you is here. You'll have plenty to eat and you'll live long enough to wear all the pretty clothes in your closet as long as you remain under my protection. If you want that protection, you must demonstrate your unwavering loyalty to the OCSD. Do you understand?"

She nodded, her expression passive.

"Go back to your room to get dressed properly. You have an appointment in an hour."

Careen held back her tears until she was in the shower. *The Resistance was the closest thing to family I've ever had. I cared about them more than I cared about myself. I sacrificed myself for nothing. Even Tommy's turned against me. How could I be so stupid?* She looked down at her battered body and a fresh wave of sobs broke over her. *I did everything I could do. I'm done resisting. Done fighting for people who are trying to hurt me. I've been alone for most of my life. It's no different now.*

Chapter 42

4:30 PM
Quadrant DC-005

Three hours before, Atari had breezed into Command Central, startling Tommy away from what he'd been reading.

He'd grabbed the game controller and let his avatar fire round after round into the air in what Tommy assumed was some sort of celebration.

"What's up?"

"Guess!"

"How am I going to guess?"

"I'll give you a hint."

Tommy sighed.

"I considered several options before I decided what centaurs must do with their arms when they run."

"What the hell kind of a hint is that?"

Atari let out an annoying cackle. "Too subtle for you, apparently, no-brain … er."

"I don't know. You figured out a way to pierce the shield without activating the Link?"

"No. How would you infer something like that from centaurs? Ridiculous! You lose." He dropped the controller on the desk and left the room.

If he doesn't want to tell me, fine. Disappearing in the middle of conversations was high up on Tommy's list of Annoying Things Atari Does.

Tommy needed a break from watching the monitors in Command Central. His dad had met with Madalyn earlier in the day, but without audio, it looked like just another boring meeting to him. Then his dad's guards had locked him back in his room and taken their posts outside the door. Tommy headed downstairs to the gym, ran three miles on the indoor track, and hit the weight room. Then he grabbed a snack, took a shower, and figured he'd check the surveillance feed one more time before he took a nap.

His dad's room was empty.

He rolled back the footage. Fifteen minutes before, the guards had entered, woken Tom from a nap, and hustled him out of the room. Tommy recognized the tall, thin man who'd met them in the hall as Hoyt Garrick, the Chief QM. Garrick led the way as the guards guided Tommy's dad to the elevator. Tommy found them on another camera and watched with growing horror as Garrick unlocked the door to the secure ward and the guards forced his dad inside.

That settles it. He'd come up with an emergency evacuation plan, just in case something like this happened. Atari hadn't returned, which meant he couldn't stop Tommy from leaving the safe house. He rolled his chair over to another computer and clicked on the open tabs until he found the map of the capital quadrant that was marked with tiny red dots, indicating the locations of the sensors and scanners. There were so many it would be impossible to travel more than a block in any direction without passing one and showing up on someone else's security cam feed.

He studied the grid of streets and the bridges over the river that separated him from the heart of the capital. It would help if he knew exactly where he was. He hadn't seen a single window anywhere in the safe house, but maybe there was another way to get a fix on his position. He headed for the stairwell and climbed flight after flight until he emerged on the roof. He opened the door slowly and stepped out into a solarium with a tinted-glass roof. The well-lit buildings of the capital were visible in the distance, and he watched the streetlights wink on in the gathering dusk. He took his time visualizing a route to the OCSD along some of the main roads he'd seen on the map.

He pounded back down the stairs to Wardrobe and found Atari's security guard disguise. He was surprised how much the short, brown wig alone transformed his appearance. Next he tried on the jacket and grinned because he didn't need Atari's padded undershirt to fill it out properly. The uniform pants were a little short, but since they were worn tucked into heavy boots, it wouldn't matter.

He rummaged around until he found a pair in his size and tugged them on, thankful he wouldn't have to limp around in ones that were too small.

The false teeth were another matter. He took the bridge to the kitchen and dunked it in boiling water a couple times before he considered putting it in his mouth. He worked it into place; it reminded him of the retainer he'd worn in high school after his braces had come off. His parents would've freaked if his post-braces teeth had turned out as crooked as the ones he now wore.

He grabbed the elevator key and ID badge Atari had tossed on the dressing table and compared the man in the mirror to the one in the photo. If no one looked too closely, he could pass for Logan Daniels.

4:25 PM
Quadrant DC-001

Hoyt Garrick swiped his ID card through the reader at the entrance to the secure ward. As the guards shoved Tom through the door, Garrick held up a hand to block their way. "I've got it from here." He pulled the door closed behind him and took Tom by the arm, steering him down the hall. He could feel the other man trembling.

"You should know I'm not a fan of the OCSD's scare tactics."

Garrick chuckled. "Yeah, well, there aren't too many places in this building where we can meet privately. I want to talk to you. Stratford saw you as a threat."

"The feeling was mutual."

"He wasn't afraid of many people. What's your theory on who killed him?"

Tom shook his head. "Stratford had Lara and me moved from the building a few hours before he died. Everything I know about the assassination I learned secondhand."

Garrick opened the door to one of the rooms. Kevin rose to greet him. Garrick saw a look pass between them, and Tom relaxed even before Garrick released his grasp. Tom pulled his arm free of Garrick's grasp and addressed Kevin.

"I hardly recognized you in that suit."

"I know, right?" Kevin broke into a grin. "You look just the same. Except for that black eye."

"Long story."

Garrick cleared his throat. "Madalyn's insisted we keep looking for the rest of the Resistance down in the BG quadrants. Unless one of you has something you'd like to share ..."

"Absolutely not. I didn't—" Tom looked at Kevin. "Well, neither of us risked coming back here to give information on our supposed allies."

"Supposed, huh?"

"I'm merely saying that perhaps the Resistance, as a whole, isn't worth trying to bargain with any longer. It might be more prudent to—"

Kevin coughed violently and excused himself, almost running out the door. Garrick stared after him. He was back in seconds.

"Sorry." He cleared his throat. "Tom, you know Trina and I believe Stratford wasn't Madalyn's original target. So that would mean she was either trying to off Garrick or she was planning to assassinate the president."

"Did Madalyn want to kill you, Chief Garrick?"

Garrick laughed. "If she did, she's going to be sorry she missed her chance."

Chapter 43

4:25 PM
Quadrant BG-098

Mitch checked the road behind him several times on the trip back from the cemetery to the diner. The last thing he needed was that marshal from Wes's old post snooping around.

Jaycee sat silently in the passenger seat. How many excuses could he come up with to keep her from leaving? Once she was on her own, he knew she'd try to claim Wes's death benefit and insurance money; then she'd have to explain why her name didn't show up in any of the government's databases. As far as the government knew, she'd never been born. She'd never registered for school or an Essential Services account. There were going to be all kinds of questions she wouldn't know how to answer. Eventually, those questions would lead back here, to him. He'd already had too many run-ins with the QM for his liking.

He parked behind the diner, and Jaycee was out of the truck before he cut the engine.

"Work clothes!" he shouted after her as she ran up the back porch steps. She slammed the door in response. He decided not to follow right away. Maybe it would help to give her some space.

Everyone holed up in the bunker was getting antsy, but it couldn't be helped. It was good that Eduardo and Lara were leaving; he, Trina, Grace, and David could work on their part of the plan for a while longer before they'd need to be on hand for the big finale in the capital.

Jaycee, dressed for the outdoors and carrying her rifle and a worn army surplus duffel bag, stormed past him without a word and headed up the path that led to the bunker. "At least wait for me! Jeez," he muttered to himself as he headed inside to change out of his funeral suit.

He was halfway up the stairs to his room when the bell on the diner's front door jingled. He hurried back down, expecting to see Wes's buddy Nelson; instead, a squad of eight unfamiliar marshals swarmed into the dining room.

"We have orders to search the premises for contraband and fugitives."

"Yeah, yeah. Go ahead. You missed a few dishes the last time you guys were here." Mitch sank onto a stool at the counter to wait it out.

4:30 PM
Quadrant DC-001

Careen followed Madalyn down the hall to a conference room, where Madalyn gestured her toward a chair and then pushed an intercom button. "Could you please send Mr. Atari in?"

The door opened and a thin man in a wide-lapelled pinstriped suit and fedora stepped into the room. He looked like he'd arrived via time machine, and Careen couldn't help staring. *No one dresses like that. Why in the world is he staring at me?* The man paused in the doorway, swept off his fedora, and raked back his dark hair before he entered the room.

"Mr. Atari, I need you to install another Link."

"Very good." He laid his hat on the table and opened the leather briefcase that completed his vintage ensemble, pulled out a tablet, and pecked away at the keyboard. "What is the recipient's name?"

Madalyn nodded at her, and Careen dutifully recited her name.

Mr. Atari kept his gaze down. "Hold out your left arm, please." As he pushed up her sleeve, his long fingers reminded her of a spider's legs, and the thought made her shudder. She closed her eyes.

She remembered the bracelet with green agate stones and the lock and key charms. For a moment, it was Tommy's gentle touch against the inside of her wrist. But when she opened her eyes, it wasn't Lara's bracelet she was wearing. A tiny light on the red plastic band was centered over the pulse point on the inside of her wrist. It flashed in time with her heartbeat. Then it bit her.

Mitch stormed into the bunker, out of breath, making everyone jump. He fixed his gaze on Jaycee.

"I'm not changing my mind, Daddy." Jaycee's defiant look softened. "But I'm glad I don't have to leave without saying good-bye."

"I know. Me, too." He opened his arms and she stepped into his hug. "I would've been here sooner, but more marshals came and searched the place again. I moved the truck to the foot of the hill, so you wouldn't have to go all the way back to the diner. It'll be safer that way, in case the QM decides to double back tonight."

He glanced around the room. "So who's up for a field trip?"

Grace looked at him in surprise. "Field trip? Where?"

"Over the next hill. I know you'd all like a breath of fresh air, and I could use your help with a job. Need to get it done right away."

"What kind of job?"

"No big deal, really. Just grave robbing in the Carraway family plot."

Chapter 44

6:00 PM
Quadrant DC-001

Tommy hunched his shoulders against the cold breeze as he trudged over the pedestrian walkway on the bridge across the Potomac River. It was a lot longer walk to the OCSD building than he'd anticipated. Though his ears and nose were numb, the security guard jacket he wore kept most of the frigid air at bay.

He'd snuck out of the safe house without running into Atari. He had no idea if he was somewhere in the building, or if he'd gone out on some clandestine, Atari-like errand. He hoped the note he'd left on the desk in Command Central would adequately explain why he couldn't wait any longer. If he could sneak his dad out of the building, they could make their escape into the darkness.

He approached the OCSD's employee entrance, passing the spot where he'd tackled the guard who'd shot Trina with the gun that now rested on his own hip. His nerves hummed with heightened awareness, but he wasn't nearly as frightened as he'd been the first time he'd broken into the OCSD.

He swiped the ID card in the reader and the door clicked open. Eyes straight ahead, he strode toward the elevator and pushed the button to summon the car.

"Hey! Hey you!"

Tommy tensed and turned around. An older guard motioned him back toward the security stand.

"I've been due for a break and my replacement's late. C'mere and hold the fort with Beatty until I get back."

"Uhh, sure." Tommy nodded as the other guard hurried past him and stepped into the waiting elevator car.

John Beatty nodded once. "Sup?"

Tommy returned the nod, intending to keep the conversation to a minimum. Atari could be pretty chatty, but who knew what he was like when he was pretending to be Logan Daniels.

They sat in silence for a few minutes before someone buzzed at the visitor's entrance. Beatty pushed a button to unlock the door and admit a crew of painters for after-hours work.

"Sign in here." Beatty turned the computer screen toward them, and one by one they keyed in their names and ID numbers.

He patted down one of the painters, and Tommy copied his movements. When they were done, Beatty printed temporary ID cards for them to clip on their coveralls and then read from a laminated card: " 'Please restrict your movements to the area in which you're working. If you need to venture into another part of the building, you must be accompanied by security. If you are found in a restricted area, you may be subject to arrest.' Do you understand?"

One of the painters nodded. "We got it." They gathered their equipment and headed for the service elevators.

Beatty pecked at the computer screen. "Give me the tag numbers on the two you patted down."

"Huh?"

"The tag numbers. You did tag them, didn't you? It's procedure."

Tommy tried playing dumb. "Dude. I forgot."

"You gotta remember to tag *every* visitor, Daniels." He handed Tommy a piece of stiff fabric about an inch square. "Here. You do the next visitor that comes in. Slip this in a pocket when you pat them down. Otherwise, how can we keep tabs on them once they're in the building? You know the security cameras are on the fritz."

Tommy rubbed the fabric between his fingers. "GPS?"

"Yeah."

"So we keep tabs on visitors for, like, ever?"

"No. The tags are short-range. Only work for a few blocks once you're out of the building."

"Oh, yeah. Right."

Beatty eyed him with suspicion. There were no new visitors, and the tense silence stretched on and on. Tommy scrolled back through the sign-in log. His dad had signed in two days ago, and Kevin had arrived the morning after they'd gone their separate ways in OP-439.

"Weren't you headed someplace else?" Beatty asked.

"Huh? Oh, yeah. I was." He was afraid to be more specific.

The older guard was shambling slowly back to the visitor's entrance. "Here comes Smitty. You can go."

"Okay. Thanks." Tommy headed for the elevator and hit the Down button before Beatty could change his mind. On the way to the basement, he stared at himself in the mirrored elevator door, reassuring himself that his disguise was good enough. Hopefully it wouldn't matter that he'd slipped up a few times.

Though he tried to walk softly, his footsteps echoed in the empty hallway. *Why does everything sound louder at night?* He rounded the corner past Kevin's old office and down the familiar corridor to the secure ward. As he unclipped his ID badge, the hairs on the back of his neck prickled. He heard a rush of footsteps behind him, and someone slammed him against the wall, twisting his arm behind his back. He dropped the ID badge.

"That wasn't Smitty." Beatty's voice was close to his ear, low and accusing.

"Ow! What the hell are you doing?"

"That wasn't Smitty. I said, 'here comes Smitty. You can go.' You agreed. But that wasn't Smitty." He applied pressure until Tommy feared his arm would pop out of the socket. "And you're not Daniels."

"I wasn't paying attention, all right? I made a mistake."

"Oh yeah? Then tell me, how'd you grow four inches overnight? And how'd you get that wicked scar on your chin? Daniels didn't have a scar two days ago when he and I were on duty together."

"All right! All right, you got me." He decided to stall and hope an opportunity to get away from Beatty would present itself. "How did you know where I was going?"

"You've still got that visitor tag in your pocket. Duh."

That stupid tag thing had tripped him up twice. "You're right. I'm not Daniels, but we look enough alike that I could pass for him—unless I ran into someone who knows him, like you. They gave me his ID when they sent me in on … on a secret mission."

Beatty relaxed his grip. Tommy winced and rubbed his shoulder as he turned around. He had Beatty's attention, so he lowered his voice and inclined his head toward the secure ward.

"You know they keep the political prisoners in there. The dissidents. The really dangerous ones."

"No."

"Well, then obviously you wouldn't have known about why I'm here. It's need-to-know stuff—and who am I to question? I'm just following orders."

"You're shitting me."

"No, I'm serious. C'mere." He gestured toward the other guard's ID badge. "Open the door and I'll show you."

Beatty swiped his ID twice, but the door remained locked. "Oh, yeah. You must not have clearance." Tommy stooped to pick up the badge he'd dropped. One swipe and the door opened. Beatty looked impressed and curious enough to follow Tommy into the dimly lit hallway.

He swiped the ID badge again and accessed one of the darkened rooms. Beatty stuck his head inside, and Tommy shoved him through the doorway, sending him sprawling, and pulled the door closed.

The hapless guard rattled the doorknob. When he realized he was locked in, he pounded on the observation window. His shouts, which were likely full of threats and truthful observations about Tommy's treachery, didn't penetrate the soundproofing, and Tommy couldn't resist motioning that he couldn't hear anything Beatty was saying. Beatty responded with a rude hand gesture, and Tommy grinned and gave a farewell salute.

He hurried down the long corridor, peering in the observation windows and opening doors, but his dad was nowhere to be found. He even checked the dungeon-like room at the end of the hall. The last time he was here, Kevin and Trina had used the forgotten emergency exit there to escape into the parking garage next door.

Where had Garrick taken his dad? He'd been stuck at the visitor's entrance long enough that they could be anywhere. He hurried back down the hall and was reaching for the doorknob when he heard voices on the other side of the door.

"There are no visitors allowed in this area. It's restricted."

"But where are they, whoever they are? The tag tracker says they're right here! There's no name in the visitor's log." Someone rattled the doorknob, and Tommy drew his hand back as though it could bite him. *Dammit!* He dug the visitor tag out of his pocket and examined it. There was no way to turn it off. He'd have to destroy it—but how?

"They can't be in there. No one has access to that part of the building."

Tommy listened at the door until the voices faded and then slipped out of the secure ward as quietly as he could and sprinted down the hall. He ducked into the nearest restroom, which happened to be the women's, and flushed the tag. Problem solved? He hoped so.

He headed for the emergency stairwell and took the steps two at a time on his way to the fourth floor.

7:25 PM
Quadrant BG-098

"Here. Dig." Mitch passed a spade to David. Grace held two flashlights pointed in different directions as the members of the Resistance, freed from the underground bunker for the first time in nearly a week, braved the December chill.

"Are you kidding? Exertion isn't good for my heart, you know."

"It's not like you gotta dig six feet down; it's not even half that. My family never trusted banks. This was their solution."

"I thought grave robbers only worked at midnight." David used his foot to help sink the spade into the moist earth.

"This place is so remote no one would see us in the middle of the day. It wasn't necessary to wait until midnight. Jaycee's busting to leave, so the sooner we finish here, the sooner she can go."

David tossed a shovelful of earth aside. "How many generations of your family are we talking about?"

Mitch shrugged. "Four, maybe five."

Trina, hard at work in the beam of Grace's other flashlight, pulled a muddy coffee can from a hole in the ground. It rattled as she set it down. "Is this really where you keep your life savings?"

"Quite an inheritance, huh? I've never needed it before. I'd better check the map to be sure we're getting it all."

David stepped closer to the flashlight beam and opened one of the cans. "Some of these coins are old enough to have some actual silver in them."

"Oh, I've got silver bars—and gold, too. But I need the coins for this plan. Just think how Madalyn will react when she realizes she can't claim her payment for the formulas without breaking her own law."

"Surely she'll figure out a way to deposit the money into her account?"

"Nah. The deadline for submitting cash to debit accounts is long past. She won't be able to deposit it, and we'll make sure she gets caught with the contraband."

Jaycee wiped her cold, muddy hands on her jeans. "This is so lame. I want my own account—something I can use—not a bunch of old coins."

Mitch looked sad. "I kept you off the grid your whole life for a reason. Once you're in the system, you could be Linked or subjected to whatever new forms of oppression the OCSD comes up with in the future."

"Then we'd better not screw up this mission." She folded her arms on her chest. "I'm sorry, Daddy, but I don't want to be stuck behind the counter at the diner my whole life, working for barter. I want to be free. I want to see the world. I've hardly ever left the quadrant."

Mitch shook his head. "You're as free as you can get right now, sweetheart. You just don't appreciate it."

Chapter 45

7:37 PM
Quadrant DC-001

The fourth floor hallway was empty when Tommy emerged from the stairwell, and he wasted no time gaining entry to the room where they were holding his father. The suite's sitting room was dark, but the bedroom door stood ajar, and a lamp within cast a dim glow. He tiptoed across the thick carpet toward the light. His father lay back against the pillows on the bed, eyes closed, arms folded over his chest. For a fleeting second Tommy thought he was dead, but then he saw his chest rise and fall. He approached the side of the bed and touched Tom's shoulder.

"Dad?"

His father woke with a gasp and rubbed his eye. "What is it?"

"Dad, it's me."

Recognition, then anger, swept across his face and he spoke in a harsh whisper. "What are you doing here?"

"I came to get you out."

"I told you in no uncertain terms when I left BG-098 that I didn't need your help. Madalyn has been willing to talk about rescinding more Restrictions. She's agreed to let me see Careen; surely you don't want me to sneak away in the middle of the night when there's a chance I can help her."

"Dad, why would you believe anything Madalyn says? Don't you see that you're in serious danger?"

"You're a fine one to criticize. There are surveillance cameras all over this building! You have no concept of what awaits you if they discover you here. You're wanted for the university bombing and Wes's murder, and you're on the Most Wanted list along with the rest of the Resistance. You'll be in as much trouble as Careen if someone recognizes you."

He shook his head. "The cameras don't work. Obviously, they don't want you to know that, but one of the guys in the Resistance has been hacking the system so the video feed gets directed to him. Besides, you didn't even recognize me, did you? I'm not in any danger." He saw no need to mention Beatty. "What makes you think you can trust the OCSD now? You've never been able to before."

"I have some information about Madalyn that she doesn't want to go public, and it turns out Chief Garrick is a potential ally. I never thought I'd resort to blackmail, but this kind of leverage will be enough to see me safely on my way. Your heroics are unnecessary."

Tommy's anger flared. "I'm part of the Resistance because of you, Dad. Like it or not, you're stuck with me. Why can't you just—"

They both heard the click of the lock. Tom gestured toward the bathroom and Tommy hurried inside, leaving the door open a crack. He held his breath and prayed whoever it was wouldn't need to pee.

"Careen refused to see you."

He'd heard Madalyn Davies's voice on television so many times that he would have recognized it anywhere.

"Take me to Careen right now and let her tell me herself, or I'll assume you're trying to renege on our bargain."

"We never had any bargain. I'm afraid there's nothing you or I can do to change her mind."

"Perhaps she'll come around after she's had a chance to think about it. Meanwhile, we can talk about the best course of action for the OCSD."

"About that … I don't think we'll be needing you as a consultant after all."

"Maddie, you left me with the impression that we might finally reach some sort of equilibrium."

"Equilibrium? Ha! You've always wanted the lion's share of the power, Tom. You just have no idea how to take it."

"Like you? Someone who gained everything she has through deception and lies? You haven't changed a bit."

"Don't act all noble. You haven't changed either. You aren't trying to help anyone but yourself."

"You're not concerned about your secrets going public?"

"No." Tommy could hear the triumph in her voice. "Your tiny

little time bomb has been deactivated. Looks like you've failed again."

"Now look here—"

"No, *you* look here. I'm calling the shots now, and I'm not as patient as Lowell was about dealing with you. Did you honestly think your mere presence here would awe us so much we'd call off the search for the rest of the Resistance? Hardly."

The silence seemed to stretch on forever. Even after Tommy heard a door slam, he stayed frozen against the wall in the bathroom until his dad appeared in the doorway.

"Dad? You know Madalyn Davies?"

"Uh-huh."

"Does Mom know?"

"Oh, yes. She knows. Madalyn was one of my students. That shouldn't matter now, but I'm afraid it always will."

Tommy followed him back into the bedroom. "Dad, seriously. We're getting out of here now." His dad hesitated for a second before he grabbed his jacket off a chair and followed.

"This late at night the stairwell's deserted." He opened the door and led his father out. Tom kept up until they reached the basement but hung back as Tommy swiped his ID badge through the reader at the entrance to the secure ward.

"Why are we going in here?"

"There's an exit. Kevin and Trina used it last time." He didn't bother to look at the observation window as they passed Beatty's prison; even if the guard saw them, what could he do about it? *Almost there.* He rushed his dad up the shadowy stairs, and a blast of chilly air hit them as he opened the door to the parking garage.

Their footsteps echoed in the cavernous space as they hurried up the ramp. His dad whispered, "I don't think I've ever left the OCSD through the regular visitor's entrance."

As they emerged at ground level, floodlights powered up at the OCSD building, casting alternating stripes of light and shadows on the garage's floor and walls. An alarm began to wail outside.

"Is that alarm because of us? Because of you?" He clutched his father's arm. "Did they pat you down when you first got here?"

"I don't remember. Oh, wait. Yes, they did."

Tommy grabbed at the camouflage jacket and tore it off his dad's back. He plunged his hand into first one pocket, then the other, and found the fabric square. "This is a GPS tracker."

A cacophony of sirens joined the alarm; quadrant marshals were closing in fast. "Come on!" He ran up the spiraling ramp, his dad at his heels, until they emerged on the second level of the structure. He led the way to the nearest wall and leaned over the side.

His father whispered, "Just throw it! Get rid of it!"

"Hang on a second." Tommy balled up the jacket and timed his release so it landed squarely on the top of a delivery truck as it lumbered past, bound away from the safe house. They ran the length of the garage, following the truck's progress. It paused at a stoplight, and when the light turned green, three patrol cars screeched in to block the intersection in front of the OCSD building. Quadrant marshals leaped from the cars and converged on the driver, guns drawn.

Tommy scouted his route out of the garage and back to the safe house, and once they'd left the shelter of the parking garage, he kept to the shadows as much as possible. He hadn't felt conspicuous on the long walk over earlier that evening, but in his security guard's uniform he appeared to belong, whereas Tom, dressed in jeans and white button-down shirt, did not. Tommy noticed him shivering long before they reached the pedestrian walkway over the river. He shrugged off his jacket.

"Here, Dad, take this. I'm not cold."

Tom zipped it up and put his hands in the pockets. The streets on the other side of the bridge were deserted, but Tommy's senses were on high alert; empty buildings weren't always empty. He'd never have guessed from looking at the outside of Atari's warehouse that it contained a luxurious and high-tech safe house. Who knew which other supposedly abandoned warehouses were actually inhabited? He held back the chain-link fence and helped his dad step through the gap. It took a lot longer to cross the parking lot on foot than in a vehicle, and Tommy breathed a sigh of relief once they'd plunged into the darkness of the unlit parking garage. He groped his way down the ramp, not daring to use the flashlight clipped to his uniform belt until they were well below ground. When he switched it on, the familiar shadows from the construction debris loomed ahead. He dug in his pants pocket and fished out the elevator key.

"Hold it right there."

They both jumped. Tommy recognized the voice behind him, but his dad did not. Tom whirled around and struck without hesitating, and the sound of his dad's fist connecting with Atari's jaw made Tommy wince.

"Ow!"

Tommy laid a restraining hand on his dad's arm and addressed Atari. "Serves you right, sneaking up on people."

Atari shoved past them and onto the elevator. "I was hardly sneaking. You left me a note, so I knew where you'd gone. You walked right past me in the parking garage. You obviously have no sense of situational awareness."

His dad was staring at Atari like he'd stepped out of an old movie or something. Atari did take a little getting used-to. "No, we didn't notice you. Dad, this is Atari. This safe house is his place. He's one of us."

Tom stuck out his hand. "Sorry about that."

Atari ignored it. "Another Bailey? Fantastic."

Tommy spoke up, hoping to downplay Atari's rudeness. "What's with the Godfather suit? Who are you supposed to be today?"

Atari ignored the questions. "Pretty sure Mitch told you to stay put."

"I couldn't wait any longer. I saw them taking Dad to the secure ward."

"You had orders. You shouldn't have gone out."

"I'm not going to apologize."

The doors opened, and Atari addressed Tom as he led the way into the foyer. "Your wife will soon be on her way to OP-439."

"How do you know?"

"Mitch said she, someone named Eduardo, and Jaycee are heading there together."

"That's good. I need to return home as soon as possible, as well."

"We've got a car service that's discreet and reliable. I'll put in a call, and they'll have you there by morning. Meanwhile, we can find you something decent to wear in Wardrobe."

Tom nodded. "I don't suppose there's any reason to linger here when we could be on our way." He looked at Tommy. "I assume you have some of your own clothes to wear?"

"I'm not leaving."

"Nonsense! We should face what happens next together, not scattered all over the country."

"Dad, I'm not going anywhere without Careen."

"You heard Madalyn say in no uncertain terms—"

"Bull! Madalyn was lying. There's no way Careen would choose the OCSD over—"

Atari broke in with a smirk. "Over you?"

"Yeah, over me. And over the Resistance, too. There's no way she's at the OCSD because she wants to be."

"Sucks for you, Wunderkind, but your dad's escape guarantees they'll be keeping a closer watch on Careen. Your heroics this evening will make it that much harder for us to get to her."

"Wait—get to Careen? Did you find out where she is?"

"Silly me. In all the excitement, did I forget to mention? I Linked her a few hours ago."

8:02 PM
Quadrant DC-001

"What do you mean Tom Bailey's gone? I was just with him!"

"Bailey's visitor tag showed him moving about the building into an area that's off limits. A guard who was on duty at the visitor's entrance left his post, and we can't find him. We picked up Bailey's signal outside, but he'd ditched his tag."

"Get out!" She watched the guard leave her office and then dialed PeopleCam.

"Run Sheila Roth's interview with Tom Bailey immediately."

Then she summoned Kevin and Hoyt Garrick. "We've had a serious security breach. Tom Bailey was here, in custody, and now he's gone."

The two men glanced at each other before Garrick spoke. "Really? How did that happen?"

"I have no idea. It would appear the security protocols for the OCSD building are insufficient."

Garrick pulled up a screen on his tablet. "I'm confused. You say he was in custody, but he's listed on the visitor's log. Do you want me to send marshals out after an escaped visitor?"

"Technically I suppose he was a visitor, because he came here of his own free will. But his being at liberty could … umm, raise some embarrassing questions. I can't have him running around in public spouting his anti-OCSD propaganda."

Chapter 46

10:10 PM
Quadrant BG-098

The group arrived back at the bunker, chilled and muddy. Lara waited her turn to wash up. She was eager to be gone. She'd been unable to do any of her own work where people might observe, but as soon as she got back to OP-439, her part of the project could begin.

Mitch and Eduardo had set up a television. In the close confines of the bunker, it was impossible to ignore its constant feed of information. Grace, now free of mud and grime, joined Trina and Lara as they watched the evening PeopleCam broadcast.

"Tonight we bring you breaking news: an exposé inside the rebel group that calls themselves the Resistance."

Silence fell in the bunker.

"These people are ruffians and outlaws who have incited unrest among law-abiding citizens. They caused the CSD riots and the food riots, and their smear campaign against the OCSD is well known. Somehow, they even infiltrated PeopleCam. No one can figure out how we were hacked! We didn't want to show the Resistance's propaganda videos, but they forced us to do it.

"In the early days of the Restrictions, the self-proclaimed leader of the Resistance, attorney and terrorist Thomas Bailey, pitted himself against Lowell Stratford, criticizing his every effort to secure our country against the threat of terrorism. Though it was always suspected his opposition of Lowell Stratford went much farther than his verbal attacks, no charges were ever filed against him.

"Bailey had supporters who believed him to be pure of heart, but in truth, there is a dark side to the mysterious rebel leader, previously unknown to the public.

"He faked his own death six months ago, in an accident that left his only son maimed for life. Heedless of the consequences of his actions, Bailey and his wife left their son for dead and disappeared, only to continue his terrorist activities from a clandestine location, where he exerted great influence over the actions of impressionable Careen Catecher.

"Bailey, who fears capture, spoke with me earlier today from an undisclosed location. I must warn you, the statements made in this brief interview are quite upsetting. I apologize in advance for the poor audio quality."

An old photo of Tom flashed on the screen, and tears pooled in Lara's eyes. *Tommy will look just like that in a few years.*

"So, Tom, why have you returned from the dead, so to speak?"

"The Resistance has the ability to destroy the OCSD ... I want to see our country torn apart."

"What?" Lara gestured at the television. "There's no way he said that."

"That's absolutely shocking, Tom. Why would your revolutionary group try to take over the United States?"

"It's in everyone's best interest to ... take responsibility away from individuals. People are not capable of managing their own lives. The Resistance will ... hobble and control their every move. Bad decisions are made ... teenagers and young adults. The Resistance will ... control their ... better than the OCSD."

"That's not even a decent editing job!" Grace looked like she wanted to climb into the television and claw Sheila Roth's eyes out.

"One more question, Tom: what do you have to say about Careen Catecher?"

"Careen was never really part of the Resistance. Kids can be idealistic and read into things. She's not important enough to bother with."

"Surely no one's going to be fooled by this." Grace wrung her hands.

Sheila faced the camera for her wrap-up. "Tom Bailey is a dangerous revolutionary and not to be trusted. I wouldn't be at all surprised if he's been working behind the scenes since his disappearance, planning more attacks—possibly even the university bombing. I'm Sheila Roth for PeopleCam News."

Trina followed Eduardo and Mitch up the stairs and out of the bunker, where she stood in the shadow of the boulders and took a deep breath. Even though they'd just spent hours digging up coffee cans full of money in the fresh air, returning to the damp underground bunker made her desperate to escape back outside, even if it was just for a few minutes. She wrapped the blanket she'd brought with her closer around her shoulders. Eduardo and Mitch had paused a short distance away to wait for Lara and Jaycee.

She was going to miss Lara and Eduardo. With them gone, she'd be stuck in the two-room bunker with Grace and David, who tended to bicker without realizing they were doing it. She was jealous of Mitch's ability to come and go at will.

"What's this?" She watched Eduardo accept a device the size of a cellphone with a short antenna from Mitch.

"It's a bug detector. Sweep every room at the Bailey's first thing, got it? And don't stay there if anything seems off. The QM might have it under surveillance."

"Got it." Eduardo slipped it in his jacket pocket.

"Kevin is expecting you at the memorial service in OP-441 on Tuesday. He'll arrange it so you have a chance to speak to the president." Mitch handed him a loaded bag. "And here—I packed you enough supplies to last you for about a week. Who knows if you'll be able to find food. It's mostly MREs and bottled water, but it won't spoil."

Eduardo slung it over his shoulder. "Thanks."

Lara and Jaycee emerged from the bunker, ready to go. Eduardo and Lara were leaving as they'd arrived, with only the clothes on their backs. Jaycee had crammed as many of her things as would fit into her duffel bag.

She dropped it on the ground at her feet and held the rifle in the crook of her arm. Mitch took her by the shoulders and spoke soberly. "Listen to me. Do not take that death benefit money. It's vital that you stay off the OCSD's radar. And do not—I mean it—do not let yourself get Linked. You're the only one of us young enough to be in danger from that. Got it?"

"Yes, Daddy! I got it. Stop worrying!" Their parting hug was brief; she picked up her bag and ran after Eduardo.

Lara started to follow, but Mitch laid a hand on her arm. "Just in case you get stopped or have issues." He handed her an ID card for Jaycee. Lara glanced at the name.

"You made her my daughter?"

"She could sure as hell pass, looks-wise. It's a smart move. It should keep anyone from questioning either of your false identities too closely. Take care of my girl."

Lara laughed. "I'll do my best to keep up with her." Then her expression turned sympathetic. "Look, Mitch, I know it's tough letting her go, but I'll look after her like she was mine. I promise."

They embraced, for far longer than seemed necessary to Trina.

"Are you sure you're okay doing this? What about Tom? Do you think he suspects?"

Trina shrank deeper into the shadows. *Whoa! What the heck?*

"Tom never suspected before." She shook him off. "Don't worry. I know what I'm doing." She ran to catch up with Eduardo and Jaycee.

There was something going on between Mitch and Lara that no one else had noticed. But what?

Chapter 47

9:40 PM
Quadrant DC-005

"The car will be here in five minutes." Atari pressed the elevator button. "I'll walk you out."

Tom, showered, shaved, and dressed in a suit and heavy wool coat, looked much more like the father Tommy remembered from his childhood. The fading black eye, however, put him firmly in the present. Tom addressed Atari first. "You'll send word to Mitch that I'm a free man? I don't want David to jump the gun and release that file on Madalyn. We'll need it later."

"I've got time to do it now." He hurried into Command Central.

Tommy crossed his arms on his chest. "Tell Mom I'm fine, and I'll see her soon."

"I think she'll be disappointed that you've decided to stay here." His tone made Tommy feel like a little kid. But he wasn't buying it. Not this time.

"No, I think she'll understand. Now that we've located Careen, there's no way I'm leaving here without her." Why was Careen so unimportant to his father all of a sudden, when just a few days ago, he'd come to the capital to try and get her released? "Dad, I'm willing to fight and sacrifice for Careen. You know, the way Mom has for you."

"You seem to think my relationship with your mother is out of balance?"

"Mom's always had your back. How could you let Stratford torture her? I don't get it. If it had been me and Careen, I'd never—"

"What? Son, you can't know what you would've done. You're involved in the Resistance, yes, but in a very limited scope. You enjoyed the adrenaline rush when you saved your old man, and now you harbor schoolboy dreams of rescuing the girl. But the fate of our country is hanging in the balance. These next few days are critical, and I can't be distracted by the search for one young woman when I can take steps to avert a much bigger disaster."

"Fine. Then I guess it's a good thing we both know what we have to do."

Atari returned, and he and Tom stepped onto the elevator. Tommy nodded once in farewell as the doors slid closed.

Tommy waited in the lobby for Atari's return. The doors slid open, and Atari stepped out. "Package delivered."

"So where's Careen? Why did you Link her? Is she all right?"

"Dude, cool your jets. I located her a couple days ago and then lost her again. Looks like they were keeping her at PeopleCam all along."

"So the protest at PeopleCam … did CXD know she was there?"

"No, but those crazy kids said they stormed the building because they saw her. Pete searched the building for hours that night but no luck. That's why I never told you. I figured you'd freak. This has been a very eventful day."

Atari launched into a dramatic retelling of how he'd tricked Madalyn into putting on a Link. When he was done, Tommy, feeling more pro-Atari than he ever had, offered him a congratulatory fist bump. "Now we're that much closer to winning."

"What do you mean?"

"You know, overthrowing Madalyn and the OCSD. Living happily ever after. Free at last and all that."

Atari studied him, serious for once. "There's no such thing as winning this game."

"Wes thought we could win."

"Wes was brought up to believe that winning—or dying—were the only options."

"Then why are we going through all this? Why does the Resistance even try, if we can't win?"

"Let me employ a football analogy. It's not about winning or even about touchdowns. It's about first downs."

Tommy sighed. "You don't have to relate everything to football."

"I haven't yet exhausted my knowledge of the game, but have it your way. You and I would prefer to live the way we want and push for a little more breathing room when we need it. We don't agree with the OCSD, but a lot of people do support the OCSD's intent. They're even willing to put up with the OCSD's methods in exchange for feeling safe.

"We don't, can't, and shouldn't all want the same thing, or behave the same way, or believe the same things. Four hundred million individuals aren't going to agree on much. We shouldn't have to pretend like we do."

"Careen believed we could fix the mess the OCSD had made of things. I didn't pay close attention or try to understand. I was still recovering from the accident. I cared more about getting back into top physical condition and learning to fight and shoot."

"Idealogically, Careen was in the infatuation stage."

Tommy still didn't want to believe him. "None of the adults ever mentioned failure."

"Well, would you lead off with 'we can't win' if you were recruiting people for your revolution? No, of course not. It's too discouraging. Mitch might be the only one of us who's fanatic enough to keep going for victory over the OCSD. Let me ask you this: are you willing to keep fighting even if you can't win in the end?"

"Yeah. I am."

"Then you're one of the cursed. There'll be plenty of days when you'll want to throw in the towel."

He shrugged as if it didn't really matter.

"What do you want, Tommy? What do you want from your life? Beyond the next fifteen minutes. Beyond the next few months."

"To do what I can to make a difference, even if we can't win."

Atari nodded and offered another fist bump. "The extent to which you resist is the extent to which you are free."

Chapter 48

6:15 AM
Sunday, December 10, 2034
Quadrant OP-439

Eduardo pulled the truck up to the Baileys' garage. Lara got out and keyed in the entry code, and he guided the truck inside. The trip from BG-098 had been uneventful, but now he felt a twinge of mixed guilt and embarrassment. He'd been in this backyard before, when Wes had tapped him to spy on Tommy and Careen. He'd trusted Wes then, because he'd thought he had no choice. Now it seemed more prudent to follow Lara's lead.

They crossed the backyard to the kitchen door. As Eduardo drew near, he could see the door was splintered near the lock. Someone had kicked it in and then pulled it closed again. Lara looked at it and nodded slowly. "I see no one bothered to look for the spare key."

"Let me go first. Wait here." Eduardo pulled a can of pepper spray and the bug sweeper Mitch had lent him out of his jacket pocket and eased the door open.

Lara stood on the threshold, craning her neck to see past the kitchen, but Jaycee waited shyly at the bottom of the porch steps and clutched her rifle, duffel bag slung over her shoulder.

Some minutes later, Eduardo appeared at the door. "The front door's been broken in, too. I can nail it shut for now and rig a way to lock this one if you want to stay here."

"Let's see how bad it is before we decide." Inside, Lara set down the bag Mitch had given them and righted an overturned chair as she surveyed the wreck of her kitchen. Jaycee laid her things on the kitchen table and gazed out the big bank of windows that overlooked the backyard before she inspected the rich wood of the cabinets. Some of the doors sagged on broken hinges, and broken dishes and glassware crunched underfoot. She touched the shiny countertop.

"I bet your house looked like something out of a magazine."

"I suppose so, but right now I'd trade it for the diner's fully stocked kitchen. These MREs your dad sent will last for a while, but I'm going to miss having fresh food."

"I wish you were my mom."

"Oh, that's awfully sweet of you, honey." She hugged the girl. "I wish I'd had a daughter like you."

"Will you help me find her? My real mom?"

Lara released her. "Well … uh, I wouldn't know where to begin."

They both jumped at a crash in the hallway, and Eduardo came back into the kitchen, trying to avoid the debris scattered on the floor. "The house was fine when we were here the night of the explosion. The QM must have trashed it when they came looking for Tommy, but it doesn't look like they've got it under surveillance now. As long as we keep a low profile, we should be able to come and go from here."

Jaycee took a few hesitant steps down the hall.

"Make yourself at home," Lara said. "Just stay inside, okay?"

The girl disappeared into the living room. Soon Lara heard the plink of piano keys. She peeked around the corner and smiled as Jaycee pressed randomly, delighted by the sounds that emanated from the scarred instrument. She settled onto the bench, her rust-colored hair spilling over her shoulders, and walked her fingers up from the lowest notes.

Eduardo was waiting when Lara came back into the kitchen. "Unless my apartment's been completely trashed, I think we should sleep there."

She nodded. "Do you want to check it out?"

"Sure. It's not far. I'll walk over. Walking attracts less attention than a car with BG plates." He headed out the back.

As soon as he was out of sight, Lara hurried down the hall to Tom's office and closed the door. She pressed a nearly imperceptible indentation in the wainscoting, and a spring-loaded panel opened to reveal a safe. She turned the dial and reached inside for her laptop. Now she could truly get back to work. She plugged it in, logged on, accessed a government website, and ran a data search. Results popped up without delay. *Looks like no one bothered to revoke my clearance after we disappeared last summer.* Her fingers flew over the keys, as she downloaded the resulting files, to be examined more closely later.

The piano noises had stopped. She slid the laptop back into its hiding place and returned to the living room, but Jaycee wasn't there. Unexpected tears welled up as she climbed the stairs, and she chided herself for getting emotional over the feel of the familiar treads beneath her feet and the smooth bannister in her hand. Their home had been happy and full of love, but over time, the secrets had crowded closer, pressing at the safe haven she'd created for her family.

She stepped over the personal items strewn on the hallway floor and paused in Tommy's doorway. Jaycee, wearing one of Tommy's sweatshirts, lay curled up on his bed with her rifle beside her, fast asleep.

My family is growing. Lara folded her arms. *If I help find her mother, Mitch will never forgive me.*

The scuffling of footsteps broke the silence. The familiar creak of the screen door on the front porch spurred Lara to action. She pulled the bedroom door closed and darted down the stairs.

In the front hall, she grabbed Tommy's baseball bat and crept to the window, chancing a look through the blinds.

7:01 AM

Tom arrived back in OP-439 tired, disappointed, and still a little angry.

The Resistance had changed. Either that or it had never been what he'd believed it to be. Initiating violence—especially against innocent bystanders—had never been part of the plan.

Things are so much more dangerous now than when I began this fight. Mitch was out of control.

He wished he'd been able to bring Madalyn around to his way of thinking. That could have diffused Mitch's plan for revolution.

The black town car turned the last corner and pulled up in front of his home. He took in the peeling paint, unkempt landscaping, and shattered front door. Their home had been a safe place. Lara had never asked him not to be who he was; her only caveat was that Tommy be sheltered from any knowledge of or involvement in the Resistance. Through his actions, he'd destroyed that bulwark against the realities of the outside world.

It would have been better if Tommy had come home with him and left the more experienced members of the team to extract Careen. He'd be crushed if Careen didn't want to return to the Resistance. Part of him sympathized with his son and found it hard to believe she'd prefer to ally with the OCSD. He wasn't as heartless as Tommy believed—about Careen or about Lara.

Tom crossed the wide front porch and tried the door, which was shut tight. Then he remembered he didn't have his keys, and headed around back through the overgrown hedges. Perhaps a spare was still hidden near the back porch.

That door hung on broken hinges, the frame splintered. It dragged against the floor, pulverizing tiny shards of glass and pottery as he pushed it open and stepped into the ruins of his home.

As he surveyed the wreck of the kitchen, his first thought was for his wife. Lara had put so much care and effort into their home, and now it was trashed beyond recognition. The destruction went far beyond material possessions like dishes and furniture. He'd sacrificed his job and his family for what he'd believed was a way to advance a just and noble cause.

But all this destruction, including the damage to his relationships with Lara and Tommy, was the by-product of his own willingness to sacrifice to the cause. Now everyone who resisted would pay the cost.

He nudged a broken vase with his foot.

"Tom?" The familiar voice meant he really was home. Lara stood in the doorway to the dining room, clutching Tommy's baseball bat. "Where's Tommy? Mitch said he was with you."

He crunched through the debris to embrace her, bat and all. "I didn't know if you were here yet."

She twisted out of his arms. "Well?"

"Tommy? He said to tell you he's fine, and he'll see you soon."

"What kind of an answer is that? Where is he?"

"At a Resistance safe house in the capital. He's bound and determined to rescue Careen. What could I do?"

Chapter 49

1:30 PM
Tuesday, December 12, 2034
Quadrant DC-001

Careen inhaled deep breaths of the biting cold winter air, glad to be outside for the first time since she'd gone to OP-439 in search of Tommy and Wes. How long had it been? She had no idea, but this was definitely wintry weather.

High heels clicking on the pavement, she followed Madalyn exactly twenty-seven steps from a rear door of the PeopleCam building to the backseat of an oversized SUV with tinted windows. Their security guard escorts sat in front.

She looked eagerly out the window during the short drive. All too soon, the SUV entered a subterranean parking garage. As she stepped out of the vehicle, Careen was treated to another blast of icy air and felt the thrill of goose bumps on her stocking-clad legs. She touched her fingers to her tousled hair as the guards hurried her inside. Her Link's light flashed, visible just inside her coat cuff.

Careen had been sent back to her room immediately after the strange-looking man had put the red bracelet on her wrist, with no explanation as to why it was there. The light that flashed in time with her pulse was distracting, and it was awfully tight, but she couldn't find a way to loosen it or take it off. Like everything else, she'd get used to it.

Two hotel security guards met them at the door and led the way up the stairs and into an opulent ballroom decorated with brightly colored balloons and wide cloth streamers, like a circus-themed children's party. A banner hung on the wall: *Forever Linked for a Happy Future*.

A group of elementary-school-aged children stood in rows beneath the banner, smiling and showing their flashing Links as a photographer captured the moment for posterity. Careen, completely absorbed in watching the children, scarcely noticed where she was until the guard tugged on her arm to urge her up a set of metal stairs onto a raised platform with a podium. She took a seat in one of the chairs set behind the podium, facing the parents, grandparents, and older siblings of the Linked children. She dropped her own gaze to her hands, folded in her lap.

The photographer finished, and Madalyn stepped up to the podium.

"You may return to your parents."

The children broke out of the orderly rows, the younger ones bobbing through the crowd in search of familiar faces.

As Madalyn began her welcome speech, Careen scanned the crowd through the fringe of her long bangs. The adults in the audience were silent and still; every one of them held their children in a protective cocoon. No one fidgeted, not even the littlest Link recipients. The moment was too solemn. She turned her full attention to what Madalyn was saying.

"From today forward, these children, and soon all American children, will never know neglect or hunger. The Cerberean Link system is designed to safeguard them and attend to their needs.

"If a child is sick with a fever, the Link will respond, and the appropriate authority will be notified immediately. If a child is lost, the GPS feature of the Link will assure they are quickly and easily found."

This bracelet thing can locate lost children? Careen clutched her own left wrist. *No wonder they all look so serious. It's an honor to be chosen.* She flashed to the memory of being trapped with her dying father in the rubble of another bomb blast, nearly ten years before. *If I'd been wearing one, they might have found us in time to save my dad.*

"No child will ever be denied access to food, health care, or other resources to which they are entitled. The Cerberean Link will train them to function independently of their parents, be responsible for themselves, and be part of the unbroken chain of our society."

Madalyn pulled back her sleeve to display the red band that encircled her own wrist, and raised her arm so it was visible to the crowd.

"Personal accountability makes responsible citizens. The Link assures if you've done nothing wrong, you have nothing to fear." She turned to Careen and beckoned her forward.

Madalyn had been in the room the only other time Careen had spoken to a large group of people. That had been at OCSD headquarters, just moments before Lowell Stratford's death. This time she wanted Madalyn to be pleased with what she had to say. Her feet carried her obediently across the platform. She took a deep breath, glanced down at her Link, and then lifted her chin.

"I was nine years old when my father was killed in a terrorist attack. As I grew up, there were many times no one noticed when I was sick or hungry. It's very difficult for a child to thrive without consistency in their life. Everyone needs someone to count on. The Link is a miracle."

Someone spoke from deep in the crowd. "What kind of terrorist attack killed your father?"

"It was a ... bombing."

Madalyn nudged her out of the way and spoke into the microphone. "Careen has been granted an opportunity to lead by example and make amends for her own mistakes."

The photographer hurried to stand in front of the podium. "A few more photos, children. This time with the young lady." Careen descended the platform and the children grouped around her, some of the older girls jostling to stand next to her.

One of them whispered, "Your hair is pretty. But I liked it better when it was pink."

"Me, too," she whispered back.

"All right everyone! Show your Links!" Lights winked on every wrist. "Now a silly one!" The children struck poses and made faces, and some of the adults in the crowd smiled. Careen saw a man with short brown hair and glasses elbowing his way past the families, his gaze fixed on her. She shrank back, but the children pressed around her, cutting off any avenue of escape. He was only a few yards away when a huge *boom* rocked the floor. She staggered against the screaming children, and they went down like closely packed dominoes.

Tommy was the only one in the audience at the Inaugural Link Ceremony who wasn't part of a family group. He'd realized it almost at once, and now he hovered close to one that had grandparents, aunts, uncles, and cousins, hoping he could blend in and avoid scrutiny. He was dressed like the other men, in wool pants and a shirt and tie. He pushed his glasses up. This disguise was good. A few minutes ago he'd seen his reflection in a mirror out in the hall and at first hadn't recognized himself.

From the moment Careen entered the room, he'd barely torn his eyes away, convinced he could read her heart and her intentions if he concentrated hard enough. She looked older in a business suit and heels. But it wasn't just the clothes that made her seem different—it was her demeanor.

She'd always been interested in what was going on around her. Sometimes it was downright annoying. This time, she'd taken a seat on the platform behind Madalyn, folded her hands in her lap, and kept her eyes cast down.

Look at me. He willed her to feel his presence. *I'm here.* He took a step closer to the podium, and when she glanced up their eyes met. His pulse quickened. She recognized him. She knew. Then she dropped her eyes again, so she wouldn't give anything away.

It was the moment right before the snap. He knew what to do. If he ran the play properly, she'd be sharing his room at the safe house tonight. *Okay, focus. First things first.*

All the parents stood silent, clutching their children as though they feared they'd have to surrender them for good. He wished he could tell them not to worry, that the Link was in the control of the Resistance, not the OCSD.

He was so keyed up that he hadn't been paying attention to anything that was said. Then Careen stepped up to the podium and he willed his heart to quiet down so he could hear her voice.

She said someone to count on. She saw me. She knows I'm here. Wait—what? The Link is a miracle? She can't believe that. It's what Madalyn wants to hear. He tried to catch Atari's eye to get his reaction, but he was too busy fiddling with the camera to notice.

Tommy moved into position while Atari assembled the children for photos with Careen.

"Now a silly one!" Atari pushed the detonator on the camera right on cue, and even though he knew it was coming, the explosion made Tommy cower. Everything began to happen in slow motion. Careen wobbled and fell into the mass of screaming children. The security guards ran to secure the exits as the parents surged forward.

He shoved his way through the traffic jam and spotted Careen huddled on the ground, arms sheltering the closest children. Many hands reached into the pile to pull the Linked to safety. Just as his fingers brushed her sleeve, he took a block in the back and sprawled on the carpet. Before he could get to his feet, a security guard had stepped in and rushed her away.

Chapter 50

2:16 PM
Quadrant DC-005

Back at Command Central, Atari and Tommy watched the People-Cam coverage of the Inaugural Link Ceremony. Atari slurped the milk in his cereal bowl. Tommy wasn't hungry.

"I was sure she knew it was me. I don't understand. Has she totally drunk the Kool-Aid? Could she really believe what she said?"

"It's easy to get all starry-eyed about the upside of the Cerberean Link."

"Why did you pick such a crazy name?"

"It's a nod to Greek mythology, of course. Cerberus was the three-headed dog that guarded the entrance to Hades."

"Right. Like Fluffy."

"Who?"

"The three-headed dog in *Harry Potter*. I just watched it for the first time last night."

"Yeah. Banned."

"They banned a lot of good stuff."

"Yeah. Anyway, Cerberus was a guardian. I thought it was appropriate because, like the real mythological creature, Cerberean Link has more than one side: it monitors your health and keeps track of all your records. It can pinpoint your location anytime, anywhere. But you see the downside, right?"

"It leaves you with no privacy."

"Bingo."

"Why did you invent the Link when you knew what Madalyn would use it for?"

"Hey, be fair. None of this stuff is new. I just integrated it all into one app and installed it on an unremovable band that links you to every detail about your life. Good ideas are corrupted in the hands of bad people. Lucky for us, it's not just good people who'll be trapped in this web."

"So how are we going to get Careen out of there?"

"Looks like she didn't want to escape. Maybe life's too good over at Death Star."

"Bull. Of course she wants to escape. We just need a better plan."

Atari mimicked his voice. "*We just need a better plan.* Why don't *you* come up with something?"

"Hey, don't forget I got my dad out. I can do it again if you're out of ideas."

"Your dad's right, you know. You lack perspective. You underestimate your opponents. You're too straightforward, too simple, and too honest. That's a problem.

"You think you know what's going on in the world because of what you see on TV. But you're wrong. Stratford and Madalyn gained control by making people believe things that weren't true. I'm a much worthier opponent for Madalyn. I'm going to turn the tables on her. Let's see how well she handles it when I mess with her reality for a change.

"There's no need to tax yourself coming up with a better plan." He nudged Tommy with his elbow. "My better plan is evolving. You'll get a kick out of this."

A few keystrokes later, Tommy's image sauntered into view on the main television screen.

"Jeez, Atari! You can't just, um, cartoon me like that!"

"It's hardly a cartoon. This is very sophisticated technology. He looks just like you."

That's debatable. Tommy scrutinized the image.

"*It was a no-brainer.*" His voice came over the speakers.

Atari grinned. "Look how well the audio is synched."

"Seriously?"

"Yeah! I've been recording voice samples ever since you got here, and I can make him say anything I want. His vocabulary is a little larger than yours, but I don't think anyone will notice."

"You're an ass."

"Sticks and stones will break my bones, but words of one syllable will never hurt me, bro. I needed to practice on someone I could observe. Oh—and hey, I've got a surprise for you. Just until we get you the real thing, of course. Thought you might like this."

He pressed a key and Careen walked into frame and struck a seductive, come-hither pose that might have been all kinds of awesome if it was real. It was a jolt, seeing her like that, and Tommy's pulse quickened. He glanced over at Atari, who seemed to be enjoying watching her a little too much.

"Not cool." Still, his eyes drifted back to the screen. Her clothing was skin-tight, her features enhanced with heavy makeup. After a moment, memories of the real Careen took the forefront of his mind, and he thought how embarrassed she'd be if she knew Atari was using her this way. "Delete it."

"No chance! It's a masterpiece." Atari wiggled his eyebrows as he pecked at the keys, and Careen tossed back her bangs and started toward Tommy with a swing in her walk he was sure he'd never seen before. The perspective shifted to his on-screen double's point of view as she drew near, batting her heavily made-up eyes. Her lips parted....

Tommy grabbed him by the shirt, but before he could haul him out of the chair, Atari hit pause.

"All right. Jeez. Chill out, bro. This version was just for us—I mean you. Mostly. But whatever." He turned off the monitor.

"Is this just a sick game for you?"

"No, it was part of the plan. I figured I could use enhanced footage to create a diversion."

"To help Careen escape?"

"Yeah, but that plan requires her active participation, and dude, I'm not sure she'd fight to save herself if she had the chance. I mean, after the way she acted when I Linked her, combined with what we just saw at the press conference, I'm thinking Stockholm syndrome. Know what that is?"

"Yeah, I read about it. It's when a hostage identifies with their captor. But Careen's too smart to fall for that."

"Smart's got nothing to do with it." He paused. "What pisses her off?"

"Madalyn."

"Not good enough. We need something bigger—something or someone that will make her mad enough to snap out of it."

Tommy nodded. "I know someone."

Chapter 51

3:00 PM
Quadrant OP-441

Tom and Lara both took care to avoid being recognized at the memorial service in OP-441. The only rust-colored curls in the crowd belonged to Jaycee. Lara had tucked hers under a knit cap. Eduardo had parked about half a mile from the hub, and as they drew near, Jaycee stayed close to Lara, staring at the hundreds of people that crowded the entrance gate. They stood with Eduardo and watched President Wright take his place at the podium, which was placed over the exact spot where the hub director had been gunned down by the QM during the food riots. Garrick and Kevin stood to the side. Tom locked eyes with each of them.

The president cleared his throat. "I wish I could say it is a pleasure to be here in OP-441 on this fine, sunny day. But this is a solemn occasion. It is a day of mourning and remembrance. A day on which I would like to promise you that nothing like the food riots will ever happen in this country again." He looked out over the crowd. "The OCSD's efforts to safeguard our citizens against the threat of terrorism have saved countless lives. But the events that transpired here on November twenty-third serve to remind us that even our best efforts to ensure safety will not always be successful."

Lara pressed close to his side and whispered, "It's really starting to work, isn't it?"

He looked down at her and nodded. Just then Eduardo began to thread his way through the crowd, and Tom shepherded Lara and Jaycee after him.

The president continued. "Change has been born of this tragedy. Though Essential Services has now resumed weekly deliveries, anyone who chooses may opt out of the program by filling out a form on a newly established website. On New Year's Day, a percentage of the distribution hubs will revert to being privately held grocery stores, where people will be able to shop for their own food. Other hubs will remain part of the Essential Services department, and food delivery shall remain available for those who wish to continue in the program."

A reporter shouted, "What percentage of the hubs will go private?"

"That depends on how many people opt out of Essential Services. Regardless, it is prudent to nurture an open food market so that the circumstances that led to the OP-441 tragedy will not be repeated."

After a short prayer and a moment of silence in honor of the fallen, the president's Secret Service detail escorted him through the crowd. Kevin opened a side door to admit Tom and the others into the hub. They watched Hoyt Garrick lead the president's detail across the room and and usher the president into an office, where the Secret Service took up positions outside the door. Garrick motioned for Tom to follow him, and together they went inside, where Christopher Wright was waiting

Garrick shut the door. "Mr. President, allow me to present Tom Bailey."

They shook hands. "It's a pleasure, Sir."

"I have to admit, Mr. Bailey, my curiosity about you has gotten the better of me."

Tom continued the introductions. "This is my wife, Lara, and Jaycee Carraway. This young lady's uncle was one of the marshals who worked with the hub director to distribute food in an orderly fashion. He was killed in the line of duty the following week. Oh, and this is—"

Eduardo extended his hand. "Eduardo Rodriguez, sir. You probably don't remember, but we met a few weeks ago. At the White House."

The president nodded. "I remember."

"We're here as representatives of the Resistance. The Restrictions are not effective. The system is starting to crumble. We want to suggest an alternative plan that can be implemented to head off a possible revolution."

Chapter 52

1:05 PM
Thursday, December 14, 2034
Quadrant DC-005

Tommy stuck his head into Wardrobe. "You ready? The car service delivered her, and the fake receptionist you hired showed her into the fake conference room. Put on the security guard uniform."

Atari grinned. "I changed the plan. I've promoted myself to Special Agent for this assignment. I'm wearing a suit."

"We had a perfectly good plan. Why are you changing it?"

"Because this is a better one. Come on, be a sport. I know you were disappointed there was no part for you in the old plan." He punched Tommy's arm. "I know you want in on this."

Tommy sighed. "All right."

Atari grinned and extended his hand. "Great! Shake." Tommy clasped his hand, and before he knew what had happened, Atari locked a handcuff around his wrist with a click. Tommy tried to pull away, but Atari fastened the other cuff to his own wrist. "Let's go!"

He dragged Tommy into the hall and down two flights of stairs. He paused outside the conference room door and grinned. "It's showtime! Just be yourself."

He opened the door, shoved Tommy in ahead of him, and addressed the woman seated at the conference table. "I apologize for your wait, ma'am. As you can see, we have a very, very recent arrest we're dealing with today." He pulled out a chair and nudged Tommy into the seat directly across from Careen's mother.

She tossed her hair over her shoulder and fixed her gaze on Tommy. "I didn't know my free trip to the capital was going to include sightseeing." She purred as she pressed her index finger to the center of the space between them on the glossy table, and slowly drew an undulating line back toward herself. "Nice to see you, Tommy Bailey."

He squirmed in his chair.

"I've always had a thing for guys like you. I must admit I'm surprised to learn my daughter does, too." She turned her gaze on Atari. "And it's quite all right. I didn't mind waiting." She twirled a lock of long hair around her finger. "That limo was very classy. Like something out of a movie."

Atari laughed. "Nothing's too good for you, Mrs. Catecher."

"Call me Jezz. I haven't been Mrs. Anyone for a long, long, time. When do I get—"

"She's not here at the moment."

She squared her shoulders, and something like annoyance flickered across her face. "The driver mentioned something about …" She leaned closer and whispered, "… finally getting the reward money?"

Tommy's annoyance turned to fury at her apparent lack of concern for Careen. He shot Atari a look, and Atari gestured toward Jezz with his free hand and said, "By all means. Go right ahead."

"Don't you care that your daughter's life is in danger? This isn't a game. She's being abused and tortured at the OCSD. It's not going to end until she's no longer of any use to them. Then they'll kill her. That's why we're here at … um … the offsite secret headquarters where we won't be overheard. He's Internal Affairs. Investigating the abuse of a prisoner."

Her expression hardened. "Offsite secret headquarters? Internal affairs? Yeah. You honestly think I'm that much of an idiot? My kid gets her brains from me."

Atari cleared his throat, and her gaze shifted to meet his. "Fine. Since we're not standing on pretense any longer, Jezz, here's the deal. We're from the Resistance, and we're going to extract Careen from OCSD custody. Do you love her enough to help us hide the body?"

3:35 PM
Quadrant DC-001

Kevin's trip to OP-441 had been productive, and a welcome respite from his constant contact with Madalyn. He'd had a quick conference with Garrick, Eduardo, and the Baileys after their meeting with the president, and he was ready to put the next phase of the Resistance's plan into action.

He tapped on Madalyn's office door, and when she waved him in, he put on a concerned face. "According to the PR department, Careen's television appearances are destroying the OCSD's approval rating. The CXD protesters are actively opposing the Link program, and their message is spreading nationwide like wildfire, even without being able to upload on PeopleNet and PeopleCam. Poll numbers say only forty percent of adults surveyed think the Link is a good idea, and that number is falling. Fast."

He waited without expecting Madalyn to offer any solution. Then he continued.

"The Inaugural Link Ceremony ended in chaos, and that didn't help. You know, I think everyone likes a happy ending, right? A story with, like, redemption and people making up and hugging and stuff. Maybe Careen needs forgiveness and redemption before people will like her again."

Madalyn looked confused. "How?"

"The PR department believes Careen is dragging you down because she's lost favor with the public. She's perceived as a bad person. Some people don't like her because of her alleged role in the bombing, and other people don't like her because they think she's a sellout for working for the OCSD. So maybe an on-camera reunion with someone she's close to—unscripted, like a surprise—would make her seem more likeable, more real. We could pre-empt regular programming and go with a prime-time special, say eight p.m. on Friday?"

Madalyn nodded. "I like it. Kevin, you're doing a great job. You're definitely starting to think like me."

It was a good thing he hadn't dropped Mitch's transmitter down the drain. This plan was going to require lots of help—and some split-second timing.

Chapter 53

6:45 PM
Friday, December 15, 2034
Quadrant DC-001

Madalyn followed Fawn into Careen's room and immediately took charge.

"No, no, no, Careen. That outfit won't do at all. It's too casual. You have a visitor coming."

"Visitor?"

"You've been a good girl, Careen. The visit is a reward."

Her heart leapt, but the happy feeling evaporated right away. The only people she wanted to see were the ones who now despised her.

After Fawn did her hair and makeup, she dressed without protest in the blouse, pencil skirt, and necklace Madalyn selected from the closet and slipped on heels so high that she teetered when she followed Madalyn down the hall. She stopped outside the familiar soundstage, but Madalyn continued around the corner.

Madalyn opened a door, and Careen stepped into a sitting room with a curved, crushed-velvet sofa in the center, flanked by royal blue wing chairs and mahogany side tables. She assumed the floor-to-ceiling drapes covered another blank stretch of wall, as she could see no light peeking in around the edges of the panels.

"Have a seat." Madalyn left, closing the door behind her, and Careen perched on the sofa and wrapped her arms around her middle, still a little dazed by the circumstances. She didn't look up when she heard the door open. She closed her eyes and prayed to see—

"There's my baby girl!"

Mom?

Jessica Catecher hurried across the room and pulled Careen off the sofa, sweeping her into a completely one-sided hug. Careen kept her arms limp at her sides, her gaze fixed over her mother's shoulder.

"Why are you here?" The words were barely audible, meant only for her mother, not for whoever else was listening in.

Her mother released her with an affected, tinkling giggle, but her smile faded for a moment as she ran her fingers over the scar on Careen's cheek. She toyed with her bangs and then fingered the fabric of her blouse. "Almost perfect. Very classy."

"Don't."

Her mother ignored Careen's whispered plea and patted her shoulder. She tugged here and there at Careen's blouse until it fit more snugly across her breasts. She took a step back, surveyed her daughter's appearance again, and then unbuttoned one more button. "When in doubt, it's best to look sexy, don't you think, baby?"

"No. Why are you here?"

"Careen, everyone has been so kind to you under the circumstances." She dropped her voice to a stage whisper. "They don't usually treat criminals this well, you know. You're a very lucky girl, to get to live in fancy rooms with pretty, new clothes. Why are you being so cold? Aren't you glad to see me?"

"Why would you think I'd ever want to see you again after what you did? You sold me out to the quadrant marshals!"

"I'm your mother, that's why." Tears formed in the corners of her eyes, and she batted her eyelashes until one slid down her cheek. "You're the only thing I ever did that turned out halfway decent. So be sweet and show me some respect." Then she giggled like a teenager, any hint of tears gone. "Besides, I couldn't pass up another chance to be on PeopleCam!"

"What do you mean?"

"Well, it makes sense for us to be on television together this time, don't you think? The new security program is all about parents and children. You know, family. Like us." She tossed back her hair, took Careen by the arm, settled her on the plush sofa, and sat beside her. "Now isn't this nice? Everyone will see us in this gorgeous room."

The royal blue drapes opened to reveal a camera crew set up on the other side of a floor-to-ceiling observation window. The stage lights powered up.

No.

A voice came over a speaker on the wall. "Ready, Careen? Mrs. Catecher?"

"Call me Jezz."

"And we're live, in five ... four ..."

No. Careen's heart pounded in time with the word that echoed in her head. *No. No. No.*

Her mother pinched her arm and whispered, "Sit up straight!" She arched her back to show off her bosom to its best advantage. "Smile, baby, and read the script."

No! Careen began to gasp for air. Too many eyes were watching her. She saw Madalyn's icy gaze over the cameraman's shoulder, and beside her ... Kevin? She couldn't tell from his expression what he was thinking. She felt faint at the thought of the millions of viewers watching at home.

Her mother reached out and squeezed Careen's wrist, above the fist that was clenched in her lap, but looked directly into the camera as she read her lines. "Sweetheart, I came here today to talk to you about responsibility. I didn't raise you to be a terrorist or a criminal. You were a good little girl. Did someone trick you or force you to do the things you did? It's all right to tell Mother. Was it a boy?"

"No. It was me. Only me." *What is she trying to get me to say?*

Her mother beamed at the camera. "I'm so proud of you, baby—Careen—for taking responsibility for your actions. It's not right to blame others for things you've done. We're all responsible for our actions, aren't we?"

Careen sat in stony silence until her mother cleared her throat and nudged her in the ribs hard enough to make her gasp in pain. It was obvious she was trying to stick to the script, because when she got no response, she ad-libbed. "Don't you have something you'd like to say to me?"

Careen shook her head.

"Yes, I think you do." Her mother inclined her head toward the camera.

She pulled out of her mother's grasp, rebuttoned her blouse, and folded her arms across her chest in defiance. Her chin jutted out as she turned toward the camera and began to read. "Mom, today you're getting the five-million-dollar reward offered by the OCSD for information leading to my capture. I want you to have it. You deserve a comfortable life, even if you have to live with the ...

shame of having a criminal for a daughter. My actions were not your responsibility. And I want to apologize—" She stopped and caught Madalyn's eye. "Are you kidding? This is absolute BS! I'm not apologizing to her!"

Madalyn pushed her way past the camera, and, just on the other side of the glass, mouthed, "Do it. Now."

Careen shook her head. Her mother turned toward her with bewildered doe eyes, moist with more unshed tears. Jezz Catecher was wearing her trademark what-did-I-do look, but Careen was immune to her mother's attempts to manipulate.

She wobbled in her high heels as she scrambled up from the sofa and pointed down at her mother as she shouted at Madalyn through the glass. "Get her away from me!" She rounded on her mother and spat out, "I wish it had been you who died instead of Daddy!"

She yanked her arm away from her mother's outstretched hand and hurried to the door. When it failed to yield, she tugged at the doorknob, screaming, pounding, all self-restraint gone. *I don't care. I don't care what they do to me anymore.* She stumbled backward as the security guard stepped into the room.

Madalyn's voice came over the monitor. "Take her to prison immediately."

The guard made a grab for Careen, but Jezz stepped between them, took Careen by the shoulders, and shook her like a rag doll.

"Stop it! I can't believe you're acting like this on television!" Her mother fixed her with an urgent gaze. "I'm only doing this because I. Love. You. So. Much."

Careen wrenched herself free and shoved her mother with all her strength. Jezz fell against the security guard, knocking him off balance, and Careen dodged past them into the hall.

"Stop her!" Madalyn's shrill voice echoed over the speaker.

Careen's blood pounded as she ran, hampered by the heels and the tight skirt. She searched for a place to hide, wishing for a change of clothes. She couldn't go back for a pair of jeans and a sweater. They'd passed a dressing room with lighted makeup mirrors and racks of clothing on their way to the studio, and she raced around the corner and ducked inside, concealed herself behind a rolling rack of clothing, and worked her way into the depths of the room. *I need Fawn. Fawn will find me and help me.*

All too soon, she heard footsteps too heavy to be a woman's. She cowered between the rows of clothing, fists pressed against her mouth, as she watched a pair of wing-tip shoes approaching. There was nowhere else to hide. The wing tips paused at the end of the aisle, and her gaze moved slowly upward.

Pete Sheridan held a finger to his lips. He whispered, "Come with me."

Chapter 54

8:15 PM
Quadrant OP-439

Lara hurried to retrieve her laptop from its secret hiding place in Tom's office. She downloaded some files and sent them to Mitch, and was just closing the secret panel in the wainscoting when Tom came in.

"You ready to leave for the night?"

"Almost. I wanted to get my laptop." He opened a cabinet. "I can't recall where I left it."

"It's probably long gone by now. The house has been searched more than once."

"Well, there was nothing incriminating stored on it. I wanted it more for composing than anything else; I can write longhand just as well, I suppose." He grabbed two legal pads out of the cabinet and shut the door. "That meeting with the president went well. And Garrick's a good man. He's determined to make the murder charges against Madalyn stick. The door is open for us to influence the president, the chief QM, and Senator Renald. We have more power players on our side than Mitch and the Resistance. It's time to go it alone."

"Tom, you do realize what you're saying? Cutting ties with the Resistance and taking on the OCSD sounds like a foolish move. The OCSD sapped all the power from the three branches of government. Are they strong enough to take it back? Don't you think it'd be better to stay the course with Mitch?"

"Absolutely not. There's something I didn't tell you. I can't, in good conscience, be a part of Mitch's grandiose schemes of revolution any longer. The man is a psychopath."

"Everything we're doing is dangerous, and changing allegiances now makes me nervous. Besides, we've got Jaycee here with us.

I promised to look after her like she was my own child. I have responsibilities and ties to Mitch because of that."

"It might be best for Jaycee to keep her distance from him as well."

"Tom, really. No one's a perfect parent. It's clear he loves her very much."

"Lara, after what I've learned, I feel compelled to sever ties with Mitch and do everything I can to circumvent his plans. I didn't want to burden you with this, but now I believe you need to know."

8:20 PM
Quadrant DC-001

Pete Sheridan helped Careen into a long overcoat. She buttoned it, and he pulled up the hood to conceal her face. She slipped on the oversized pair of sunglasses he offered her, and pulled them down her nose so she could peer over the top of the frames as he spoke to her.

"Ever since the Tom Bailey interview aired, Sheila Roth wears this disguise when she comes and goes from the studio. She says it's for her privacy, but personally, I think she's terrified of being kidnapped by the Resistance and held for ransom." He chuckled. "No one will look at us twice if we walk out together."

He took Careen by the arm and led her through another makeup area and out into a hallway on the opposite side of the soundstages. He glanced both ways and drew her into the stairwell.

Pete was the Resistance's spy at PeopleCam. Careen hesitated at the top of the stairs, uncertain whether to follow or turn back and face her punishment.

Where could she go if she left her life in this opulent prison behind? She had no friends. The remaining supporters of the Resistance and even the violence-eschewing CXD activists wanted her dead. *Madalyn was right. She's the only one with the power to protect me.* The Link flashed at her wrist. *Ironic. It's supposed to keep me safe, but they'll use it to track me down.*

Pete gave her arm a gentle tug. He was no different from her guard. Not really.

They reached the ground floor, and he hurried her along a hallway until they came to a metal fire door. Careen put her hand on the doorknob and spoke in a whisper.

"You'll get in trouble for this. Take me back upstairs. Tell them you found me trying to leave the building and I'm very confused. Maybe Madalyn won't send me to prison if I apologize to her and my mother."

Pete shook his head. "Young lady, don't ever give up that easily." He pushed her out into the darkness and locked the door behind her.

8:25 PM

Atari and Tommy, dressed in black from head to toe, waited in the van, which Atari had concealed in the deep shadows at the rear of the parking lot.

Atari's phone rang, and played a song Tommy had never heard before.

Every breath you take, every move you make, every claim you stake, every smile you fake, I'll be watching you.

"Dude—that's a creepy ringtone."

"It's Madalyn—right on cue." Atari had the phone on speaker, and her shrill, panicked voice filled the space around them.

"Quick! Enable the Link! Careen's disappeared somewhere inside the building!"

Atari grinned at Tommy before he spoke with affected surprise. "What? Right now? I'm sorry, Madam Director, but I can't make any guarantees as to the Link's accuracy if the subject is inside a building."

"Just do it!"

Atari picked up the tablet and swiped over to the Link's login page. A few keystrokes later, Madalyn exclaimed, "Find her! Where is she?"

"I'm monitoring it now. If she tries to leave the building, the outside sensors will pick up her signal. Putting you on hold until I know more." He punched a key on his phone, cutting off her protest in midsentence.

Atari set the phone on the dashboard and turned his attention to the tablet. "I jammed all the security cameras inside the building and substituted a loop of old footage. She won't be seen on any of the monitors."

He looked at the clock on the van's dashboard. "It's showtime." He picked up the phone and reconnected with Madalyn.

"I've picked up her signal. She just exited the west side of the building."

Atari held the phone at arm's length as Madalyn shouted, "Send security after her! Kevin! Get my coat!"

He disconnected the call and held out his fist for a congratulatory bump. Tommy returned it but appeared hesitant. "Isn't it a little early to be celebrating? We don't have her yet."

"No worries. I got this." He put the van in gear and coasted around the perimeter of the building without turning on the headlights.

8:28 PM

Kevin followed Madalyn onto the elevator and held her coat. She fidgeted as they descended to the lobby.

"What a disaster! Good thing it wasn't really live."

Kevin nodded, though personally he thought it was a shame the viewing audience would never see what had just happened.

"Stall her. Slow her down." Mitch spoke in his ear.

As soon as the door slid open, she hurried out. Kevin fumbled with her coat and let her arm miss the sleeve twice as he helped her into it.

"Okay, you're clear. Let her go."

She dashed across the lobby and outside. Kevin kept his expression sober as he summoned another elevator.

Pete Sheridan was already in the car. The door slid closed, and both men spoke at the same time. "She's gone."

8:29 PM

The van rolled in a slow arc across the parking lot; Tommy and Atari pulled ski masks over their faces. Atari coasted to a stop and pointed around the side of the building. Tommy slipped out the passenger door and took off into the darkness.

As he rounded the corner, a woman in a long coat stepped out of the building. He closed the distance between them so quickly that she didn't notice his approach until he was almost upon her. She cried out once in surprise and struck at him ineffectively, wobbling in her high heels. He wrestled her into submission, turning her back to him and locking his arms around her to pin hers to her sides. Her knees buckled, but she still fought to wriggle out of his grasp as he half-dragged her toward the waiting van. He felt his grip beginning to slip as they struggled, and she clamped her teeth on his forearm, just above his wrist.

It hurt like crazy, but he didn't dare yell out loud. He shook her loose, and while she was off balance, he picked her up, slung her over his shoulder, and carried her the rest of the way to the van.

Atari rolled down the driver's side window and hissed, "Quit messing around! Let's go!"

Tommy whispered back, "Shut up, you idiot! What do you think I'm trying to do?" He deposited his captive in the van and scrambled in after her. Atari hit the gas before he had time to close the door.

She scuttled backward until she was pressed into the far corner, still looking around for some means of escape. He pulled off his ski mask and crawled toward her on his hands and knees.

"Hey, it's me. Take it easy."

Careen gasped; her mouth twisted like she was going to cry. "Tommy?"

"Yeah." He pulled her toward him, a hand on either side of her face. His kiss was charged with a mixture of desire, relief, and a healthy shot of adrenaline, and they were both breathing hard when he released her. She drew a sobbing breath, and he gripped her shoulders. "You knew we wouldn't give up until we got to you, right?"

She nodded, her eyes brimming with tears. He kissed her again, and she trembled in his grasp.

Atari called from the driver's seat, "Hey, I'm averting my eyes and everything, but you two might want to hold onto something besides each other." He hit the gas and turned the wheel hard to the left.

The van hurtled through the streets of the capital, in and out of darkness punctuated by the yellow glow of the street lamps, pursued by an impressive number of vehicles containing OCSD security guards and quadrant marshals.

The driver negotiated tight corners and ignored the traffic signals, forcing the pursuers to abandon caution as well. DC-001, with all its government workers, had more cars on the roads per capita than any other quadrant in the country. Horns blared as the van and its pursuers flew through an intersection, and one of the OCSD cars collided with a hapless motorist.

The GPS on the dashboard indicated just a few more blocks until they'd be out of the quadrant. There was no guarantee the pursuers would give up once the van hit the open freeway, but there was also no question that this was the only way to permanently free Careen. Tires squealed as the driver skidded around the last corner; the entrance ramp was in sight.

"Our blessed lady of acceleration, don't fail me now."

The driver chuckled and floored it, so focused on the goal that a QM vehicle went unnoticed until it made a kamikaze move and T-boned the van's passenger side. They sliced across several lanes, and though the van's driver tried desperately to spin out of the skid, both vehicles came to rest in the ditch on the far side of the road, bringing the chase to a halt.

The guards and marshals piled out of their vehicles, guns drawn, and approached the van. "Hands where we can see them!"

The driver rolled down the window and held up both hands.

"Out of the van!"

Jezz Catecher opened the door, a mischievous grin on her face.

<h1 style="text-align:center">Chapter 55</h1>

8:37 PM

Tommy braced himself against the side of the van and sheltered Careen in his arms while Atari negotiated a sharp right turn and hit the gas. Horns blared, and he slammed on the brakes and wrenched the wheel to the left. Tommy heard the *whoosh whoosh whoosh* of cars passing them by as Atari slowed down, changed lanes, and made three left turns, reducing his speed each time.

Once Atari quit slamming them against the walls with his crazy turns, Tommy could feel Careen's trembling cease, but every muscle in her body remained taut, poised to bolt. The dim glow from the street lamps disappeared when Atari turned the van into the parking garage. As they spiraled down into the blackness, she pushed away from him and huddled against the far wall, curling her knees into her chest. She didn't move when Atari opened the sliding door. He played the flashlight over them both.

"Come on, Princess. Welcome to the tower." He reached out a hand to her, but she shrank away, her eyes huge, like a frightened animal's.

"Back off, okay?" Tommy crawled over to the doorway and drew Careen toward him. "Let's go."

Together they steadied her as she stepped out. Tommy slid the passenger door closed, and Careen exclaimed at the familiar symbol on the door.

"This is a quadrant marshal van?"

"Well, not exactly. Not anymore. They're so careless with their toys." Atari pulled off his ski mask with a flourish, and he leered at her as he taunted her with the flashlight, the beam illuminating her body from head to toe in an appraising sweep of her figure. She balled up her fist and swung at him, then tried to dodge past Tommy as Atari groaned, dropped the flashlight, and brought both hands up to his face.

Tommy grabbed her around the waist to stop her flight, and still she fought his grasp. He pulled her close and locked his arms around her. "You're safe here," he whispered in her ear. "I swear. Count on it." Then his voice turned teasing. "You wore me out back there. Don't make me carry you again."

She stopped struggling, and after a moment, he opened his arms and let her right herself, but he kept a firm grip on her shoulder as he guided her to the elevator.

Behind him, Atari muttered, "She hits harder than your old man. I think she broke my nose. If I were you, I'd stick to the sim version of her. Lots less trouble than the real thing."

8:55 PM

Careen's pulse pounded in her head and her stomach churned; her fight-or-flight reflexes were in overdrive. She'd been too shocked to even think about refusing Tommy's kiss, and now she was confused. *That Atari guy works for Madalyn. If the members of the Resistance are all in prison, how is Tommy here?* She gazed around, even more confused, as they stepped out of the elevator into a room that looked like some kind of art gallery and smelled of popcorn.

Atari, fingers pressed to his nose, disappeared down one of the hallways.

"Where are we?" She was afraid to speak above a whisper.

"Atari's place."

She bit her lip and clutched at the Link on her wrist. Tommy noticed the gesture and smiled. "Nice left hook, by the way. You should follow up a knockout punch like that with an ice pack." He gestured to one of the black leather sofas. "Have a seat. I'll get one."

She stayed on her feet and edged toward the elevator, but he was back, ice pack in hand, before she got up the nerve to press the Down button and flee.

This had to be another, albeit more elaborate, test of her loyalty. But how did Tommy fit in? Was he on CSD, doing Madalyn's bidding under Atari's supervision? Until now, it had been too dark to see his face clearly. *Once I get a good look at him, I'll be able to tell if he's been dosed.*

She kept a wary eye on her surroundings as Tommy led her down a hallway, fearful that Atari might be lurking around any corner. Tommy opened the door and gestured her into a spacious bedroom. The furniture was glossy-white and streamlined, with navy bedding and chrome accessories. It was different, but every bit as expensive-looking as her rooms at PeopleCam. She sat on the edge of the bed. He pulled the desk chair over to face her, took her hand, and gently laid the ice pack on it. She looked into his eyes for the first time. They were clear. Just as she remembered, his left eye, a tiny bit more heavy-lidded, hinted at a playful wink.

"Better?"

She nodded. "Why are we here?"

"Atari's place is also a Resistance safe house. You remember Atari from the day we broke into the OCSD, right? He's kind of a jerk. You can't pay attention to anything he says, okay?"

She nodded again, studying his face. *Okay, so even if he hasn't dosed, maybe it's some kind of test for him, too.* She didn't want to get him in trouble; could she get him to give her a clue or a sign?

"Where is everyone?"

"Not here. But they're fine."

"How did you get here?"

"I'm here to find you. Danni brought me."

"Danni?"

"Yeah. She's been organizing the CXD thing. It's totally gone viral."

So Danni's organizing the hoards of protesters who want to kill me. Why am I not surprised?

He removed the ice pack and sandwiched her cold hand between his own. "I'm so sorry about everything. I wish I'd never agreed to go to OP-439 with Wes."

She touched his lips to silence him and shook her head, fearful he'd say something incriminating. He leaned in, and she moved her fingers to brush his cheek. *If this is part of the test, I'm going to fail.* When their lips were so close that no surveillance camera would be able to tell she was speaking, she whispered, "Are they watching us?"

There was a sharp knock on the door, and she pulled away.

Atari shouted from the hallway, "Debriefing. Kitchen. Half an hour."

Tommy rolled his eyes, and Careen took the opportunity to change the subject. "Do I have time to take a shower?"

"Yeah, sure."

"Do you have any clothes I could borrow? Something more comfortable?" *Something I can run in if I have to.*

"Sure. I'll go raid Wardrobe and see what I can find. There are towels, extra toothbrushes, and anything else you need in the bathroom." He rolled the chair back to the desk on his way out.

Chapter 56

8:59 PM

Atari stalked away as soon as the elevator doors opened, pinching his nostrils to contain the blood flow. He was loath to let Careen see how much she'd hurt him.

Even though the primary objective had been achieved, the mission felt tainted. He should be enjoying the rush from having outsmarted Madalyn. He peered at his face in his bathroom mirror. His nose was definitely crooked. He wet a washcloth at the sink and dabbed at the blood. Getting socked by a girl was humiliating—especially after all he'd done for her.

One thing he knew for sure: he wasn't willing to forego the thrill he knew he'd experience when the Link went live, nationwide.

He'd just pulled a roll of gauze out of his first aid kit when his phone rang.

Every breath you take …

He answered, and Madalyn's voice shrilled in his ear.

"Where is she? How did she get away?"

"Madam Director, I explained to you the system wasn't ready." He couldn't breathe through his nose, and his voice sounded thick even to his own ears.

"Are you crying?"

"No. I just have a bit of a cold. Anyway, it crashed when I brought it online. I'll need time to make the necessary adjustments. Right now it's impossible to pinpoint her location."

"Well, she can't get far. Once you fix the Link, it will be easy to track her down. How long before it's ready?"

"There's no way to estimate until I assess the extent of the problem."

"There was a plot to help her escape. We have one of the conspirators in custody."

"Interesting. Well, no one could've foreseen that. We might never find her. Until the Link goes live, of course."

"Hmm. I imagine the five-million-dollar reward would spur you to give it your best effort."

"Madam Director, it's not a matter of money."

"It's always a matter of money. Produce Careen Catecher and the five million dollars is yours. No questions asked."

9:08 PM

As soon as the door closed behind Tommy, Careen searched the drawers in the nightstand, dresser, and desk for evidence to suggest he was being drugged or kept there against his will. She gasped when she found his gun in the bottom desk drawer. The thrill that ran through her body at the sight of a weapon turned instantly to dread. If Tommy was armed, he was here in this strange place of his own volition. He couldn't be trusted any more than Atari.

She closed the drawer and hurried back to her spot on the edge of the bed. Moments later, he returned carrying a stack of sweaters, jeans, and leggings.

"These okay?" When she nodded, he set them on the bed beside her.

"Thank you." She stood and slid her arms around his waist, laying her head against his chest. His lips brushed her hair as he wrapped her in the embrace she recalled so well. His arms had been the safest place in the world. *Until now.* She gently pulled away and chose a sweater and leggings. As soon as she was inside the bathroom, she locked the door and turned on the shower, gripping the edge of the countertop as she tried to control her panic. *I have to act like I don't suspect. I have to pass the test—whatever it is.*

She shed her clothes and stood under the steamy spray for as long as she dared. She rushed as she dressed, tugging the leggings and sweater on over her damp skin. The half hour was nearly up.

Tommy was lying on the bed reading when she emerged. He'd never seemed interested in books before. She tried to not stare as she towel-dried her hair.

He looked up and closed his book. "You want socks?" She nodded, and he grabbed a pair out of a dresser drawer and tossed them to her. "Come on, I'm sure Atari's dying to tell you how brilliant he is." She padded down the hall after him to the kitchen and watched as he rummaged around in the well-stocked refrigerator.

She had to convince him she didn't suspect anything. "Are you going to make one of your famous peanut butter and pickle sandwiches?"

He laughed. "I actually enjoy peanut butter and pickle, especially when it's not my only option. You want turkey?" She nodded. Tommy layered the sliced turkey, lettuce, and tomato, and finished the sandwiches with a drizzle of Italian dressing. "Another Essential Services life hack. I like it this way better than with mayo."

They carried their plates into the dining area, and the simple act of sharing a meal with him seemed so right and so normal that she almost let her guard down. Her trepidation returned stronger than ever when Atari joined them at their table. Purple bruises had erupted under both his eyes. He'd stuffed both his nostrils with gauze and stabilized his nose with a strip of first aid tape. He reached across the table and took Careen's arm. His long, tapering fingers felt like spider's legs as they caressed her Link, but she resisted the urge to pull away, afraid to antagonize him further.

"You're the one who Linked me, right?"

He nodded.

"Can you really use the Link to find missing children?"

"Yes."

She bit her lip. "So when is the QM coming for me?"

"They're not. Yours isn't turned on."

"But it is! The light has been flashing the whole time."

"That's just for show."

Careen looked at Tommy, who nodded.

Atari continued. "When things light up, people believe they're working. The system's not online yet, and besides, I'm the only one who knows how to work it."

"Wait. How—"

"Would I go to all that trouble to extract you if I were just going to turn you in again? That makes no sense at all. Don't you want to hear about the rescue?"

None of this makes any sense. But she nodded, and he continued.

"We went with a variation on my stock plan: create a diversion and set off an explosion. But we needed a catalyst big enough to get you to explode, and in this case, Tommy assured me he knew just what to do." He paused, folded his arms, and leered at her.

"Excuse me?"

Tommy shot Atari an exasperated look before he turned to Careen. "It wasn't all that hard to convince her to help."

"Who?"

"Your mom, of course." He laughed. "Nobody on earth makes you as mad as she does."

"You know my mom?"

"Yeah. She was part of the plan. The setup was pretty simple. Kevin arranged for the broadcast and wrote the script. Pete Sheridan was in on it, too, but the Academy Award goes to your mom."

Careen's eyes filled with tears. The conspiracy was farther-reaching than she'd imagined. It was more like her mother to act without thinking than to engage in calculated treachery, and knowing she was part of the test devastated Careen more than all the accumulated hurt and neglect from her childhood. In the studio, she'd hoped that, just for a moment, her mom had been on her side. She covered her face with her hands. She could check her childhood home off her list of possible refuges.

Atari continued. "Once you were loose in the building, I correctly anticipated that Madalyn would insist I use the Link to locate you. All it took was a little sleight of hand and some split-second timing to lead the QM and Madalyn on a wild goose chase after the wrong van."

"Wait—what? I thought they were chasing us!"

"So did they. We were driving a QM van, which made it unlikely we'd be stopped and searched. We started out in their convoy, in pursuit of the fugitive. Then, when everyone was looking the other way, I turned a corner and came back here. You know the rest." He touched the tape across the bridge of his nose.

"No, I don't! If they thought they were chasing me, who—"

"Jezz was the decoy driver."

"What?"

"That was the one part of the plan we couldn't control. Once she was in the van, we couldn't intervene."

Tommy put a protective arm around Careen. "That's enough for now."

Atari cleared his throat and stood up. "Well, duty calls."

Chapter 57

10:12 PM

As soon as he was gone, Careen drew a shuddering breath.

"Your mom agreed to the plan. She said to tell you she owed you one." Tommy stood and extended his hand to her, but she sat unmoving, stunned. *Everyone's against me. What does Madalyn have planned for me next?*

"Come on. You could use a good night's sleep. I'll clear out and give you some space."

She wanted him with her, hoping his presence would keep Atari away. "Would you stay with me and just … stay?"

"Yeah, sure. Whatever you want."

With actions calculated to seem helpless and acquiescent, she leaned against him and yawned as they crossed the foyer and headed down the hall.

Atari stuck his head out the door of Command Central and caught Tommy's eye as they passed, so he left Careen at the bedroom door. "I'll be back in a minute."

"I'll be waiting."

He dashed back to Command Central. "What? What's happened?"

"The QM took Jezz straight to prison. No word beyond that. I'm working on getting more information, and while I'm working on it, you keep an eye on Million Dollar Baby in there. She's pretty confused, and that was a lot to take in. I see why Mitch wasn't keen on extracting her."

"Screw Mitch. Careen is fine, now that she's away from Madalyn."

"If you say so, bro. She's your responsibility."

Tommy headed back down the hall, opened the door a crack, and peeked inside. The bedside lamp cast a soft glow, throwing the corners of the room into deep shadow. He could hear her brushing her teeth.

When she was finished, she stood silhouetted in the bathroom door, waiflike and fragile in the leggings and loose black sweater. He was glad she hadn't sent him away.

"Sleepy?"

"A little." She turned off the bathroom light and joined him. "Do you remember when we were escaping from the OCSD, and you asked me if I trusted you?"

His heart sank. "I said I'd never let anything bad happen to you." He gently touched the scar on her cheek with his fingertips. "Maybe I was being sappy. And unrealistic."

Tears sparkled in her eyes as she looked up at him, and she laid her cheek against the palm of his hand. "I trust you. This wasn't your fault."

She's the only one who doesn't blame me, and I've hurt her so badly. He pulled her up on tiptoe, and she shuddered as he folded her into his arms. His lips played over hers, and though they'd been apart nearly as long as they'd been together, the kiss was anything but awkward. It took about two seconds before he forgot his invitation to stay didn't include picking up where they'd left off back at their secret cabin in BG-098. He tightened his hold on her and she winced.

"What's the matter?"

She shook her head, lips pressed together, staring up at him like she was trying to memorize him. "Your hair's getting really long." Shivers radiated down his spine as she ran both hands through the golden strands.

His hand slid under her sweater, seeking the curve of her breast. She tensed up and turned her back, and he kicked himself for moving too fast. He realized why she'd held him off as she lifted her sweater over her head, revealing a mass of half-healed bruises and abrasions on her pale skin.

"Oh wow! Why didn't you say something? I didn't mean to hurt you."

"It's not as bad as yours were during that awful combat training. Most of them don't hurt any more, but my ribs are still pretty sore."

He brushed his fingers over the marks on her back, crisscrossed by her bra straps. *Oh God, is that a boot print?* He kissed a green-and-yellow-tinged bruise on her shoulder. "I'm afraid to touch you now."

She turned around to face him, clutching the sweater over her heart. "You could never hurt me the way they did."

His blood ran cold as he considered. "Did they … I mean, you don't have to tell me, but did they … were you …"

She shook her head with the tiniest of smiles. "No, not like that."

He sighed and relaxed, but she seemed to tense up again. Anxious to do the right thing, he whispered, "That doesn't mean we … I mean, we don't have to—"

She looked up at him, tears in her eyes. "I can't. Not yet."

He drew back the covers and helped her settle against the pillows, leaving the lamp burning, just like she preferred. He slid in beside her, kissed her softly on the cheek, and stroked her hair until her eyes fluttered closed and she drifted off. He'd never get enough of watching her—her breathing slow and steady, her cheeks flushed and warm. So often in sleep she was clutched by night terrors, but now she looked as relaxed as he'd ever seen her, asleep or awake. It reinforced his view that he, and not Atari, was more attuned to her present state of mind. Satisfied, he brushed a wisp of hair off her face and settled onto his pillow.

10:15 PM

On the far side of the safe house, Atari scrolled through the day's news feed on his tablet.

"Children over the age of two and under the age of eighteen, whose last names begin with A through L, must report to the designated Distribution Center in their quadrant to receive their Cerberean Link on Monday morning. Those whose last names begin with M through Z may report beginning at one p.m."

"What the … ?" Atari paused the broadcast, leaving Sheila Roth frozen, her mouth gaping open like a fish. He dialed Madalyn Davies's line.

"What's going on? PeopleCam's announced that nationwide distribution of the Link begins next week. How can that be? I just told you it's nowhere near ready for a full rollout!"

"We've got to move forward. The protests against the Link are more widespread than ever. Better to get the Linking over and done with, even if the system's not operational yet. We've rehired all the workers and told them to report to the Distribution Centers first thing on Monday."

"But you understand the sensors won't be installed for some time."

"There's no need to mention that. It's just an unannounced grace period. The children will be used to their Links before the system actually goes online."

Chapter 58

12:30 AM
Saturday, December 16, 2034

Careen played possum until she was sure Tommy was asleep. He didn't stir as she slid out of bed, pulled on her sweater, and tiptoed out of the room. She'd had time to search his room for clues, and now she meant to learn more about Atari. Light from the foyer guided her as she crept down the long hallway. The safe house was huge; so far, she'd only seen a small portion of it. She'd watched Atari disappear down a different hallway off the foyer when they'd arrived, so she assumed his rooms were on that side of the building.

The singsong chirps of the video games and the gurgling water gave the impression that she'd wandered into some bizarre electronic zoo, but the constant babble of sounds was helpful in that it masked any noise she might make. She hurried past the fountain and down the third hallway, peering around the corner into the room with all the computers. No one was there.

She sat in the tall, black-leather chair, which might help to conceal her presence if Atari happened by. She shuddered. The last thing she wanted was to be alone with him.

She tapped one of the keyboards to wake it up, though she wasn't even sure what she was looking for. A second tap brought up a grid of surveillance cameras on one of the big screens. She recognized the atrium and lobby of the OCSD.

One touch on another keyboard brought up a paused video game. Other tabs were open on the toolbar, and one of them was labeled CAREEN.

With shaking fingers, she moved the cursor and clicked on her name. The video was a little dark, but she could see a woman running full-out down a city sidewalk.

Two quadrant marshals intercepted her at a corner, and she struggled wildly in their grip, kicking and screaming. One of them lost his hold on her, but just as it looked like she might break free, the other marshal shoved her against the wall, pinning her there while his partner zip-tied her hands behind her back. As the camera zoomed in, Careen clamped her hands to her mouth to keep from screaming. The woman in the video was her. *But how is this possible?*

She breathed in panicky gasps, wishing she'd never seen any of it but unable to look away. The onscreen Careen tried to pull free of the marshal's grasp, and he slammed her against the wall one more time before flinging her to her knees. A third figure stepped out of the shadows, gun in hand, and the marshals stood aside as Tommy, a look of stony determination on his face, fired point-blank into the back of her head.

That must be Tommy's test. If it is, he's the one who's going to fail.

12:55 AM

Movement in his bedroom startled Tommy awake. He rubbed his eyes as he reached for Careen in the darkness, but the space beside him was empty and cold. *I thought I left the light on.* He fumbled for the switch. "Hey!" He sat up slowly, hands out in front of him.

Careen stared at him over the barrel of his gun; if he could've removed the 9mm from the scene, he'd have perceived her as cute and cuddly, with her tousled hair, in the slouchy sweater and socks that were way too big for her. The tiny light on her Link flashed in time with her racing heartbeat. "Take me back. Take me back right now."

"I thought that went without saying. I never wanted to break up." He tried cracking the lopsided smile that she'd always seemed to like before. "What happened to my girl—you know, the one who can't condone violence?"

Her expression hardened even more. "Shut up. You don't … you *can't* know what I've been through, so you don't get to be cute and make jokes. When I was being interrogated and beaten and humiliated, I swore if I had a gun I'd shoot whoever I had to, no regrets. I'm never going to let anyone hurt me again."

His brain was working on the double-quick. He wanted to tell her that she shouldn't put her finger on the trigger until she was ready to fire the weapon, but he figured it might be more prudent not to spout off any unsolicited instructions. Instead, he tried to get to the root cause of her distress.

"I'd never hurt you. Just put the gun down so we can talk, okay?"

She shook her head.

"A little while ago you said you trusted me."

"I was lying. Duh."

"Careen, ask me anything, and I promise I'll tell you the truth. You'll feel better if you talk about it. What did they do that's making you so upset now?"

"They? You're all 'they.' This is some sort of test of my loyalty, but now I see that no matter what happens, I fail."

"Do you know how nuts you sound right now?" He slowly drew back the covers. "Give a guy a break. Don't shoot me in my boxers, please. At least let me put some pants on first."

She shook her head again, and he froze with one foot on the floor. The contrast between the sleepy Careen who'd nestled beside him just a short while ago and this wild-eyed harpy who seemed determined to shoot him with his own gun was so great that he wouldn't have believed it if he hadn't seen it with his own eyes.

"Everything you and Atari said makes sense now. This place is part of the OCSD, isn't it? Madalyn said the CXD protesters tried to kill me—once at PeopleCam and again at the Link press conference. I bet Danni loved turning them against me! Madalyn said the Resistance has been destroyed, and everyone involved has been sent to prison. So the only way you could even be here is if—"

"Madalyn said, Madalyn said. Listen to yourself! Madalyn's been lying to you, like she lies to everyone. The CXD groups aren't violent. They're not trying to kill you. They got excited when they saw you at PeopleCam, and it turned into a riot. Madalyn may wish the Resistance had been destroyed, but it's not true! Mom, Dad, Trina, Eduardo—everyone's fine."

"How do I know *you're* not lying? There's video of you and me—or people who look just like us. What is it, another trick? Or some kind of instruction manual?" Her nostrils flared.

Dammit, I told Atari to delete that video. He looked as apologetic as he could. "Atari said that video was just a test to see if he could make the images of people—of us, in this case—look realistic. And you gotta admit, it was pretty realistic." She looked even more furious, and he cringed. "He was going to create more doctored footage to use when we extracted you. That plan got scrapped a few days ago. But I told him that video was *so* not okay."

"Not okay? Is that the strongest objection you could muster about a video of you murdering me?"

"Back up the bus for a second. I'm confused. There's a video of me doing *what*?"

"You shot me in the back of the head!"

"So there's more than one." *How do I explain this without making her even madder?* "Did you find the video in Command Central?"

"Yes."

"It's the middle of the night. Atari's probably asleep. Show me?"

"Okay."

"Will you put down the gun?"

"No chance."

"Can I get dressed first?"

A tiny smile touched the corners of her mouth. "Yeah."

He pulled on a pair of jeans and a hoodie, and soon she was following him down the long hallway, gun pointed at his back. A trickle of sweat ran down his cheek, and his fear was for his safety and her sanity. *She doesn't know what I know—that everything changes in the time it takes to pull the trigger.*

When they reached Command Central, she closed the door behind them and tapped the keyboard to bring up the video.

She'd paused it after the kill shot, and even without the replay he could barely look at his doppelganger on the screen, standing over her body, gun in hand. He was sure he hadn't looked like that—triumphant and heroic—when he'd killed the marshal. His stomach lurched. "Please. If we have to watch this, I'd appreciate it if you'd put the gun down."

She pointed the muzzle at the floor, which he considered a major step in the right direction. "We don't have to watch it. I don't want to see it again. What was on the other video?"

"It was ... Atari called it a dating sim."

"Sim?"

"Simulation. It was you and me. I made him pause the video before we did anything too embarrassing."

"Eww. He did that to both of us?" She looked like she was going to cry.

"I know it seems bad, but the videos were for practice."

"But don't you get it? If Atari can fool people with an enhanced video, the Link won't be reliable or honest. Someone who can produce "evidence" like that can use it against anyone.

"Atari fooled Madalyn. And me. We're never going to be able to trust or rely on him. As long as what we see with our own eyes can be falsified, altered, and manipulated so easily, we're never going to be able to trust anyone. We'll never know what's real and true."

"Atari's got mad skills."

"But his capabilities make him just as likely to do evil as good." She stared down at the Link on her wrist. "They said the Link is to protect children. I believed it was true! It would be such a good thing to know nothing bad could ever happen to the defenseless. But the thing itself is bad. Oh my God, it's almost too late. Tommy, we're trapped here with him. What are we going to do?"

Chapter 59

1:15 AM
Quadrant OP-439

Jaycee had been headed for bed when she heard Tom and Lara's voices coming from Eduardo's living room. The tone of Lara's voice made her slow down and creep closer to listen in. She was a spy now, after all.

"Are you absolutely sure? How do you know it was him?"

"In a speech I gave. He quoted me back to myself. It's been what, sixteen or seventeen years? But he apparently took it to heart when I said, 'we must be prepared to spin, deceive, or manipulate if it champions the cause. Revolution means breaking the law and using force if necessary. Casualties are to be expected.' "

"So it really wasn't the OCSD setting up bogus terror attacks?"

"It appears the ones orchestrated by Mitch opened the door for the OCSD to stage their own. The most notable one to Mitch's credit is the one that killed Careen's father. Once I realized that, I felt doubly responsible for the poor girl. That's why I was so adamant about trying to help her."

Lara made an angry noise. "I can scarcely believe it. Mitch was to blame for everything we've been through? You'd think he might have mentioned it at some point!"

"Well, it's not exactly something you bring up over coffee."

Jaycee didn't want to listen anymore but she stayed frozen on the spot, afraid the floorboards would creak and give away her presence.

"We trusted him."

"He didn't do *all* the things the OCSD accused me of, but he certainly made me the scapegoat. And just last week he had the audacity to say that we were all expendable. He could continue on without any of us, should we be apprehended."

"You never would have condoned that kind of violence."

"Of course not. Mitch was aiming to accelerate the downfall of the OCSD. But when Stratford blamed those attacks on me, who knows if he believed I was truly responsible, or if I was simply a target that could be eliminated."

Jaycee realized she'd been holding her breath. She felt dizzy, and Lara's response faded into a meaningless buzz. She steadied herself against the wall as she crept into the bathroom. She needed a moment to think. She slid down the wall, holding her head in her hands.

If her father had really killed Careen's dad, he was a terrorist, not a noble revolutionary.

There was no way to undo the past, but from now on, Jaycee vowed to take charge of the future.

ACKNOWLEDGEMENTS

To Susan Hughes of My Independent Editor, who is not just my editor, but also my friend. Thank you for everything you do, before, during, and after each book finds its way into the world.

To Shelly Dippel, my friend, sounding board, and writing groupie. It would have taken much longer to finish *Ignite* without your input. Thanks for listening to the story, in all its incarnations, until it was done.

To Mike Reid, my most awesome stagehand on *Between the Covers with Tracy Lawson*, who shall now also be known as King of the Formatters. Thanks for calmly handling all my technical glitches!

ABOUT THE AUTHOR

Once upon a time, Tracy Lawson was a little girl with a big imagination who wanted to write books when she grew up. Her interests in dance, theater, and other forms of make-believe led to a career in the performing arts, where "work" means she gets to do things like tap dance, choreograph musicals, and weave stories.

Her greatest adventures in musical theatre included creating disco choreography for forty middle schoolers on roller skates in *Xanadu*, building cast members' endurance during an extremely aerobic jump rope number in *Legally Blonde*, and wrangling a cast of amazingly enthusiastic teenaged tap dancers in *Crazy For You*. She can also spin plates on sticks while she tap dances. Just ask her. She'll be happy to demonstrate!

Though teaching dance and choreographing shows was a great outlet for her creativity and boundless energy, Tracy never lost her desire to write. Faced with her only child leaving for college and her husband's simultaneous cross-country job relocation, it seemed she'd found the perfect time to switch her focus. But fear not— she has maintained her ties to educational theatre by returning to choreograph shows each year at Bexley City Schools in Columbus, Ohio, so she can continue to nurture students and share her passion for putting on a great show.

In her spare time, she blogs about YA and classic dystopian books and hosts *Between the Covers with Tracy Lawson*, an author interview program on the Liberty.Me network.

Tracy, who is married with one college-aged daughter and three spoiled cats, splits her time between Dallas, Texas and Columbus, Ohio.

To learn more about Tracy and all her books, visit `http://tracylawsonbooks.com`

For the inside scoop on Tommy, Careen, and the Resistance Series, visit `http://counteractbook.com`

OTHER BOOKS BY THE AUTHOR

Counteract: Book One of the Resistance Series (2014) is the story of a guy, a girl, the terrorist attack that brings them together, and their race to expose a conspiracy that could destroy their country from within. What Tommy Bailey and Careen Catecher learn about the true nature of the terrorist threat spurs them to take action, and their decisions lead them to run afoul of local law enforcement, team up with an underground resistance group, and ultimately take their quest for the truth to the highest reaches of the United States government.

Resist: Book Two of the Resistance Series (2015). Tommy and Careen are no longer naïve teenagers who believe the Office of Civilian Safety and Defense's antidote can protect them from a terrorist's chemical weapons. After accidentally discovering the antidote's real purpose, they join the fight to undermine the OCSD's bid for total control of the population.

Being part of the Resistance brings with it a whole new set of challenges. Not everyone working for change proves trustworthy, and plans to spark a revolution go awry with consequences far beyond anything they bargained for. Tommy and Careen's differing viewpoints threaten to drive a wedge between them, and their budding relationship is tested as their destinies move toward an inevitable confrontation with the forces that terrorize the nation.

Winner Best YA Fiction for 2016 in the Texas Association of Authors Book Awards

Fips, Bots, Doggeries, and More: Explorations of Henry Rogers' 1838 Journal of Travel from Southwestern Ohio to New York City (2012) is based on a journal written by Lawson's great-great-great grandfather, who kept a daily account of his family's fifty-five-day journey by horse and wagon. He notes in the journal that he endeavors to record everything he finds interesting, and the journal is a treasure trove of information about the social and political environment of the times, emerging technology, agriculture and topography, sites of interest, and his family's health and comfort.

After receiving the journal as a Christmas gift, Lawson conducted research to lend context to the journal, and ultimately made most of the same trip herself by automobile, with her young daughter in tow. They kept their own journal, and the book compares and shares information about both trips, taken over a century and a half apart.

Winner Best Nonfiction History for 2012 in the Ohio Professional Writers Association Book Awards

Pride of the Valley (coming in 2017) with Steve Hagaman. After she finished writing *Fips, Bots, Doggeries, and More,* Lawson was curious about what happened after her ancestors returned home from their 1838 journey to New York. Their working vacation was partly to visit relatives, and partly to observe mills and determine how best to add grist milling to their sawmill business.

She happily dug into the research, and even picked up a coauthor along the way.

Though their efforts to locate business ledgers or miller's journals came to naught, they found clues in land and census records, a poem, and a stereoscope image from the 1860s. It might not sound like much, but it was enough to go on, and those clues directed them to other long-forgotten information both enhances and challenges accepted accounts of the mill's history.

Pride of the Valley tells the story of the beginning, life, and eventual demise of the Mount Healthy Mill, which operated on the banks of the West Fork of the Mill Creek in Springfield Township, Ohio for over one hundred and thirty years. But the story is only half-told without also getting to know the families who owned the mill and discovering how their lives were interwoven with pivotal events in our country's history.

Tommy wiped his sweaty palms on his jeans as he stood outside his bedroom door. Atari stuck his head around the corner and made an impatient face. "Why are you lurking in the hall?"

He shrugged. "Girls take forever to get ready."

"Ready for what?"

Tommy let the insinuation pass, determined not to let Atari bait him. "We have dinner plans."

"Well, you have to eat sooner or later to keep up your strength. You've been behind the Do Not Disturb sign ever since she got here." He wiggled his eyebrows "So, just between us dudes—was it worth the wait? Or is she too much for you?"

Tommy forgot he was playing it cool and responded with a rude gesture. "Hardly."

"Ha! I see what you did there. You don't have to get testy about it. By all means, ply the pretty lass with food. I've got better things to do." He disappeared, and though Tommy heard the door to Command Central slam shut a moment later, he wasn't fooled by Atari's feigned disinterest. He was watching them closely. Was it jealousy or suspicion?

Tommy was sure Atari had plans for the Link—plans that Mitch and the others knew nothing about—but he hadn't figured out exactly what Atari intended to do or how to summon help. Even though Atari called the safe house a communications hub, his reign over Command Central cut off Careen and Tommy's ability to send an SOS to headquarters in BG-098. There was no way to contact his parents in OP-439, either. They'd ruled out trying to get in touch with Kevin for fear of blowing his cover at the OCSD. For better or worse, they were on their own.

He hated to admit it, but he was even reluctant to rely on Careen for help. Since they'd rescued her, she was prone to fits of crying and moody silence and refused to talk about what had happened to her while she'd been imprisoned. It was clear she didn't trust him, but that was nothing compared to her fear of Atari, which was so paralyzing that she wouldn't venture out of their room alone. Tommy imagined himself the lesser of two evils in Careen's eyes, and that hurt.

He'd let her set the boundaries with regard to their interactions and even agreed to let her keep the gun, provided she not point it at him all the time. She'd commandeered the bed, too. Sharing it—even without any of the implied benefits—was definitely off the table, even though he'd be glad to resume their relationship whenever she gave the word. He just hoped Atari never found out he'd been sleeping on the floor. He'd never hear the end of it.

Hiding out in his room might suit Careen, but it made it impossible to learn more about Atari's secret plans. He'd been surprised when she'd agreed to venture into the other parts of the safe house and pretend to be on a date. If they were visibly wrapped up in their feelings for each other, Atari might not realize they were also spying on him.

At seven p.m. sharp, she emerged wearing jeans and an emerald-green sweater with a neckline that did more than hint at her cleavage. She'd swept her hair up into an artfully messy ponytail with a few loose strands framing her face and concealed the last tinges of yellow-and-green bruising around her eye with makeup she'd found in the well-stocked bathroom. She'd applied a hint of eyeliner and lip-gloss and powdered over the nearly healed gash on her cheek, but it would be a long time before the scar faded enough to be inconspicuous.

"You look great." He tilted her chin up for a strawberry-flavored kiss. He knew he was taking an unwelcome liberty, but Atari was almost certain to be watching. "Hungry?"

She nodded and took his hand, and as he led her into the dining area, she sniffed the air. "Is that pizza?"

"Yeah."

"It's been—"

"Forever. I know."

He led her to a table in a corner of the room and pulled out her chair. She smiled as she sat. He saw Atari duck back around the corner as he headed into the kitchen.

As Tommy returned with the pizza, he scratched the side of his nose with his free hand, which was their agreed-upon signal that they were being watched. She applauded as he slid the pan onto the table, and they both dug in as if they didn't have a care in the world.

A few bites later, she popped a bit of crust into her mouth and wiped her fingers on her napkin. "So … you've got this first-date thing handled. Should I be jealous? How many other first dates have you had?"

"Umm … none. Not really. Unless you count our Essential Services smorgasbord."

"I don't think you can have two first dates with the same person."

Oh, good. A little teasing banter. She's in there, somewhere. "Fair enough. This one counts as our official first date. I've been watching lots of old movies I found in the library here. Pretty sure this is what people did on dates when our grandparents were kids." He served them each another slice.

The video games whirred and chirped in the background as they ate. Careen looked over his shoulder into the gallery. He asked, "Have you tried any of those games?"

"No, I've never seen any of them before."

"You finished? Let's go play one."

They left the table and she wandered around the room, looking at the brightly colored images on the screens. "How about Asteroids?"

"Okay." He stood close behind her, reached his arms around her to take the controls, and settled his chin on her shoulder. The first round was a tutorial, and he spoke near her ear as he played.

"The object is to break up the asteroids before they hit your spaceship. Use the roller ball to rotate the ship, and hit this button to fire." His lips brushed her cheek as he pushed the reset button. "Your turn."

At first she giggled helplessly as the asteroids threatened, but it was so good to hear her laugh that he didn't care if she never caught on. As soon as she mastered the controls, her demeanor hardened until the competition felt more like a power struggle than a friendly game.

Seriously? No way was he going to knuckle under and let her win. "Ha! Beat you again."

She stuck out her tongue at him like a child. "Fine. Let's try a different one this time."

"Centipede? Q*Bert? Pac-Man?"

"I want a fair chance. Which one haven't you tried? Or do you know how to play them all?"

"I've tried most of them. I've been here a lot longer than you."

"Okay. Then let's play Centipede. The controls look the same."

"Yeah. Use the roller ball to move the garden gnome and shoot the centipede before it gets to the bottom of the screen."

"Me first." The game started off slowly, and she yelped when the pace increased. "Whoa! It just split in two!" She tapped the Fire button as fast as she could.

"Blast those mushrooms out of the way. That'll slow down the centipede."

He smiled at the focus and concentration on her face.

"Look out for the spider!"

She zapped it into oblivion.

She beat him at Centipede—by a lot. While she tried to figure out how to add her name to the list of high scores, he wandered over to the jukebox, flipped through the playlist, and made a selection.

She turned around. "All this and music, too?"

"Yeah. Most of the tracks are pretty cheesy, but this one's good." He took her hand. "Wanna dance?"

She stepped into his arms and laid her head on his chest, and they swayed in time to the music. "I like your hair this way." He brushed his fingers against the side of her neck. *How could something as simple as slow dancing be so hypnotic?* If only he could freeze time until she felt it, too. To hell with Atari, Madalyn, and the rest of the world. Right now all he wanted was a lifetime of ordinary moments like this.

As soon as the song ended, she slipped out of his embrace and beckoned him over to Wild Gunman, where she posed with the plastic six-shooter. "We have to try this one next." He watched while she drew down against caricatured desperadoes of all descriptions. The guy in the serape was too quick. "See if you can beat me this time." She held out the gun.

As Tommy hesitated, Atari's voice came from behind him. "Dude, when you gonna get back on that horse?"

Tommy's anger flared. "Mind your own business for once, will ya?"

"What does he mean?"

"You mean you didn't tell her?"

"I didn't tell you, so why would I tell her?"

Careen laid down the toy gun. "What are you talking about?"

"No secrets here, remember?" Atari flashed his wolf-like smile at her. "Careen, Danni's clothes flatter you. That sweater's a particular favorite of mine. Clingy. Sends all the right signals." Atari's eyes raked her, and she retreated behind Tommy, digging her fingers into his arm.

"Leave her alone." Tommy gave Atari a look that meant business, and he shrugged and disappeared down the hall. Then he muttered to Careen, "He's got no right to talk to you that way. I'm this close to breaking his nose again." He pulled her back into their slow-dance cuddle.

She pushed against him. "The music's over."

"Doesn't matter. Please stay." After a moment she relaxed a bit, and they swayed on the spot until he mustered the courage to speak. "I never told you why I'm here instead of with the rest of the Resistance. Some bad stuff happened to me, too." He took a deep breath and kept his gaze fixed over her head. "A couple days after I got back to BG-098, they announced on PeopleCam that you were in custody and cooperating with the OCSD's investigation into the bombing. We figured the quadrant marshals would be coming for us sooner or later, so we evacuated. But my dad decided to turn himself in and give the rest of us time to get away. I couldn't let him do that. He's too idealistic, you know?

"Jaycee and I got everyone else to safety, and then I took off after my dad. By the time I got back to the diner, marshals were already there. Apparently, Dad managed to convince them he was on his own and had never met Mitch before. A local marshal backed Mitch up, said there was no way he was in the Resistance, so the rest of them put my dad in handcuffs and took him to the capital.

"At least that's what Mitch said. He told me not to go after my dad, but I didn't care. I was ready to go. I had the keys to the truck in my hand. Then, all of a sudden, one of the marshals was there. He'd thought something was fishy and doubled back.

"He held us at gunpoint and demanded to know where the others were. Made some crack about looking forward to finding my mom."

He shuddered. "Then Danni burst through the door with a big box of groceries and startled him. There was no time to think about it. I drew and fired. And I killed him."

She stared at him, tears glistening in her eyes. He sniffed and turned his face away, trying not to cry. "It happened really fast. Before I knew it, Danni had me in the truck, and we were on our way here."

"You've been here nearly the whole time?"

"Yeah. I had a chance to leave with my dad and go back to OP-439, but I said no. I wasn't going anywhere without you. I've been stuck with Atari for weeks, and I've suffered plenty." He took both her hands in his. "But there's no point in comparing my situation to what you went through. I'm nervous around guns right now. I'd rather not shoot for a while, and ... well, when you point the gun at me, it freaks me out. A lot. I hope you understand."

"I'm so sorry," she whispered. "Can you ever forgive me?"

"It's not your fault. You didn't know."

"But it is my fault! I caved and told the people who interrogated me how to find the diner. If I hadn't—"

"No." He fixed his gaze on hers. "That doesn't matter."

"I tried to protect you. I just ... couldn't. "

"I know. It's okay now."

A single tear rolled down her cheek. "Tommy, I didn't realize how angry I was at you for leaving me in the blown-up building. Do you know how terrified I was when I woke up in the hospital to find Madalyn Davies gloating over me? I lied to Madalyn and tried to protect you even though you'd left me behind. They told me over and over you and Tom and the others didn't care about me. Eventually I believed it."

"Don't apologize. For any of it."

"But I am sorry. So sorry." Her lips sought his, and as they clung together he forgot about Atari's treachery and the Resistance's revolution on the horizon. At this moment there was only Careen, warm and soft and miraculously unbroken. They were both unbroken, despite everything they'd endured. The video games around them chirped and whirred in victory as she whispered an invitation in his ear.